Daughters of Riga

by

Marian Exall

Cover Art by *The Wild Rose Press, Inc.*

The Wild Rose Press, Inc.
PO Box 708
Adams Basin, NY 14410-0708
Visit us at www.thewildrosepress.com

Publishing History
First Edition, 2024
Trade Paperback ISBN 978-1-5092-5387-6
Digital ISBN 978-1-5092-5388-3

Published in the United States of America

Dedication

Edith Zwartendijk,
whose memories of her father's courage
inspired this novel

Prologue: *2003*

The waiting area was nearly empty. Only four people sat, spaced far apart in hard plastic chairs along the sides of the room. They thumbed through magazines or gazed blankly at the National Health Service posters advocating flu shots or listing the warning signs of depression. A receptionist sat behind a screened-in counter, the muted clack of her computer keyboard and her occasional telephone conversations the only sounds.

It was already dark outside—as dark as a London winter afternoon gets under the glare of sodium streetlights, lighted shop-fronts, and neon signs. The waiting room was uncomfortably warm, yet the old woman seated closest to the receptionist had not taken off her coat, or even unbuttoned it. Although she sat still, with ankles neatly crossed, energy seemed to hum around her. Dark green tweed strained across her well-upholstered bosom, thick gray hair sprang in short unruly curls from under a knitted hat, and her face, deeply etched with wrinkles, was rosy. This might have been the result of the heat in the room or of the medical condition that brought her here, but the flush suggested youth, as did the piercing dark blue eyes with which she observed her companions-in-waiting as they made their way one by one to the sanctum behind the screened desk.

"It won't be long now, Mrs. Nesse." The receptionist leaned around her computer screen to reassure the now-solitary patient.

"That's all right, dear. It gives me a chance to catch up on my reading," the woman replied, lifting up the magazine in her lap. The rhythm of her speech and the slight buzz around the sibilants indicated a European accent, though it was too faint to point to a particular country of origin.

The minutes passed, each marked by a dull click from the wall clock mounted over the receptionist's desk. The old woman selected another magazine and began a desultory review of its contents, flicking the pages from the back. Suddenly her body tensed, and the hand turning the pages froze. After a moment, she smoothed out a page and lifted it to within inches of her eyes. The face in the photograph was at least a couple of decades older than when she had last seen it, the formal pose and shading of the black-and-white portrait dating it to the early sixties. The article headlined "Righteous Among The Nations" explained that some of the stories about gentiles who saved Jews during the Second World War were only now coming to light, and profiled half a dozen of the most recently recognized. The caption of the photograph that arrested her attention read, *"Richard Vandercam, Professor of History at Amsterdam University until his death in 1971."*

A nurse framed in the doorway to the examination rooms had to repeat her name twice before the woman stumbled to her feet.

"Yes, I'm Danielle Nesse." She held up a finger, requesting a moment's indulgence, as she turned to the receptionist.

"Could I borrow this? There's something I want to copy. I'll bring it back."

The receptionist glanced at the cover of the magazine extended toward her.

"That's okay. It's an old one. You can keep it."

"Thank you." She rolled the magazine carefully into a cylinder and slid it into her handbag. Then, squaring her shoulders, she followed the nurse through to see the doctor.

Part One: Dani's Story

Chapter 1

Dani woke early and lay listening to the birdsong. Through the window of her tiny bedroom under the eaves of her grandparents' cottage, she could see a strip of pearly sky on the cusp of turning blue. Peaceful. Until memories of the preceding days intruded.

She got out of bed and dressed. Downstairs, she looked at her grandfather's old pocket watch hanging from its stand on the mantelpiece, as it had since Opa's death at the beginning of winter. No one had wound the watch for days, and the time it told was useless. She grabbed her jacket from the hook by the door and went outside. Dandelions had sprung up overnight in the path's cracks. Their brightness challenged the morning chill to be gone. A bitter winter, but it was spring now, and the war would soon be over. Walking around the side of the cottage, Dani saw signs of the season's advance. Several red tulips stood straight as soldiers along the garden border. She bent to pick them, adding a few dandelions for contrast. She remembered her mother— long ago, before the war—explaining that weeds were just flowers growing in the wrong place.

High above the clouds, Allied planes droned eastward, flight after flight. The waning German resistance meant that bombing raids could be carried out in daylight now. Dani raised her head to listen to the planes. She closed her eyes and imagined flying east with them, over the ravaged Rhineland, the fires of Dresden, and the ruins of Warsaw, over the advancing Russian lines, denuded farms and bombed-out churches, on and on, like a bird returning to its summer home.

Inside again, she climbed the stairs to her grandparents' bedroom. Two women from the village had come the day before to help lay out, wash, and dress her grandmother's body. Dani peeled back the sheet that covered Oma's face. The once-rosy cheeks looked gray now, her periwinkle eyes hidden behind papery lids. Dani placed her brilliant red-and-yellow bouquet—the only color in the room—under the cold hands clasped across the old woman's breast.

Back in her bedroom, she dragged her suitcase out from under the bed and wiped off the dust. The last time she had packed the case was in Riga, five years before, her mother guiding her on what to select. Now the choices were simple: she had only one spare dress, a couple of sweaters, no shoes other than the ones she wore every day. She added socks and underwear, a nightdress. There was plenty of room for the framed photograph of her parents on their wedding day: Nellie looking like a schoolgirl with her curly dark hair and broad smile, her eyes half-closed as she gazed up at her new husband. Henrijk's hollowed cheeks already showed signs of the tuberculosis that would claim his life when Dani was a small child, prior to the move to Latvia.

Dani slid out the envelope hidden under the frame's cardboard backing. She emptied its contents onto her bed: a business card with the name Richard Vandercam in ornate script and an address on Herengracht in

Amsterdam, and a piece of paper bearing the names of Sarah and Piotr Peleç, her aunt and uncle, and their home, a farm in Suffolk, England. At least, it had been their home in 1940, when they first escaped from Riga and could still correspond with the family left behind. Dani considered the two addresses. She was uncertain whether the Germans had withdrawn from Amsterdam, their last stronghold in the Netherlands. Travel to the north might still be unsafe. But England was another country, another language. Both seemed impossible destinations. Sighing, she replaced the card and the paper in the envelope, which she stowed in the pocket of her dress. She carried the most important documents she owned—two letters received from her mother nearly five years ago—with her always. They lay next to her heart in a linen pouch under her clothes, the multiple franking on the envelopes indicating the circuitous route they had taken to reach her from Latvia. She knew their contents by heart now.

Dani wrapped the framed photo in her nightdress, but there was still too much room in the suitcase for it to be protected from damage. She looked around her bedroom for something to fill the space. Her eye fell on the doll lying on the top of her chest of drawers. At thirteen, Dani was too old to play with dolls, but this one had traveled with her from Riga, and she kept it from a sense of obligation: it did not belong to her but to Richard Vandercam's daughter Berta, who had been her friend. She had no expectation of seeing Berta again, but she couldn't bring herself to discard the toy. Anyway, it fit nicely on top of her clothes and provided a cushion for the photograph. She clicked the clasps closed and lifted the case. It wasn't heavy.

In the kitchen, she found the cake tin where their official documents were kept. She took her Dutch passport and ID card, leaving Oma's card on the table for whoever might come by later. There were a few guilder in the bottom of the tin. She thought about leaving them too—a contribution toward the funeral she trusted the villagers to provide—but then stuffed the notes into her pocket along with her aunt and uncle's address and the consul's business card. Jacket buttoned, she grasped the handle of her suitcase. She closed the door of the cottage behind her, but she did not lock it. She had made no friends, her grandparents fearing that any casual interaction might lead to her exposure to the German occupiers. Even in their small village, she had learned not to speak to others in the street, to tuck her curly, almost-black and decidedly un-Dutch hair out of sight under her hood. Having lived apart from the local community, she didn't care now if the neighbors claimed the contents of the cottage, or moved some bombed-out relative into what had been her father's childhood home. There was nothing left here that mattered to her.

The roads were still empty. Dani walked fast for fifteen minutes, every so often changing the suitcase from hand to hand. The instinct for secrecy was still strong, and she waited until she had put sufficient distance between herself and the village before she climbed up the slope to the top of the dyke. From here she could see the dark smudge of Rotterdam on the horizon, three or four miles away. The canals and roads formed a grid, and she could easily map out a route for herself. She set off again, determined not to look back over her shoulder.

About noon, she came to the edge of the built-up

area. The roads here were in poor repair, potholes and bomb craters filled with muddy water. Some of the houses were damaged and vacant, but people went about their business, seeming undisturbed by the destruction. Dani saw a Jeep with soldiers on board and a red cross on the side disappear into a gateway. She followed it and found a school that had evidently been taken over by the Allied forces who had liberated the city only days before. She stood inside the gate, trying to decide whether this was where she should seek help. The brick building was two stories high with an imposing main door at the center. A ragtag column of civilians curled down the steps from the entrance and spread across the schoolyard. They seemed tired and disillusioned, some sitting on suitcases, some staring suspiciously at Dani, none of them talking. The line didn't move.

After a minute or two, Dani strolled around the side of the building. Her first inclination had been to join at the end of the queue, or at least to inquire what they were queuing for, but the people in line made her uncomfortable. She sensed hostility, and noting there were no young people of her age, she decided to explore further before making an approach.

At the back of the building several military vehicles were drawn up, including the Jeep with the red cross. Three men in uniform bent over the open hood of another vehicle, and two more were unloading boxes from the back of a truck. Dani noticed a white leaf insignia against the dull green of the vehicles' bodywork, but then her eye was drawn away to another soldier sitting on some steps leading to a door, a less impressive entrance than the one at the front of the school. He was the first Black man Dani had ever seen, and she couldn't help staring as he took a bite of an apple and chewed it, his face and the red apple catching the sunlight, providing vivid spots of color in the otherwise drab scene.

The soldier caught sight of her, smiled, and beckoned her over. She froze in panic for a second before reminding herself that this was why she had come to the city: to find help in reaching friends or family who might take her in. She advanced cautiously. The soldier said something in English. She shook her head to show she did not understand. The man jerked a thumb toward his chest and spoke slowly.

"I'm Joe. You are…?"

He was asking her name.

"Danielle—Dani."

"Well, Danielle-Dani, how old are you?"

Again, she shook her head. Joe repeated the jerk of the thumb toward himself and held up ten fingers twice.

"I'm twenty. How old are you?" He grinned.

Dani smiled back at him, feeling a small sense of triumph. She could understand English!

"Thirteen," she said in Dutch, holding up ten fingers, then three more.

"Thirteen," he repeated in English, then several more words that mystified her. Joe pulled a packet out of his breast pocket and extracted a slim rectangle wrapped in foil.

"Gum?" Another mystery to Dani. Seeing her confusion, Joe unwrapped a piece of grayish material and popped it into his mouth. He started chewing with an exaggerated expression of pleasure. "Here." He pulled out another foil-covered stick and handed it to Dani. Nervously, she peeled back the wrapping and sniffed the gum. It smelled sweet. She put it in her mouth and bit down: an immediate rush of saliva, accompanied by a sugary, minty taste unlike anything she had eaten before.

"Thank you. That was good." She hoped he understood.

"No, wait! Don't swallow it!" He mimed mastication. Puzzled, she copied him, continuing to chew the rubbery substance in her mouth. They watched each other working the gum for a few moments.

"So, where are your mama and papa?" The soldier could see by her stricken face that the girl understood the words "mama" and "papa." Dani's gaze fell to the ground between them as she struggled for a response. How could she explain that, although she knew her father was dead, she still had hopes of finding her mother. Her hand crept instinctively to her chest, to the packet of letters.

Joe waited a moment, then fluttered a hand from his body to the sky, like a bird flying away, a surprisingly delicate gesture.

"Gone," he said. Dani nodded.

"All right, come with me." Joe stood up and opened the door behind him, signaling for Dani to follow. Another brief moment of panic before Dani stiffened her shoulders, picked up her suitcase, and stepped from the sunshine into a dim corridor. Joe led her to a door on which was pinned a hand-printed card: "Major F. C. McArdle." Before knocking, Joe neatly spat his gum into the foil wrapper and placed it in his pocket. Dani did the same.

Receiving permission to enter, Joe marched into the room, bringing his heels together and saluting. Dani stood close behind him, remaining invisible to the man behind the desk, who engaged in an exchange with Joe from which Dani could only pick out her name. Finally, Joe saluted again, turned, and with a wink at Dani, left the room.

Major McArdle looked to be about forty, with grizzled hair shaved close to his scalp. The dark shadows under his eyes bore witness to his exhaustion. The Canadian army unit he commanded had been dropped behind enemy lines in eastern Holland several weeks ago. They had clawed their way west, canal by canal, village by village, until they reached the Rhine delta. Then, six days earlier, the German troops had melted away, retreated in the night, or surrendered. As the last days of April wound down, the war was ending. The major's job had turned from fighting and killing to sorting through the chaos left behind and establishing some kind of civil justice amid competing claims for reparations and revenge.

He surveyed the girl standing in front of him. Skinner had said she was thirteen, but she looked much younger. Thin—well, wasn't everyone who had survived the last cruel winter?—with black curly hair and blue eyes. She didn't look Dutch. He began his litany of questions—name, age, last address—wishing his Dutch was better, writing down the child's responses on a fresh sheet of paper. When he asked about her parents, she remained silent for a few moments, then bent to open her suitcase and take out her passport and identification card.

Dani watched him as he examined the documents.

"It says here your father is Dutch, and your mother is Latvian?" That was unusual. It might explain her coloring. Then he had an inspiration. "Is your mother Jewish?"

Her grandmother had insisted over and over that she

never admit to being Jewish. It would be very dangerous, Oma said. Because they lived at a distance from Rotterdam, they could avoid the frequent demand for ID papers that happened in the towns and cities. Her grandparents had always kept to themselves and instilled the same habit of independence in Dani. She wanted to trust that things were different now, that this man would help her if she told the truth, but she hesitated, deciding to say nothing.

The major adopted a more oblique approach.

"Is your father alive?"

Dani shook her head.

"And your mother?"

Dani remained quiet. Major McArdle raised his eyes from the papers on the desk and looked directly at Dani.

"When did you last see your mother?"

Dani felt a lump form in her throat. She looked away from the officer and concentrated on the sky outside the window. She was determined not to cry, but the hope that her mother was still alive felt like a thorn in her heart.

"In 1940."

"Where was that?"

"Latvia."

The silence that followed Dani's answer seemed to press down like a weight. Major McArdle rubbed his forehead with slow strokes as if to erase the thoughts that gathered in his brain. If this child's mother was still alive in Latvia, she would have had to survive three brutal invasions: the Russians in 1940, the Germans in 1941, and the Russians again last year. If the mother was indeed Jewish, the chances of her survival were virtually nonexistent.

He cleared his throat.

"Any other family? Alive, I mean." He knew he sounded brusque, but he could see the girl was fighting back tears and he wanted to avoid any show of emotion, hers or his.

Dani pulled the envelope out of her pocket and handed over the paper with Sarah and Piotr's address on it.

"My aunt and uncle," she said.

"Hmm." He copied down the information, then handed back the paper, together with the passport and ID card. "I can't make promises, but I'll pass this on to the proper agency to see if we can connect you with your uncle and aunt." Dani's face lit up. The major resumed. "It will take a while, weeks, maybe months. That is, *if* they can find them. In the meantime, we need to find you somewhere safe to live." He raised his voice. "Private Skinner!"

Joe stepped back into the room. He had obviously been waiting just outside. Another fast exchange in English, and then the interview was over.

Dani was left on a bench in the corridor, with some crackers, an apple, and several reassuring nods and smiles from Joe. After he left, Dani ate the food, listening to the rat-a-tat of a typewriter and occasional voices from behind closed doors. A wave of tiredness overtook her. She hoisted her suitcase onto the bench and lay down, using it as a pillow. Her last thought before sleep was that she must learn English.

Chapter 2

Dani spent three months with the Sisters of the Immaculate Conception. She joined a dozen other children, most of whom had lived in the orphanage on the edge of Rotterdam for the entirety of the Occupation. The Sisters had given them new names—saints' names—and schooled them to genuflect and cross themselves at appropriate places in the daily mass. The youngest had no memory of a life before, and relied on the whispered reminiscences of older children after lights out to understand their Jewish heritage. Now that the war was over, the Sisters relaxed their insistence on Catholic observance. They opened up hiding places under floorboards and behind cupboards to extract packets of letters, photographs and other small souvenirs left when the children had been delivered into the nuns' care. The children pored over this evidence, learning or re-learning faces, names, and addresses, then peppering the Sisters with questions.

"When will they come for me? Where have they been all this time? Why can't I go home now?"

Dani waited to be reclaimed with the others. As one of the oldest children and the most recently arrived, she enjoyed a privileged position. Although her grandparents had sheltered her from much social contact, she had knowledge of the world the others lacked. Their experience was limited to a cloistered routine, shielded behind the convent walls from any outsider's notice. The children gathered around Dani, asking timid questions about her grandparents and the village school she had sporadically attended. Their admiration increased when Joe, her Canadian soldier, turned up with gifts of sugar and tinned ham for the Sisters, and chewing gum and chocolate for them.

Joe visited as often as he could, and always made time to separate Dani from the trailing crowd of children who followed him. At Dani's request, he was teaching her English, using colorful comics as textbooks. In spite of the food parcels he brought, the Sisters viewed this activity with suspicion, and insisted their language lessons take place on a bench out in the central courtyard under their eye. As April turned to May and the weather improved, they relished their open-air classroom. Dani acquired some proficiency in a slangy, energetic kind of English. The comic book stories of superheroes and villains flavored her conversation with "gee-whiz!" and "shazam!"

Then, in June, Joe's unit pulled out.

"Will you write to me?" Dani asked, distraught at losing her friend.

"Sure, honey, but you won't be here forever. Your folks'll find you and take you away, and I won't know where to write. Chin up!" Joe's smile always made her feel better. "Here, you can have all these. I can get new ones as soon as I get back home." He handed her a pile of comic books, his entire library. "Make sure you keep studying!"

After Joe left, there was nothing to do but wait. Now that the orphanage's isolation was not strictly enforced, rumors started to spread about the Nazis' wholesale deportation of Jews, and the labor camps that were in fact extermination centers. The nuns' insistence that patience and prayer would be rewarded when the children's parents or other relatives returned to claim them, began to wear thin. Some of the older children became rebellious, loudly refusing to attend mass, and, against Mother Superior's strict orders, strolling out into the city to bother the Allied soldiers for candy.

Dani kept her silence. She had overheard her grandparents whispering about people disappearing overnight to the camps in Germany. She wondered how the Sisters, who must have known what had happened to the parents of their charges, could maintain their serene optimism, but she understood that it would be cruel to crush the hope every child nurtured that *their* family at least had survived.

As time passed, and especially after Joe left, her own hopes wavered and dimmed. She was therefore unprepared when summoned to Mother Superior's office to see her smiling broadly. The nun emerged from behind her desk to give Dani a warm hug.

"They've found your uncle and aunt!" she announced. "I have a letter from the Red Cross. It's in English." She handed it to Dani. "Can you translate?"

The words danced in front of Dani's eyes. Gradually, she picked out their meaning.

"Sarah and Piotr live in London now. They will meet me at…" she stumbled over the word, "Harwich? Where is that? In England? A Red Cross person will escort me from Hoek—that's near Rotterdam, isn't it?—on a transport ship leaving on July 16. That's—"

"The day after tomorrow!" Mother was thrilled. "The last to arrive, the first to be reclaimed! This will cheer the others too. Let's share the news."

When she said goodbye to the other children at the orphanage, Dani's excitement at finding Sarah and Piotr was tinged with sadness at the knowledge that they would not be so lucky. As she returned their hugs, she also felt a gnawing worry that leaving Holland put her farther away from her mother, reducing the chance of finding her again. But she waved and grinned at their shouts of good luck, and thanked the Sisters for their kindness, hiding her anxieties.

****

Piotr—"Call me Pete. That's my name now"— looked the same as when Dani had last seen him in the Riga apartment: a flop of fair hair falling over his forehead, high cheekbones, and a long neck with a prominent Adam's apple. She recognized him across the customs hall before he spotted her. When he did identify her, probably because of the Red Cross nurse standing at her side, he crossed hesitantly, and stood staring for a moment before speaking.

"Little Danielle! So grown up, I can't believe it!"

There was some paperwork to take care of before the nurse said a cheerful "Good luck!" and left. Pete guided Dani through the crowds of returning servicemen to the railway station attached to the docks and onto the London-bound train. The carriages were already quite full, and it took several minutes to find two seats together. The train left the station and was soon chugging through flat countryside dissected by hedgerows and ditches, not unlike the Dutch landscape on the other side of the North Sea.

"There's so much to tell you. I suppose I should start at the beginning." Pete spoke in Latvian. Dani hadn't

17

heard the language for five years, but it was immediately familiar, conjuring memories of her mother's voice. "When we arrived in England, the only jobs we could find were on a farm in Suffolk. The work was very hard, especially for Sarah. She missed her family so much, and her music. At first, we tried to practice every evening, but Sarah was too exhausted. Sarah became…sad. We were miles from town. The rooms we had were cold and damp. I knew we had to leave. By the next spring my English was better, and I managed to get a job as a delivery driver in London. I found a little flat in Camden Town, and, even though it was more dangerous than the countryside because of the bombing, we moved to London. It's better there, with people around. I picked up some work playing clarinet with a dance band. After the American GIs arrived, there was dancing every night, even when the bombs were coming down." He paused to look at Dani, and his voice turned serious. "What about you? Have you heard anything, I mean, about Sarah's parents? Your mother?"

Dani shook her head, her throat tightening. She looked down at her clasped hands to avoid Pete's gaze. He rushed on.

"Sarah was certain the consul would look after you and Nellie. After all, you're Dutch citizens. What happened? How did you get separated?"

Dani hesitated, searching for words in Latvian to explain that she didn't feel ready to talk about that ghastly sequence of events five years ago. Besides, she had noticed the curious, even hostile glances of the other travelers in the compartment as Pete had been talking.

"Can we speak English?" she whispered.

"Of course. Yes, we *should* speak English. At home

now we only speak English for the baby's sake."

"The baby!" Dani squeaked, eliciting a smile from the man in uniform sitting across from her.

"Oh, I wasn't supposed to tell you. It was to be Sarah's surprise. Don't let her know I said anything."

"A baby? Is it a girl or a boy? When was it born?" Dani was delighted to think she had a cousin.

"It's a girl: Victoria. Born on May 6, VE Day. She's beautiful!" Beaming with paternal pride, Pete had forgotten his question about Nellie. Dani was relieved. It was painful to think about the past. "We've moved to a bigger flat in a nicer area. I'm full-time with the orchestra now. We've even done a couple of BBC broadcasts."

The reticent Piotr, who had followed the exuberant discussions around the Kutners' dinner table with wide eyes but without contributing an opinion, had been replaced by Pete, the confident family man and full-time band member who spoke English with a London accent.

Within an hour, they were passing through the outer suburbs, row upon row of tidy red-brick houses. Half an hour later as they approached Liverpool Street Station, the London terminus, Dani saw the results of the Blitz. In places, entire streets had been leveled, leaving nothing but piles of brick and lumber; in others, a gap like a missing tooth showed where a bomb had taken just one building from a row of otherwise apparently unscathed houses.

"Cor! Look at that." A soldier sitting by the window, returning from years of service overseas, had not seen the devastation before.

"You should see Berlin!" responded another.

With Pete carrying her suitcase in one hand and

Dani holding onto the other, they fought their way through the crowds at Liverpool Street Station. The noise made Dani want to cover her ears: so many people all chattering at speed. She realized her carefully compiled comic book vocabulary would not be enough. Would she ever be able to understand the various accents, or speak as fast as everyone around her?

"Our bus stop's over there. Whoa!" Pete pulled Dani back onto the curb before a black taxicab sped by. "Look right, look left, then right again," he chanted. "They drive on the left here, and everyone's in a hurry to be somewhere else."

They caught their bus and rode north without further incident to Highgate where the Peleçs now lived. Dani said little. She was amazed by the number of people in the streets, the traffic, the noise. Following closely behind Pete, she got off the bus in front of a terrace of once-elegant Georgian townhouses, now divided into apartments.

"This is us: number 33A, ground floor."

Sarah must have heard the key in the front door, because she was standing in the entrance hall as Pete ushered Dani in front of him.

While Pete was physically unaltered by the war years, Sarah appeared a ghost of her former self. The chestnut-colored hair that had gleamed gold when Sarah tossed her head was now cut short and a mousey-brown color. The hands that flew to her mouth when she saw Dani were red and rough with housework. Even her voice, once she had controlled the tears that choked her, seemed like an echo.

"My God. You look exactly like her!"

Chapter 3

Dani adored Victoria: her super-fine gold hair that lifted in the breeze, her blossom-soft skin, her giggles and smiles—she was an easy child to love. With Pete's big-band career taking off, he was rarely home before the early hours of the morning. Occasionally tours kept him away for days. Sarah began to rely more and more on Dani's help with the baby. They shared the excitement of Vickie's first words and first steps, the teething tantrums and the frustrations of potty training, becoming more like sisters than aunt and niece. If Pete felt closed out of this feminine cabal, he disguised it behind exuberant expressions of pride in his new daughter, his reclaimed niece, and his revitalized wife.

"Are you sure you don't have school today?" Sarah was attempting to bundle a wriggling Vickie into her coat. Although the sun shone, the morning was still springtime chilly.

"We have the day off for VE Day, your birthday!" Dani bent to bestow a kiss on Vickie's nose, eliciting a squeal of delight. Standing up and speaking to Sarah, she added, "I've packed some raisins for a snack, but maybe the ice-cream van will be there." She mouthed the words "ice-cream," knowing Vickie's excitement might defeat her mother's efforts completely.

Vickie had graduated from a perambulator to a folding pushchair from which she observed and commented on the passing world.

"More! More!" She ordered her slaves.

"It's uphill! I can't go faster!" Dani laughed, breathless.

"Let me take over," said Sarah. This was a frequent outing for the trio: up the hill from the flat to Hampstead Heath, where the ground flattened past the bathing ponds, then a gentle decline to the Parliament Hill lookout point. There, Vickie was freed from restraint and could totter about on the grass while Dani and Sarah sat on a bench to take in the view over London. Brownish smoke hung in a pall over the city. Through it, they could just make out the dome of St. Paul's, the OXO Tower on the South Bank, and in the distance to the right the green swathe of Hyde Park and the Houses of Parliament.

"It's amazing, isn't it?" Sarah said. "All those people—millions of people we know nothing about."

Dani made a hum of agreement. She liked the distance the view gave them. She had a better sense than Sarah of the millions of people moving around Europe, rootless and homeless. She felt grateful for her small niche, the limited community in which she lived. She had no desire to explore that wider world. She waited, tense; she knew what Sarah's next thought would be.

"I wonder where they are now: Mama, Papa, Nellie, Pavel—all the people we knew in Riga. Do you remember those suppers? Mama's goulash? The discussions we had? The music!"

Dani nodded but said nothing. When Sarah and Pete left Riga, the family was still intact, living much the same bohemian life as always. For Dani, Sarah's frequent flights of nostalgia for Latvia led to only one image: her mother, growing ever smaller through the rear window of the car taking Dani and the consul's family away. She stood up, looking for a way to escape the conversation.

"Vickie, come on! Let's see if we can find the ice-cream man."

****

When she was pregnant with Victoria, Sarah had started going to a local synagogue. The congregation was a mix of recent refugees from Europe and families who had been members for generations. She had found a welcoming community there. Vickie's birth had forced a hiatus in her attendance, but after Dani's arrival, the rabbi had persuaded Sarah back to undertake a course of religious instruction, making up for her secular childhood. Sarah urged Dani to join her.

"Come on, you'll enjoy it. The rabbi's really kind and a good teacher."

Dani was reluctant. She was uncertain whether the years of coaching to deny her Jewish heritage or her innate shyness led her to refuse the invitation.

"No, I'll stay at home and look after the baby. You can't study with her in your arms. Besides I get enough learning at school."

Sarah shrugged. "Well, please yourself, but I think it would be good for you to get out and meet other people."

Dani was relieved that Sarah accepted her excuses without further argument. Possibly Sarah was relieved not to have to engage a stranger to babysit.

Pete also refused to be drawn into Sarah's newfound spiritual journey. As a nominal Christian, he had a ready defense, although he appreciated the change that membership in the synagogue had produced in his wife.

"She's so much happier than she used to be," he confided to Dani. "I know you and the baby have a lot to do with that, but it's the people she meets at Temple Beth Israel too. They seem to understand what she's lost—well, what we've all lost." Pete paused, struggling to express his emotions in words. "I can't talk to her about it. It's too…close somehow. But it's like they've been living with it for generations; they know what to say, what not to say." He shrugged, then fell silent. After a few moments, he brightened. "Has she told you about the string quartet?"

Sarah had at last welcomed music back into her life. Two German-Jewish refugees in the congregation played the violin, a third woman, long retired from teaching the instrument, played cello, and Sarah, clearly the best musician of the four, adapted her fiddle skills to the viola. They played together a couple of times a week for their own enjoyment without any idea of performing for an audience. Sarah anticipated these sessions held in the community room of the synagogue with delight.

"Are you sure you're okay to look after Vickie for a few hours?" Sarah asked. "Don't you have to go to school today?"

"It's the half-term holidays. Go on! Vickie and I'll be fine." Dani waved her aunt out the door. She paused to listen to the footsteps receding down the stairs, then let out a long breath.

"Come on, Queen Victoria. Let's play hide and seek."

****

Pete was the one who discovered that Dani was routinely skipping school.

He returned from a tour of northern cities, catching

the overnight train to arrive at King's Cross Station at nine a.m. He took the tube to Highgate and rode the lift to street level, barely able to keep his eyes open. His route to the flat took him past Highgate Hill Secondary Modern School, an ugly building thrown up cheaply in the year before the war. It was a mild day in October. A girls' P.E. class was playing netball in the playground. Pete stopped for a moment to see if he could spot Dani amongst them. Disappointed, he picked up his instrument case again in one hand, grasped his suitcase in the other, and trudged forward. Through an open window, a teacher's voice droned. Pete glanced in at the rows of heads bent over their desks. He thought about the bed waiting for him, and hoped he would have the place to himself. A few hours' sleep and he'd be ready to resume his role as father of the family.

When he reached the flat, he put his bags down inside the front door and closed it quietly.

"Dada!" Victoria tottered toward him, arms extended wide. Dani followed her out of the living room.

"Hello, sweetheart," Pete picked up his daughter and gave her a kiss. "What's up? Where's Sarah?"

"She's practicing with the quartet. It's half-term, so I can look after Vickie." Dani had already turned back to avoid Pete's eyes. Lying to Pete was harder than lying to Sarah. Sarah believed anything; Pete was worldly-wise.

After a few minutes, Vickie settled down on her father's lap with a rag doll. Pete looked steadily across his daughter's head until Dani met his gaze.

"It's not half-term. You should be at school."

For a second, Dani struggled to come up with another excuse, but she realized with a kind of relief that lying was futile.

"I hate it there. The other kids—they're all so loud and rough. They make fun of my accent. The teachers don't care. No one notices if I go to school or not."

Pete sighed. "But it's the law: you have to stay at school until you're fifteen." He felt a wave of sympathy: Dani looked small and childlike compared to the well-developed young women he'd seen playing ball. "Look, Sarah and I'll get into trouble if you don't go: the truant officer will come around to the house. As refugees, we can't afford to break the rules. It's just until next summer. Please?"

Dani nodded. "All right," she said in a quiet voice.

The next morning Pete walked Dani to school.

"Don't come inside," Dani said, in a panic that Pete would embarrass her. It was bad enough arriving late when classes had already begun. She had been deliberately slow getting dressed in the hope that Pete would give up his plan to accompany her. She realized she had only increased her humiliation.

"Okay, I won't." Pete watched her push through the entrance and make her way along the corridor. She hesitated at an open door. Pete couldn't resist following her into the building; she seemed so vulnerable. He was still a dozen feet away when he heard the cold tones of a male teacher emerge from the classroom.

"Well, Diane. Glad you could finally join us. Don't stand there dithering. Come in and sit down."

Dani disappeared into the room, and Pete turned to leave.

"Just until next year," he told himself.

****

Dani left school for the final time on her fifteenth birthday in March. Pete did not insist that she finish the school year. He remembered the bullying he had suffered, a musical prodigy born into a primitive farming community on the Latvian borders. Although Dani was not physically abused as he had been, he saw how the other students intimidated her. Many of these teenagers had grown up without supervision, dads away in the armed services and mums working in factories to help the war effort. Their manners were rough and their language crude. There was no point in complaining to the teachers: that would only make Dani a target. Anyway, the teachers were mainly disengaged and cynical, exhausted from trying to control an overcrowded classroom where few students seemed interested in learning. Pete had done what he could when he wasn't at work: walking Dani to school in the morning and hanging around the gates at the end of the day; attending the occasional event for parents. He had not shared his concerns with Sarah. She was pregnant again, feeling unwell and exhausted much of the time. He worried that fretting about Dani might push her back into the dark mood of her earlier years in England.

To celebrate Dani's birthday, Pete surprised the family by taking them out to dinner at a restaurant in the West End. He had arranged for a fellow band member to look after Vickie, who was already fast asleep for the night by the time they were ready to leave.

The evening was not a complete success. Sarah, now in her seventh month, felt large and ungainly. She worried out loud about Vickie. They had never left her with a stranger before. She picked at her food and grimaced after the first sip of wine.

"This doesn't taste right. You finish it, Pete."

Dani wore a new dress that Sarah had made for her.

She'd liked the fabric's pink-and-mauve floral design when they selected it at the store, but now she felt as if she was wearing the loose cover for a sofa. The French menu baffled her. Finally, she asked Sarah to order on her behalf, and was relieved when she was served a recognizable lamb chop with peas and creamy potatoes.

Pete alone seemed at ease in the elegant dining room. As they waited for dessert to arrive, he poured the last of the bottle into his glass and leaned back with a satisfied smile.

"Well, Dani, now you're finished with your education, what do you want to do with your life?"

Dani looked alarmed. "Can't I just stay with you, and help Sarah with Vickie and the new baby?"

Pete laughed. "Of course you'll stay with us. We're not throwing you out. But you don't want to be a nursemaid forever. You need to get out and meet people, do something, have a career. Look at you: pretty as a picture and speaking three languages! There must be something you want to do?"

Dani considered the question for a moment, then shrugged. "Not really. I like looking after babies."

Before Pete could press further, Sarah spoke up. "Leave her alone, Pete. It's her birthday—let her enjoy it. Look, here comes your Cherries Jubilee."

But Pete had sown a disturbing seed in Dani's mind. She had refused to think about the future just as she avoided thinking about the past. Pete was right: she couldn't stay at home for ever. Sarah and Pete's children would grow up. They wouldn't need her anymore. They might even come to resent having to provide for her.

When they left the restaurant, Sarah decided that Pete was a little too drunk to manage the Underground, and they took a taxi home, the first time Dani had ever ridden in such a luxurious and expensive mode of transportation. Pete soon dropped off to sleep, his head on Sarah's shoulder, his hand on her distended stomach, and snuffling noises emerging from his sagging mouth. Sarah smiled down at her husband.

"He's going to regret this in the morning," she whispered, the affection in her voice contradicting any implied criticism. Dani nodded, but her thoughts were elsewhere. She watched the nighttime streets roll past, brightly lit store windows, laughing couples coming out of a cinema. What *did* she want to do with her life?

Chapter 4

Katherine—named for Sarah's mother Ekaterina, the Russian soprano and prima donna—arrived three weeks early, a wrinkled red monkey of a baby who cried pitifully much of the time. The contrast with peaches-and-cream Victoria, a full-term infant, took Sarah by surprise.

"I thought the second one would be easier," she confided to Dani. "Thank goodness you're here to help."

To compound the difficulties, Vickie resented no longer being the center of attention and regressed to wetting her pants and throwing tantrums if she didn't get her way. All this during the coldest, rainiest spring on record. Damp nappies steamed on a clothes rack in front of the perpetually lit gas fire, and the smell of regurgitated milk permeated the small apartment. Nobody was getting enough sleep.

A bright spot was that Pete's dance band had landed a weekly radio program. This meant more money and more regular hours. In addition, he had taken on the task of musical arranger for the band. His reputation in the popular music business was growing.

One June day, about noon, he rushed into the flat with an announcement.

"We're moving! I've found a house in Muswell Hill, three bedrooms and a garden, but we've got to move fast. Sarah, get dressed."

Sarah was still in her dressing gown, hair uncombed. "I've just managed to get Kathy down for a nap, and Vickie hasn't had her lunch yet. I can't go out now. You go with him, Dani."

Pete frowned at her for a moment, then shrugged. "Come on, Dani. The agent's meeting me there in half an hour."

The house was semi-detached, red brick, with bay windows and a small front garden.

"There's a garage," Dani said.

"Yes, I'm thinking of getting a car," responded Pete airily.

The agent was sheltering from the drizzle by the front door. A young man with brilliantined hair and a bow tie, he launched into his sales patter without pausing for introductions. "An ideal family residence, close to schools and shops, and very well maintained. No bomb damage." Turning to Dani and seeming not to notice her youth, he inquired, "And do you have children, Mrs. er…?"

"This is my niece," Pete replied through gritted teeth. "My wife's at home with our daughters."

"Oh." Chastened for only a moment, the young man resumed. "The kitchen has all the modern conveniences, of course, and the reception rooms are unusually spacious." He led them through the downstairs. "Now this is a bonus: a conservatory!" With a "ta-da" gesture, he indicated glass doors at the back of the sitting room leading to a small extension with windows on three sides. Through the glass, Pete and Dani could see a lawn bordered by bushes and small trees. Pete and Dani looked at each other and smiled; the same thought occurred to both of them.

"A music room for Sarah," Dani whispered.

Upstairs there were two similar-sized bedrooms, one with a bay window to the street and the other looking out over the back garden. The bathroom was twice the size of the one at the flat. The door to the third bedroom was down a couple of steps from the landing.

"This would be your room, Dani," said Pete, stepping into the center of a rectangular space with a sloping ceiling, and windows at both ends.

"But it's huge! The girls could use it as their playroom. And Sarah could have her sewing table here too." Dani, who shared a small bedroom with Victoria and her toys, couldn't imagine having this much space to herself.

"No." Pete's voice was stern. "It's for you, no one else. A room of your own."

****

An offer was made and accepted. As if an unseen hand had thrown a switch, the rain stopped and the sun came out. The doctor's suggestion that Sarah give a supplementary bottle of formula at bedtime cured Katherine's colic and allowed everyone a better night's rest. Victoria discovered words, and not just words: complete sentences. Freed from the frustrating inability to vocalize her resentment of her sister, that resentment vanished; she became a cheerful child again.

In advance of moving day, the whole family paid a visit to the new house.

"Look, Mama, flowers!" Vickie rushed past the "modern conveniences" of the kitchen and ran through the back door into the garden. "I get them for you."

"Not that one!" Sarah cried too late. Vickie grasped the stem of a rose, then pulled back, her face crumpling.

Dani reached her before the scream emerged, distracting her by leading her farther down the lawn and pointing out other wonders. By the time they rejoined Pete, Sarah, and the baby, they were standing in what the pretentious agent had called the conservatory.

"Yes, it's perfect. Thank you." Sarah reached over Katherine in Pete's arms to give her husband's cheek a kiss.

"A fresh start," Pete said. "We're going to get all new furniture. Leave that tatty utility stuff for the next tenants at the flat. You and Dani can start shopping tomorrow."

In spite of Pete's assurances that they weren't to worry about money, Dani did worry. She overcame her reluctance to venture far from home to accompany Sarah to the antique and used furniture stores in the Camden Market. They identified well-made pieces that needed a little touch-up but were cheaper and superior to the new furniture in the department store showrooms. Besides, they could buy secondhand furniture without using ration cards, still required for most goods even three years after the end of the war. Sarah had an eye for quality, having been raised in the elegance of an Art Deco apartment in Riga, and plunged into the project with enthusiasm. Pete was initially dismayed but won over when he saw the purchases in place after they moved in.

Dani refused to allow Pete to pay for any furniture for her room beyond a single bed. Since her birthday dinner she had been turning over ideas on how to earn money, buy her own things, and make a financial contribution to the household. She needed a job but feared she was unqualified for anything other than looking after babies. Sarah, seeing Dani's restlessness, kept telling her how essential she was to the little girls' care, how much she was valued. The reassurances did not soothe her. She knew *her* mother had worked outside the home—she had a clear image of Nellie in crisp white blouse and dark skirt setting off to her job at the consulate—and Sarah too, before the war, had a career as a musician with a symphony orchestra. In contrast, Dani had no talents, no skills, very little education, and a foreign accent. Thinking of "before" only increased her frustration. For the first time since coming to London, she felt the lack of someone to confide in. Loneliness crept up on her unrecognized. After all, she had the constant company of an active toddler and the frequent demands of a baby's care: how could she be lonely?

A row of small shops catering to their everyday needs was situated at the end of the street: a butcher, a greengrocer and a bakery. There was also a hairdresser—Carol's Cut and Curl—and a florist shop, stylishly named *L'Amour des Fleurs*. Doing the morning shopping, Dani paused outside the florist to breathe in the floral scent that wafted out of the open door. The August sun was warm on her back, and her basket was heavy. She stepped under the green-striped awning that shaded the shop window and looked into the dim interior. She saw ranks of buckets, each containing a different selection of flowers, leading back to a desk set between large houseplants. Her eyes met those of a woman in a white apron, standing behind the desk. Dani started to back away, embarrassed, but the woman smiled and invited her in with a gesture.

Well, I suppose I could buy a few flowers for the house, Dani thought, *although we already have lots in the garden.*

"Come on in, luv, and take a look. I haven't had a customer all morning, and it gets a bit lonely." Dani had half-expected the shopkeeper to speak with a French accent, but her voice indicated she was a Londoner.

"I expect people have plenty of flowers in their own gardens now," Dani replied.

"Yeah, you're prob'ly right. What I need is a big funeral; people don't want their garden flowers for that." The woman came out from behind the desk and started fussing with some of the arrangements. "You're new 'round here, ain't cha? I know most of 'em that lives here. Done the flowers for their weddings and funerals. *You're* not plannin' on gettin' married, are you?"

Dani laughed. She felt strangely at ease. The damp green smell and the shadowy interior suggested an overgrown garden, a pleasant contrast to the dusty street outside. Thinking she ought to buy something to justify staying longer, she looked around for a small bunch of flowers. She caught sight of a white square of card attached to the open door, unnoticed when she had entered. It read, "Part-Time Assistant Needed."

The woman saw the direction of Dani's gaze. "You lookin' for a job?"

****

Dani started at a pound a week for three days' work: Friday and Saturday, the shop's busiest days, and one other day as needed. An ideal schedule, as Pete's radio show aired on Thursday evening and he took Friday off. Even if he had another engagement on Friday or, more often, Saturday evening, he didn't need to leave until the late afternoon, so Sarah still had consistent help with the children.

Esmée—she was christened Elsie but renamed herself when she purchased the shop—and her husband Stanley lived in the apartment upstairs. Stanley was a morose man. He rose at four a.m. every day to drive the van to Covent Garden, where he selected the freshest blooms from the wholesalers. Then he returned to Muswell Hill, unloaded, and disappeared upstairs with the morning paper and a cup of tea. He reappeared at lunchtime to receive a list of deliveries from his wife, and departed again in the van. He rarely spoke to Dani. Esmée, on the other hand, loved to talk.

"Stan knows his flowers, but he's no help with customers. The war done it; before that, he was a different chap. Anyway, that's why I need an assistant. I can't be in two places at once, can I? Can't be makin' up bridal bouquets in the back room and servin' in the shop at the same time. Plus I like the company."

Esmée undertook to train Dani in all aspects of the florist business. If it were up to Dani, she would have stayed in the back room working on the special orders, but Esmée insisted she help out front as well.

"Customer service is an art, luv, and I'm an *artiste*. It's more than just ringin' up sales. It's about understanding what people want, even if they don't know it themselves. You watch me and learn."

One of the first things Dani learned was that Esmée was not good at numbers. The record of sales—top copy to the customer as a receipt, carbon copies to be totaled at the end of the day and reconciled with money in the till—was almost illegible, with scratched-out figures and multiple recalculations. Stan had provided a cheat sheet showing the correct change from one pound and ten-shilling notes for the standard prices of the flowers on sale. However, if a customer bought two bouquets or proffered a half-crown, Esmée would become flustered. If she knew the customer or he or she "looked like a decent sort" she would ask them to calculate their own change. Nevertheless, the amount in the ancient brass cash register at closing was only ever a poor approximation of the day's sales.

Before Dani's hire, Stanley would make a point of returning before five-thirty to carry out the ritual of counting up the takings and attempting to square the total with goods sold. As soon as Dani demonstrated her facility with figures, that task devolved to Dani, at least on the days she worked. In addition, several times during the day Esmée summoned Dani from the back room where she was assembling funeral wreaths. "Can you come and ring this gentleman up, please, Dani?" Having spent the requisite time discerning what the customer wanted, even if they didn't know it themselves, Esmée, the *artiste,* looked on with a smile while Dani dealt with the sordid business of payment and making change.

Toward the end of a busy day in September, Esmée drew Dani's attention to a young man hovering outside the shop window. He was neatly dressed in a tweed jacket, white shirt, and tie. He had short, sandy-brown hair and a broad open face.

"Now here's an opportunity for you to turn a casual customer into a regular. See, he wants something, but he doesn't know what. Go on, show me what you've learned."

Dani was about to point out that the young man outside wasn't even a casual customer yet when he peered in through the window, catching her eye. He smiled, and she reddened.

Esmée nodded, as if she had orchestrated his appearance. "He's comin' in. Off you go."

Dani took a breath and stepped forward. The boy—he couldn't have been older than twenty—stood hesitantly just inside the door. She could now see he had freckles, and his clothes although clean were well-worn. "Can I help you, sir?" she said in a small voice. She heard the door close as Esmée retreated to the back room.

"Yes, please. I want to buy some flowers for my aunt. She has me over for dinner every Friday. I took chocolates last time, but..." He trailed off, looking around at the tiers of buckets, each holding a single variety of blooms. "Perhaps these?" He pointed to the display nearest to the door, bunches of what Esmée called her "cheap and cheerful." Dani had assembled these little bouquets herself earlier in the day from off-cuts and leftovers of the more expensive arrangements. Priced at one shilling and sixpence, they were a colorful bestseller. Dani knew they would wilt within a day or two.

"Yes, well, how about gladioli?" Dani indicated the tall flowers, a delicate shade of mauve, that Stanley had brought in that morning. She'd been glancing at them throughout the day, a memory nagging at the edge of her consciousness. Now it came into focus: a dark room, afternoon light shafting through narrow windows onto tall flowers. The image vanished, and she blinked, returning her attention to the young man.

"They'd look smashing in a vase in front of a mirror. It'd magnify the effect, see? Very elegant." She blushed again, shocked at her own volubility.

"Oh, yes! Aunt Celia would love those. How much are they?"

"Two and six for a half-dozen stems," Dani replied.

The lad looked crestfallen. "I don't think I have enough money."

Esmée bustled in from the back, holding a bucket full of the same mauve colored gladioli like a trophy in front of her. "Dani, luv, would you mark down those old glads for me? We need to put these fresh ones out for tomorrow." She looked meaningfully at Dani, who stood confused. "I think one and six for half a dozen should shift them. Oh, do excuse me," she said, putting on a posh voice for the customer, "I didn't mean to interrupt." Having placed the "fresh" gladioli next to the "old" ones, she exited again.

Dani wrapped the flowers in tissue, adding a purple ribbon. She accepted the money for the discounted purchase, keeping her eyes lowered. Repeating his enthusiastic thanks, the young man left.

Esmée sidled up to Dani's side. "What's 'is name then?"

Dani looked at the shopkeeper in astonishment. "I've no idea."

"Never mind, luv. He'll be back. You can ask 'im then."

Chapter 5

The following Friday at closing time, Dani's head
was bent over the till drawer as she totted up the day's
takings. She looked up in surprise when the door
clattered shut. She was sure Esmée had already turned
the Open sign to Closed. The young man from the
previous week stood grinning next to the "cheap and
cheerfuls."

"Go on, I'll finish up here. You've got a customer."
Esmée nodded toward the lad.

"But…" Dani's protest faded away. She'd probably
have to start the count all over again, but she didn't mind.
She walked forward with a shy smile.

"Hello, I wanted to tell you: my aunt really loved
those glads you sold me, and that tip about putting them
in front of a mirror? It works!" He laughed. "So, I
wonder what you think I should take her this week. I'm
Sam, by the way, Samuel, well, everyone calls me
Sammy." This came out in a rush and he laughed again,
embarrassed.

"Roses are always nice," Dani replied. Sammy
looked at the long-stemmed blood-red blooms Esmée
had placed prominently near the entrance. "Guilty
flowers" she had called them, positioned to attract the
attention of a remorseful husband on his way home, and
priced accordingly. "No, not those." Dani crouched to
push aside some buckets. "I think we've—yes, these are

40

called Peace roses." She brought out a bunch of creamy blossoms, the outer petals edged in pink. Sammy leaned forward to breathe in their fragrance.

"They're lovely!"

"Yeah, they're my favorites. They're a new type of rose, named for the end of the war." Dani repeated the information Esmée had given her. She felt obliged to add, "They don't last very long as cut flowers, though, better left in the garden."

"They'll last through Shabbat dinner anyway. I'll take them. How much?"

Dani looked back at Esmée for guidance. "They're the last bunch."

"Oh, one and six then," Esmée called out gaily. "Ooh, look at the time. Take this young man's money, Dani, and then you get on home. No," when Dani gestured toward the still-uncounted cash, "I can handle this."

Dani took off her apron and hung it up in the back room. When she left the shop, she found Sammy waiting outside.

"Do you mind if I walk with you a bit? Dani, isn't it?"

She nodded, suddenly speechless without the prop of her salesgirl role.

"Is that short for something?" Sammy asked.

"Danielle," she replied.

"That sounds French. Are you from France?" He had picked up on her accent.

"No, Holland." It was too complicated to explain about Latvia, so she lapsed into silence again.

Sammy didn't seem to notice her nervousness. He lifted the roses to his face again.

41

"My Aunt Celia'll love these. I've got four aunts. They all want to look after me, since my parents died. Celia gets me every Friday, though." He chatted on, explaining that he lived with his unmarried Uncle Fred, and worked for him too, in his shoe shop in the West End. Dani looked down at her scuffed slip-ons.

"Size three, narrow. Am I right?" Sammy said.

"Yes!" She laughed.

"But I don't want to sell shoes forever. I want my own business. Have you ever seen a television?" Dani shook her head, and Sammy continued. "Soon everyone will have one, like radios now. The news, sports, entertainment—it'll all be on television. That's what I want to do, sell televisions. And record players too. They're coming out with new electrical stuff all the time, and people will want it."

Dani could think of no response. They had turned the corner into her street, and soon they would be at her front gate. She slowed her pace a little, searching for something to say. *He must think I'm an idiot,* she thought. *He won't want to see me again.*

"My parents are dead too," she blurted, then shut her mouth quickly, aghast at what she had said. It had nothing to do with televisions. *Now I've ruined it.*

But Sammy looked down at her with a look of concern. "In the war?"

She nodded, unable to find the words to explain that her father had actually died *before* the war, and she had never received proof that her mother had died at all, just disappeared in the chaos of the Nazi invasion of the Baltics in 1941. Although she still shied away from the memory of their final separation, she had gradually accepted that Nellie was lost to her.

"Mine too. A bomb. Direct hit on our house in Hackney. Both killed outright. I was at my Aunt Helen's when the air raid warning went off. So I went down the shelter with her family. Next day, when I went home—well, it was all…gone." He looked off into the distance, reliving that moment of realization.

They reached Dani's house. She stopped, still unable to think of anything to say to detain him. For the first time, Sammy looked uncomfortable, staring around at the houses and shifting his feet.

"Look, would you like to go to the pictures?" He spoke so quickly that Dani did not understand him at first. Was he asking if she liked art? When she didn't immediately reply, Sammy continued. "On Sunday? I could come and pick you up about two? We could go to a matinee."

"Oh." He was asking her out! Her stomach gave a little lurch. "Yes, yes, that would be nice. Sunday at two. Goodbye, then." She turned and floated up the path to the front door. He was still standing looking after her. She gave a little wave, and he waved back, smiling broadly.

"Who was that boy who walked you home?" Sarah was waiting inside the hall.

"His name's Sammy. He's a customer, and he wasn't walking me home; he was just coming along in the same direction." Dani felt a need to protect her nascent relationship from Sarah's inquisition. She wanted to keep it to herself and go over everything Sammy had said to make sure she wasn't mistaken: he had asked her out!

"Well, why did he turn around and go back down the street, if he was 'just coming along in the same direction'?" But Sarah was smiling, pleased that Dani had found a friend. "Don't worry, I won't tell Pete. He'd tease you to death."

****

On Sunday morning, Dani washed her hair and polished her shoes. At lunch, she pushed the food around, too nervous to eat much. Pete noticed and was about to comment when Sarah shot him an angry glance. He shrugged and speared another carrot.

When the doorbell rang at exactly two o'clock, Dani flew to answer it, calling over her shoulder, "I'm off now, see you later!" leaving Sarah to explain to Pete where she was going and with whom.

In the end, they decided the weather was too nice to go to the cinema. Summer had extended its lease into September, so they went for a stroll on Hampstead Heath instead. Dani had not been there since the move to the house in Muswell Hill. The walk was longer than from Highgate, but Sammy filled the time describing his extended family. Celia, Helen, and Barbara were his mother's sisters. Celia and Helen were married, but Dani instantly forgot the husbands' names. Barbara was unmarried, the bluestocking: "Really clever, got a university degree. She teaches science at Godolphin and Latymer School." Dani had never heard of the school but she gathered it was a prestigious academy for girls in West London. Uncle Fred, Sammy's employer, and another aunt were on his father's side. There were hordes of cousins, too, like a litter of puppies, tumbling over each other. Dani lost track of names and who was married to whom; it sounded lovely and chaotic at the same time.

They had reached the gender-segregated bathing

ponds on the edge of the Heath. Some swimmers, especially in the men's pool, splashed and shouted, while others attempted sedate laps. They watched for a while, enjoying the sun on their backs as they leaned over the fence.

"We should have brought our bathing suits. There's mixed bathing at the Parliament Hill Lido," Sammy said.

"I don't know how to swim," Dani answered in a hurry.

"I can teach you."

"I don't have a swimsuit." Dani began to panic. The water looked dark and bottomless, a threatening and unknown element.

"I'll buy you one," Sammy offered with a grin.

"No!"

Realizing he had pushed too far, Sammy retreated into silence. He had never met a girl like Dani before. The girls he grew up with in the East End gave as good as they got. If they didn't like something they let you know about it, and reinforced their opinion with a shove. Dani was a forest animal, easily scared, quiet and careful in her words and movements. He needed to be careful too if he wasn't to frighten her.

They strolled up the hill toward Kenwood House and turned to enjoy the view over the city. Dani remembered Sarah's surge of nostalgia for Latvia when they had come here before with Vickie, and how she had walked away. Sammy talked so easily about his extended family. She wished she could reciprocate, but memories of her grandparents and her mother were still wrapped up with the pain of separation; she was afraid she would break down in tears if she started to describe them to Sammy, and that would be embarrassing. Still, she felt she owed him some information in exchange for his sharing, so she told him about Sarah, Pete, and the little girls, about the move up from a rented flat to their own house, and Pete's job with the band.

"I love that program! I listen to it every Thursday!" Sammy was thrilled to discover that Dani's uncle was a radio star.

"My Aunt Sarah's a musician too," Dani said, happy to have landed on a subject that impressed Sammy. "She used to play violin with a symphony orchestra before the war. Now she just plays with her friends at the synagogue. They're very good, but it's not for the public."

"So you're Jewish too. I thought you might be." Sammy was pleased.

"Well, I don't know. I suppose I am because my mother was Jewish—Sarah's her sister—but we never did Jewish things, holidays and stuff, and when I lived with my father's parents in Holland, we were Christian." She did not add that her grandparents instructed her that she must not even talk about her mother: it was too dangerous.

The benches were all full, crowds of Londoners enjoying a Sunday out on what might prove to be the last warm day of the year, so they sat on the grass. Sammy picked up her hand and held it gently in both of his.

"You've lost so much. I used to feel resentful that I was never left alone after my parents died. I was swept up by the family, wrapped in great blankets of love, not allowed the time to *feel* grief or loss or... I don't know. I was probably just a sulky teenager, angry at the world." He looked at her, his face serious. "But you've gone through so much more, and even younger than me. I'd like to know about it, about your mother, about *you*."

He was close, eyes still fixed on hers. She could feel his breath on her face. Then he kissed her. His lips were soft. She leaned into him, and his arms came around her. When the kiss ended, she fitted her head against his chest under his chin. She felt secure, protected by his encircling arms, his heartbeat strong and steady in her ear.

"I will tell you. I'll tell you everything, I promise. My mother's name was Nellie…"

Chapter 6

Dani wanted a quiet wedding, but Sammy's family didn't know the word "quiet." She had hoped the King's death in February might have toned down the aunts' expectations for "a real knees-up," but they entertained no opposition to their plans for a party.

"Sammy's the first of the kids to get married and we're going to do it up right," said Aunt Helen. "We've waited long enough."

The engagement had lasted four years. Not because either Dani or Sammy had any doubt about their love for each other, but Dani didn't want to start married life in a relative's spare bedroom and it had taken that long for Sammy's name to edge up the London County Council's housing list. As he had been bombed out of his home in 1941, Sammy had a right to public housing, but so did many others, and families took priority. In January 1952, the notice finally arrived: on April 1, they could take possession of a two-bedroom flat in one of the new blocks in Stratford, the borough just east of Sammy's former home in Hackney. The wedding date was set for the following Sunday, April 6.

After a skirmish over who would pay for what—"The bride's family pays, it's traditional," Pete insisted—it was settled that Sammy's family would cover the catering, and the band, flowers, and dress would be Sarah and Pete's responsibility. Pete selected five of the best-looking members of his usually invisible radio dance orchestra to play for the reception in exchange for a free meal and all the beer they could drink. In spite of the early season, Esmée found enough pink and white blooms to decorate every horizontal surface in the hall, and to construct a bouquet as big as a centurion's shield for Dani.

Sarah took charge of the dress. Rationing was finally over, but fine fabrics were still hard to find.

"I'm not having you wed in parachute silk," Sarah declared. During the war, German parachutes from downed bomber crews had provided a popular dress material. "I'll ask around." She discovered that one of her string quartet colleagues had inherited a wedding gown, an Edwardian confection of ivory lace.

"It's a good thing you're skinny. This was meant to be worn with a corset." Sarah pinned and tucked, then stood back with head tilted to judge the effect. "Lovely! What's the matter?" Dani's shoulders were shaking and her eyes were screwed shut. "Oh, sweetheart! Wedding nerves, I expect." Sarah helped her niece down from the stool on which she was standing for the fitting.

Dani sniffled. "It's not nerves. I just—I miss her— Mama. She should be here," she sobbed. Sarah, now weeping too, wrapped her arms around the girl. Dani was usually so self-contained, never talking about her losses. When Sarah reminisced about life in Riga before the war, Dani turned away or changed the subject. Of course, Sarah reasoned, Dani had only spent a year with the Kutners. Perhaps those memories were overlaid by her experiences in Holland, which had continued much longer, but Sarah always worried that Dani was nursing her wounds in silence, suppressing the pain and anger in an unhealthy way. Now she was relieved as well as moved by Dani's tears.

"I know." Sarah pressed her cheek against Dani's lowered head. "They should all be here."

A week later, as Dani stood between Sarah and Pete waiting for the signal to approach the wedding canopy where Sammy was waiting, she whispered their names: *Mama, Papa, Grandkat, Grandfather, Oma, Opa...* Then, searching her memory: *Berta, Ivan, Marta, the consul, Madame...*

****

The Stratford flat, their home for eight years, began to manifest signs of its shoddy post-war construction: window frames buckled and cracks radiated down the walls. They hid the worst with art posters, and re-covered their hand-me-down furniture with inexpensive fabric to make the place their own. Dani missed the garden at Pete and Sarah's Muswell Hill house, but she did her best with house plants and fresh flowers from the shop. She continued to work for Esmée, increasing her hours and becoming ever more indispensable. They saved her earnings and as much of Sammy's as they could toward the electrical appliance store he dreamed of owning. Looking back, these were happy years in spite of the lack of money. Family parties provided their entertainment, and summer days out to the coast at Southend substituted for an away-from-home vacation.

The only sadness was their childlessness. Dani suffered three miscarriages, the last in 1959 when she was three months along.

"Perhaps we should look into adopting," Sammy suggested. He had brought Dani home from the hospital in Pete's car, almost carried her to their only armchair, and now hovered with a blanket to tuck over her lap. Dani had hardly said a word on the way home.

"I don't need that." She motioned him away. "I'll be all right in a bit. I just want to rest."

"Maybe it's this place," Sammy looked around the cramped living room. "You can't get the windows open for a breath of fresh air, and the racket from the neighbors all the time...We should move."

"Well, we will, just as soon as you get your shop started. I can go back to work next week—"

"No!" Sammy's voice was firm. "On your feet all day, and two buses to get to and from; I don't want you to go back. Your health's more important than scrimping every last penny for the shop. I've made up my mind."

Dani sighed. They'd had this discussion before, but nothing had changed. They were trapped in a circle of rising property prices and tight credit. Whenever they thought they had identified a suitable retail space, preferably with living quarters above, the bank manager informed them regretfully that the down payment needed was fifteen percent not ten, or the estate agent told them another buyer had offered cash. Their nest egg was not growing fast enough.

They'd talked about adopting a child before, too. Dani had gone as far as picking up some literature from the Jewish Adoption Agency. Because there were so few newborn babies available for adoption, the requirements were daunting: proof of income level and savings, standards for living accommodation, references and home visits. The agency showed a clear preference for middle-class couples who owned their own home.

"Sammy, I just want to sleep. Let's not go over all this now."

In spite of Sammy's declaration, Dani returned to work at *L'Amour des Fleurs* the following Monday. Esmée mothered her, making endless pots of tea and keeping up a stream of chatter that required no response. At first, she insisted Dani sit to assemble floral arrangements in the back room, rather than stand to serve customers in the shop, although soon her need for Dani's skills at calculating change and cashing out the till overcame her solicitude. Stanley, morose as ever, continued to drive the pre-dawn runs to Covent Garden and made deliveries in the afternoons. Over the years he had become more comfortable in Dani's presence, stopping occasionally to watch her at work and nod his approval before disappearing upstairs to their flat. Esmée confided that she and Stanley were childless "because of the war." Stanley had been a POW for four years, first in Italy, then Germany.

"He only weighed seven stone when they liberated the camp. Had to stay in a military hospital in Belgium for six weeks before they'd bring him home. He's never been the same since."

Although she never expressed it, Dani felt a sort of camaraderie with Stanley. They both kept their emotions to themselves and found comfort in the daily routine of work. She thought their wartime experience was similar in a way. She had also been confined—not in a prison camp, but by the secrecy and isolation necessary to keep her Jewishness from notice by the occupying Nazis. She knew that Londoners endured privations and danger too, but their war bound them together and created community—the famous "Blitz spirit." Sammy's family easily shared their memories, even of the terrible night when Sammy's parents were killed; talking about the past seemed to cheer rather than distress them. Dani remained silent, not because she didn't remember, but because she hoarded her memories, especially of her mother, afraid that telling them out loud would dilute them somehow, cause them to fade like colored cloth left out in sunlight.

The months slipped by; a new year and a new decade began. January was always a slow month for flowers. No one had money left after the Christmas holidays for exotic imported blooms—the only ones available. It was not a popular month for weddings, and only the regular demand for funeral wreaths kept the shop afloat. Sometimes Esmée told Dani not to come in until lunchtime. "You enjoy a nice lie-in, dear. I can manage."

Dani was surprised but not upset to find the sign in the shop door turned to "closed" when she arrived at one o'clock. She used her key to let herself in, and went through to the room at the back where they assembled the floral arrangements.

"Esmée! I'm here," she called up the stairs. There was no response. She went through the motions of opening the store, checking the till for change, and rearranging the few buckets of flowers, with increasing unease. She was on her way up the stairs to Esmée and Stanley's flat when the telephone rang in the shop. She hurried back down to pick it up.

"Dani?" Esmée was crying. "It's Stan. He's had a stroke. I'm at the hospital. I can't leave. Can you—" She broke down.

"Of course, I'll look after things here. How is he? Is he conscious?" Dani pictured Stanley's face, pale against white hospital sheets, his thinning hair, his eyes closed.

She thought of Oma, that last morning, laid out on her bed in the cottage near Rotterdam, the flowers Dani had gathered to place in her grandmother's cold hands.

Esmée took a moment to regain control.

"He hasn't spoken. They don't know if he'll ever— we just have to wait."

Stanley didn't die, but he lost the power of speech, and his ability to walk. He could move one hand and make twitching movements with his left eye, a kind of suggestive wink that was completely out of character. These limited abilities allowed him to communicate basic needs and answer yes-no questions.

Esmée struggled on through the spring, relying on a local greengrocer to add her order to his early morning run to Covent Garden Market, and on Dani for managing the shop and making up the arrangements, bouquets, and wreaths while she looked after Stanley upstairs. By June, she faced the fact that the situation was unsustainable.

"I'm exhausted. You're exhausted. The customers are drifting away. We can't offer deliveries. Bill—bless his heart—doesn't know a peony from a petunia. We can't go on like this."

"Maybe I could learn to drive," Dani suggested. She wanted to help, but the London traffic scared her, and she really hoped Esmée would find another solution.

"No. I've made up my mind. I got a letter from my sister in Sussex. Now my niece is married, she's on her own and has plenty of room. She runs a little farm shop; I could help her with that. And with whatever we can get for this place..." Esmée looked speculatively at Dani. "I don't suppose you and Sammy would like to take over the business?"

"What?" Dani's mouth fell open. Sammy and

flowers? "Um, well, I don't know…"

It had all fallen into place with a rapidity that made Dani dizzy. No, Sammy was *not* interested in investing their nest egg in a florist shop, but the location was perfect, and the living accommodation above the shop was spacious and well-maintained. Nesse Appliances' flagship store opened in November, in time for the Christmas shoppers. That year, everyone wanted a television set, and Sammy could hardly keep them in stock. Refrigerators were another novelty that sold well: little waist-high cabinets with a tiny freezer compartment to store an ice tray. He sold toasters and electric kettles too, but these were slower to catch on with a public used to boiling water on the stove and toasting bread on a fork over a coal fire. Sammy enlisted one of his male cousins to help steer customers around the cramped displays.

Dani kept busy too, redecorating the flat, making new curtains and cushion covers. The apartment possessed the same number of rooms as their Stratford home, but these were much bigger and airier, with tall ceilings and sash windows that opened. Sarah came with her to the Camden Market where they searched for finds amongst the second-hand furniture, as they had done when furnishing the house in Muswell Hill twelve years before. Victoriana had become fashionable in the interim, and restorable pieces were scarce, but the outings were fun for both of them. With Vicky and Kathy now in school, Sarah regained the energy and enthusiasm Dani remembered from Riga. Pete's career successes continued to mount up, so she had the money to indulge her niece and her own good taste.

Dani's sense of guilt that she and Sammy were benefitting from her friends' misfortune was dissipated somewhat by a Christmas card from Esmée. On the outside, a plump robin redbreast sat on a snowy branch; inside Esmée's familiar scrawl filled the white space around the pre-printed greeting.

Hope you are well. We are settling in lovely at Mabel's. We got a wheelchair from the Women's Voluntary Service and on nice days I push Stan into the village. Everyone knows us here now and stops to chat. In the spring I will do floral arrangements out of Mabel's shop. She has a big garden and I talked to some of the locals who grow flowers too. It will keep me busy. Stan sends his love.

Dani waited until March, until she was quite sure, before writing back.

Dear Esmée and Stanley,

Thank you for your Christmas card. I am glad you are well and country life suits you. The shop is doing well. Sammy is very busy but happy. I have some good news. I am going to have a baby in July. I feel well, different from the last times, and I think this time it will be all right. Fingers crossed. Much love, Dani.

Sammy came up behind her as she licked the flap of the envelope. He bent to wrap his arms around her and kiss her hair.

"Does this mean I can start telling everyone?"

Dani laughed.

"Don't you think they've already guessed? Your aunt Helen's been dropping hints for weeks, and Sarah's started knitting again."

Sammy's smile nearly split his face.

"It's like we've turned a corner, come out of a tunnel, like—I don't know…"

"Happiness," said Dani. "I wish my mama could be

here, so I could tell her the news." And for the first time, the memory of her mother's face did not hurt.

Part Two: *1939*

Chapter 7

Seagulls hovered above a monochrome landscape, pinned by swirling winds against a gray-white sky. The top of the dyke etched an arrow-straight line between the dark tumble of gravel down to the canal on one side, and the empty fields on the other—fields that stretched to an indistinct horizon where the land gave way to the Rhine estuary and ultimately the North Sea. The monotony of the landscape was broken here and there by clusters of low buildings—farms and small settlements. The day—Sunday—and the wintry season kept workers from the fields. Except for the lone cyclist on the dyke, no human forms were visible. It was hard to believe the city of Rotterdam with its busy port was only a few kilometers away.

Nellie Loesseps leaned forward over the handlebars of her bicycle, trying to present a smaller target to the keen March gusts. Over the whine of the wind and the tick of the spokes, Nellie heard her daughter's sudden laughter. Dani was crammed into the slatted wooden child seat fixed to the back wheel of the bicycle. At six years old, she was really too big for it. Nellie glanced over her shoulder and caught a glimpse of Dani's head angled back to watch her mother's hair as it finally escaped the restraint of hair pins to stream out like a dark pennant. Dani's red coat was the one spot of color in this grayscale landscape; her pleasure in their wild ride lifted Nellie's heart.

Nellie started singing—wordless songs thrown into the wind. When her husband Henrijk had been alive, and weather and time permitted, the little family would often bicycle across the neatly gridded Dutch countryside, stop at a village market for beer, bread, and cheese, then pedal on to the coast. In the lee of the sand dunes, they would spread a picnic, and the child would nap on a blanket while her parents took turns reading aloud to each other, poetry or nineteenth-century novels. On the journey home, Nellie's singing used to lull Dani, resting against her back, into a doze that lasted until she was tucked into her own little bed at home.

Thoughts like these were an indulgence that Nellie allowed herself sparingly. She had come to Holland from her native Latvia at the age of seventeen and was widowed before she turned twenty-five. The early years, with their sweet memories, were separated from the present by a cruel gulf: months of watching Henrijk die of tuberculosis, then the fight to keep a struggling printing business afloat. They once had dreams of converting it into a publishing house—he had loved literature as much as she did—but now all she could do to eke out a living was print church newsletters and advertising flyers. Rather than dwell on the past, she forced herself to concentrate on building a future for herself and Dani.

Although widowhood had compelled her to become practical, Nellie had been a romantic dreamer in high school. She did well enough in her academic work but disappointed her intellectual father and artistic mother because she lacked the fire—either for politics or music—that animated their lives. Instead, she hid herself away in the bedroom she shared with her younger sister Sarah, "her head stuck in a book," as her mother said dismissively. So, when she graduated from high school, her parents suggested she go to live with relatives in Rotterdam for a year or two, to help with the young children of the household and to see something of the world, in the hope that she would come back to Riga energized and engaged, ready to plunge into her studies at the University.

Her family was Jewish, but of a liberal variety. The traditional observances lay lightly on their lifestyle, as they did on the majority of Latvia's large Jewish population. Since the Teutonic Knights had granted them a safe haven in the thirteenth century, Latvian Jews had integrated themselves peacefully into every area of society. However, the cousins with whom Nellie went to live in Rotterdam were much more conservative. Except for the necessity of carrying on their jewelry business, they kept themselves separate from the wider community, and took seriously the religious rules laid down by their rabbi. They were scandalized by Nellie's forays into the city and further afield to go to concerts and visit museums. When she announced that she had met and fallen in love with a *goy*, a man twice her age who owned and ran a small printing business, her uncle wrote to her parents of his shame and distress. That Nellie, while in his care, should so stray away from their tradition hurt him much more severely than it did Nellie's parents. They were inclined to see this adventure as the awakening of passion, a quality they had long hoped for in their dreamy-eyed, reclusive daughter.

"Hold on tight. We're going down!"

Dani gripped the belt of Nellie's navy-blue raincoat. They reached a ramp and coasted down from the top of the dyke to join the road as it approached a cluster of whitewashed houses, the village where Henrijk's parents—Dani's Oma and Opa—lived.

"Not far now, my love." Nellie stopped the bike and, without dismounting, twisted her hair back into a rough bun, skewering it with the few hairpins that had not been lost to the wind. "Are you all right?"

"Yes. That was fun!"

They went on more sedately now, protected from the wind. After a hundred yards or so, they stopped outside the gate of a cottage with blue shutters and door. While Nellie lifted Dani down and secured the bicycle inside the low stone wall, the door opened and a small elderly woman with white hair held out her arms in welcome. A man of similar age and coloring with a matching smile appeared behind her. Dani ran up the short path and launched herself into her grandmother's embrace.

"We came along the top! The wind went whoosh and undid Mama's hair!"

"Run along to the kitchen and get warm. I've made a cake for you!" Laughing, Oma turned to her daughter-in-law and kissed her heartily on both cheeks. Then she drew back and reached a finger to brush off some moisture from Nellie's cheek.

"What is it?"

"Nothing. The wind. It made my eyes water, that's all."

"Well, come on in." The women followed Opa and Dani down a short hallway to the kitchen at the back of the house. This was the obvious center of activity, with its old-fashioned tiled stove and walls lined with shelves on which copper saucepans, jars of preserves, blue-and-white Delft pottery, and mysterious dark glass bottles jostled each other in colorful confusion. The table was spread with a red-and-white-checkered cloth, and in the center an apple cake sat, glazed with honey, still warm and fragrant from the oven. Dani's eyes widened and her mouth formed an O of pleasure. The adults laughed again, and once Nellie and Dani's outer clothing had been dispensed with, they all settled around the table to enjoy the treat.

Conversation followed its familiar pattern. Between mouthfuls of cake, Dani gave a detailed account of her kindergarten activities, and showed off her skills with numbers and letters in the exercise book Oma produced. Nellie and Oma discussed Oma's plans for the garden when the weather finally warmed up. Opa remained quiet as always, his hands working on a little carving of an animal—a fox or a dog perhaps, it was too soon to tell—his bright eyes glancing up to rest on his granddaughter's face for a moment, then back to the wood and whittling knife in his lap. Second cups of coffee were poured, more compliments paid to the apple cake—"Oh, no, I couldn't eat another bite, delicious as it is"—and finally, they lapsed into a comfortable silence, punctuated by small noises from under the table where Dani was playing with the cat.

"What is it?" Oma asked again, this time not to be put off with an excuse about the wind. Nellie started. She had been gazing at nothing, thinking of the decision she had made. Although this was the reason she and Dani had come today, she was still uncertain how to broach the subject. Now Oma, gentle as ever, but persistent, was forcing the issue.

"I've had an offer for the press. It's not a lot of money—they just want the machinery for spare parts, I think." She hesitated. Oma looked at her steadily. Opa's hands were still. Even Dani, under the table, was quiet. "I'm thinking of accepting. I...I've decided to move back to Riga."

Keeping the printing business going was more than she could handle, even with help from Henrijk's parents. She was too young, too foreign, as well as the wrong sex to earn the trust of conservative Rotterdam customers. Even operating the unwieldy iron letterpress was too much for her small frame, and she could not afford to pay a helper. When the owner of a rival print shop visited her at the end of a frustrating week, she had initially demurred. The offer was ridiculously low, and she wanted time to explore other options. But several days later, when she arrived at the shop to find "Jews Out!" scrawled across the door, she panicked. Anti-Semitism had been growing in Holland since the Nazis had taken over in neighboring Germany. The relatives Nellie had lived with when she first came to Holland had decamped to New York more than a year before, but she had never been directly threatened until now. After cleaning off the offensive lettering, she called the would-be purchaser and accepted his offer. She had said nothing of this to Dani or the old people, and had debated the decision to move back to Latvia for some weeks while the sale went forward, accusing herself of cowardice.

She rushed on now, hurrying to justify what she knew would be painful news. "We can live with my parents. I think I'd be able to find work with one of the trading companies. It's been such a struggle here since

Henrijk... I miss Latvia, my family—I don't mean that you aren't family, you've both been so kind—it's just that..."

Nellie was crying in earnest now. Oma folded her into her arms, weeping too. Dani emerged from under the edge of the tablecloth, her eyes wide, and joined in the embrace.

"It's all right. I understand. Holland has become a sad place for you. I wish it wasn't so, that you would stay. We will miss you so much." The old woman hugged Nellie and Dani to her for a moment longer before she pulled away, attempting a smile. "But you will always have a home here, if you ever need one. And we'll write to each other, won't we? Dani, you too. I want to hear all about your new life in Riga. Do you promise to send me drawings?"

Dani nodded solemnly.

"And I'll write too. Mama will help me, won't you?"

"Yes, of course we'll write. We'll never forget you!"

Nellie was relieved that she had broken the news. She had been worried that Henrijk's parents would try to convince her to stay in Holland, and unsure whether she would be able to resist them. Now, she felt a rush of optimism and confidence. She chattered excitedly about the journey: they would go by boat from Amsterdam, through the Skagerak, the strait between Denmark and Sweden, and into the Baltic Sea. She described her parents' apartment and reminisced about life in Riga.

Only Opa cast a shadow over the afternoon. He had said nothing at Nellie's announcement, returning eventually to his carving. The twilight was advancing, and Nellie was helping Dani into her coat for the return journey to their little flat over the printing business when he spoke.

"That madman Hitler will never be satisfied until he rules all Europe. Someone must take a stand against him, but that means war. I worry for all of us."

Nellie paused in buttoning Dani's coat and looked up into the old man's face. She wondered if he understood more than he said about her situation.

"Henrijk worried about another war too. Surely, it won't come to that? After the last one, how could anyone—especially the Germans—allow it to happen?"

Opa sighed and shook his head, but said no more, retreating into his customary silence.

Nellie went to kiss her father-in-law goodbye.

"We must hurry to get back before dark. At least the wind will be at our back this time."

Chapter 8

After the move to Riga, Nellie no longer sang wordless songs into the wind. She and her daughter were city dwellers now. No bicycle rides along windswept dykes, just noisy streets and tall apartment buildings. Her mother, Ekaterina, was the singer in the Riga household. She had trained in Vienna during *la belle époque* and often stopped whatever she was doing to break into a Verdi aria, hands clasped beneath her bosom in traditional soprano stance, although her voice had drifted into the *mezzo* range now. She was Russian by birth but declared herself "Italian in spirit." She had named Nellie after Nellie Melba, the most famous singer of her youth, and her younger daughter Sarah after Sarah Bernhardt, an actress not a singer but one whose histrionics provided a model for Ekaterina's performance style.

When Dani first arrived in Riga, Ekaterina told her that she didn't want to be called "grandmother."

"I find it hard to believe I'm a mother sometimes, much less a grandmother," she said. After some experiments, they settled on Grankat, "Kat" being her husband Simon Kutner's pet name for her. She had given up her operatic career when the family moved back from Paris to newly independent Latvia in 1920 so that Simon could take up his professorship at the National University, but she remained in all essentials a *diva*. A large woman, taller than her wiry husband, she favored long scarves and fringed shawls, which she would fling dramatically over her shoulder to punctuate her pronouncements. She had a circle of friends in what passed for Riga's artistic set. As she was a spectacular cook, these polyglot characters often crowded the apartment, swapping stories of their glory days in Paris or Vienna before age, penury, or pure chance (but *never* lack of talent) washed them up in Latvia. After the meal, guests usually staged an impromptu musical or dance performance.

The music lessons that Nellie's sister Sarah and her husband Piotr taught to add to their slim salaries as musicians in the Latvian National Symphony Orchestra contributed to the cacophony in the apartment. Sarah was a violinist and Piotr played the clarinet. They occupied the second bedroom in the apartment, while Nellie and Dani shared a sleeper sofa in the room that otherwise served as Simon's study. The living arrangements were not as cramped as they might sound. The building was a turn-of-the-century *art nouveau* masterpiece, with high ceilings and generous dimensions. The Kutner apartment was on the second floor and enjoyed views over the Esplanade, one of Riga's many parks.

In addition to music, the rooms reverberated with animated discussions led by Nellie's father. His subject was political philosophy. If no colleagues or students dropped by to put the world to rights over cigarettes and homemade vodka, he continued the argument with himself. A lifelong socialist, as well as a Latvian nationalist, he existed in perpetual conflict. In the absence of an adult audience, he explained his dilemma to little Dani, who, fascinated by her grandfather's eyebrows which gyrated independently like drunken caterpillars, would creep up onto the professor's lap.

"You see, child, my heart is full of pride when I think of Latvia's independence, after all those centuries of occupation and exploitation by Tsarist Russia, the German aristocracy, the Poles! But my head remains convinced by the Marxist premise that nation states must wither away in the full fruition of the Revolution!"

Dani nodded, her gaze fixed on his forehead. But, lacking a sufficient grasp of Hegelian dialectic, or, more likely, an understanding of German, which Simon had chosen as sufficiently close to Dutch to be the best language to communicate with his granddaughter, she could only stroke his wild gray hair in an attempt to calm his evident frustration.

Dani had adjusted to the carnival of life *chez* Kutner with the flexibility of childhood. She delighted in the attention of four adults who, in addition to her mother, were ready to entertain her or answer her questions. However, Nellie found it more difficult to adapt to the noisy chaos of the apartment after the quiet domesticity of the rooms that she, Henrijk and Dani had shared over the printing business. When she could, she retreated to the study-bedroom, intending to read, but often sitting with a book unopened in her lap, rehashing the reasons for leaving Holland, her thoughts bouncing between regret for the past and conviction that she had acted for the best.

****

As they had returned to Latvia so close to the end of the academic year, Nellie decided that Dani should not enroll in school until September. In the meantime, she tutored Dani in Lettish, the Latvian language, so that she would be able to keep up when she started her schooling.

Dani understood some Lettish—Nellie had chattered to her in her native tongue since Dani was a baby—but she did not speak it. Nellie's family spoke Latvian and Russian interchangeably at home, often mixing the languages in a single sentence and adding a French or German expression when it seemed apt. Dani soaked up this mélange with childlike ease, but Nellie feared her daughter might be disadvantaged and perhaps ridiculed by schoolmates with a less international background. So she instituted a routine of extended morning walks during which mother and daughter conversed only in Lettish. These rambles also served to introduce Dani to her new home: the red brick columns of the National University where Simon held his position as Professor of Political Philosophy, the art museum and the opera house, built in the same gracious nineteenth-century style, and the many churches, Catholic, Lutheran and Orthodox.

For all her eagerness to see Dani adjust to Latvian life, Nellie was also determined that her daughter not lose touch with her Dutch roots. A few weeks after their arrival in Riga, she announced that they needed to register formally as Dutch citizens.

It was springtime. The parks that striped the city wore a kaleidoscope of greens. The annual choir festival was in progress, and beautiful sounds flowed from every open church door. The freshness of new growth infected everything. Even Nellie seemed eager to invest fully in a new beginning, as they dressed for their visit to the Netherlands consulate.

"There! Now you look like a proper Dutch schoolgirl." Nellie had selected a blue dress for Dani, with puffed sleeves and smocking on the yoke, and had forced her wild curls into braids tied with matching blue ribbons. Nellie wore her usual uniform of dark blue skirt and white blouse, to which she added a brimmed straw hat with a red-and-white band. "Dutch national colors," she pointed out.

They left the apartment, crossed Elizabetes Street, and entered the Esplanade. The park, with its willow-lined sandy alleys now looking their springtime best, was a gathering point for Rigans. Soldiers drilled weekdays on the central plaza, bands played Sunday afternoon concerts there, and firework displays marked each national holiday. The sun glinted off the cupolas of the Orthodox cathedral to the south, and birdsong eclipsed the traffic noise. As she walked hand in hand with her daughter, Nellie thought it would be impossible not to feel optimistic on such a day.

Leaving the park, they crossed a busy boulevard and soon reached another park, one of a string bordering the Pilsetas Canal. The waterside parks formed a shady green barrier between the New Town, its buildings ornamented with *art nouveau*, and the Old Town, a warren of winding narrow streets with fragments of medieval fortifications and gothic church towers appearing above the rooflines like random jagged teeth. The far boundary of the Old Town was the River Daugava, broad and slow-moving, Riga's artery to the Baltic Sea.

On this day, they were not going as far as the river. They penetrated only a few yards into the Old Town before Nellie, consulting the paper on which she had written the consulate's address, pointed to a forbidding stone edifice, a couple of centuries old. The Dutch tricolor fluttered above massive double oak doors opening directly onto the street. As Nellie paused, considering the large iron bell pull, one of the doors opened and an elderly man, dressed in peasant smock and trousers tucked Cossack-style into felt boots, emerged carrying a straw broom. He acknowledged them with such a solemn bow that, for a moment and in spite of his costume and the broom, Nellie thought this might be the consul himself. She spoke rather diffidently in Dutch.

"Sir, we are here to register as Dutch subjects."

The old man nodded, then confusingly shook his head. Finally, he said a greeting in Russian and, with a sweep of his arm, invited them to enter.

"That's not the consul." Nellie whispered as she led Dani inside. They found themselves in a large entrance hall, tiled in a checkerboard of black and white marble. An imposing stone staircase curved upward. Nellie noticed a small figure seated on the top step, but because of the obscuring banisters, she could not tell if it was a boy or girl, or make an estimate of the child's age. Dani followed her mother's gaze and locked eyes with the figure peering through the gap. Meanwhile the Cossack—as Nellie named him to herself—was speaking through a door to the left of the entrance to whoever occupied the room beyond.

At first glance, the consul was not a prepossessing figure. He emerged from his office still struggling into his suit jacket. His face was round and shiny, his fair hair receding, and his pale eyes blinked rapidly behind wire-rimmed glasses. Then, as he approached them with his hand outstretched, he smiled, a disarmingly boyish smile that immediately put Nellie at ease.

"Hello, I'm Richard Vandercam. It's so good to

meet you."

"Nellie Loesseps. Yes, good to meet you too." If puzzled by his enthusiastic welcome, Nellie was determined not to show it.

"I'm afraid everything's in a terrible mess, but I'm sure you'll soon sort it out." Then, turning to Dani with that charming smile, "I didn't know you were bringing an assistant, but she's very welcome, and there's plenty of room. Come, let me show you to your office."

With a hand under her elbow, and still apologizing for heaven knows what, he guided Nellie into the room that twinned his office on the other side of the entrance. Dani followed. Nellie finally managed to interject a protest.

"I think there's been a mistake. I came to register my daughter and myself as Dutch subjects. I've brought our passports. Here they are." She extracted the documents from her purse and thrust them at the consul.

"Oh, dear! I'm so sorry! I thought—I was expecting…You see, I've been looking for a secretary, and someone was supposed to come today. At least, I was told there might be someone…You can't imagine how difficult it is to find anyone in Riga with secretarial skills who speaks Dutch. Well, maybe you *can* imagine. Anyway, I do apologize for the mix-up. Come into my office. Would you like some coffee?" He broke off to speak in Russian to the Cossack, who had been watching the whole exchange with amusement, and who now, with a theatrical sigh, made his way to a door at the rear of the entrance hall that evidently led to the kitchen quarters. As they trailed the consul back to his office, there was a movement at the top of the stairs.

"Berta! Are you hiding up there? Come down and

meet our visitors." They heard a high-pitched giggle and the pit-a-pat of a child's retreating footsteps. "My daughter's rather shy, I'm afraid."

The consul had not exaggerated when he said the place was in a muddle. Every surface and much of the floor of his office was covered with piles of books and files. He cleared off two chairs for the visitors and then rummaged through the layers on his desk until he found the ledger he was searching for. He transcribed the details from their passports into it, together with other information that he extracted in an easy, conversational way, interspersed with self-deprecating and humorous comments, taking care to include Dani without talking down to her. He seemed excited to learn that Nellie's father was a professor at the University.

"I wonder if he could help me get a library pass? I'm trying to track down some sources, and I've a feeling the University might have them. I should explain: most of this"—he gestured at the mess—"is my research into folk tales. I've been collecting them for years at different postings around Europe, but the Baltic is a new area for me, and a particularly rich one, I think." The consul sighed. "I'm afraid you'll think I'm not very professional, going on about my hobby like this, but frankly, my diplomatic duties in Riga are not especially challenging and leave me with time on my hands." He appeared to pull himself together, clasped his hands, and leaned forward. "What are your plans, now you're back in Riga, Mrs. Loesseps? Are you going to look for work?"

"I hope so, once Dani is settled in school. I handled the correspondence and accounts for my husband's business, and I speak Russian and French as well as

Dutch and Lettish, so maybe one of the trading companies in town might have something I could do."

"I believe destiny brought you here today! I need someone with exactly the qualifications you possess. Why not come and work for me? It would be about half consular clerical duties and half research assistant work—my folklore studies. What do you think?" The consul turned pink in his excitement.

Nellie hesitated. "I really hadn't planned on looking for a job until September. We've only just arrived in Riga. I want to spend as much time with Dani as I can before she starts school here." She reached for Dani's hand and squeezed it. The consul's offer was tempting, perhaps too good to be true. She told herself to be cautious.

"Dani could come here with you! It's perfect! My daughter is so often alone. While you work, the girls could play together. Berta's four years old. There's a large garden, and Ivan and Marta—they take care of the housekeeping—would keep an eye on them." A shadow passed over the consul's face. "Of course, I need to talk to my wife, but I don't see why she'd object. What do you think, Dani?"

Nellie interrupted before the child could respond. "I need to think about it, and talk to my parents, and Dani too. I'll ask my father about those library privileges. Should he telephone you?" She pressed her lips together to suppress a smile. The job did sound perfect, but it would be unwise to seem too enthusiastic.

"Here's my card. Yes, please have him contact me. And will you telephone me too and let me know what you decide about the position?"

Nellie nodded, and, after a quick examination,

placed the card in her purse. She rose from her seat. Dani rose too, reluctantly. She didn't want to leave without meeting the consul's daughter, and she longed for a glimpse of the garden. But Nellie shook the consul's hand and moved toward the door. With a lingering look over her shoulder toward the top of the staircase where they had glimpsed the little girl, Dani could do nothing but follow her out.

"He seems like a nice man." Nellie stepped lightly across the street, almost skipping.

"Does that mean you'll go to work there?" Dani asked. "And I'll come with you?"

"Would you like that?"

Dani gave the question some thought. What if Berta turned out to be a brat? What if the consulate was a gloomy prison, not the fairytale castle she imagined? But she liked the consul, and if he was nice, maybe his daughter was too. It would be quieter than the apartment with its constant stream of music students and other visitors, her grandmother's operatic outbursts, her grandfather's political rants, the cooking smells and the cigarette smoke. Perhaps less interesting, but she would have her mother close by.

"Yes!"

Chapter 9

A week later, Nellie began work as secretary at the consulate, and Dani met Berta properly. The consul left Nellie to get settled into the office to the right of the front doors and led Dani up the grand curving staircase to the living quarters on the second floor. Dani wished her mother was with her, but the consul had not suggested it, and Nellie had turned away from Dani's pleading eyes.

The consul led her into a large, rather dark room, which Dani later learned to call the salon. It extended across the entire width of the front of the consulate, with two windows in deep embrasures facing onto the street. The morning sun slanting through cast a halo of light around a woman seated in an armchair in a grouping in the middle of the room. She was looking down, writing in a small, leather-bound book on her lap. With the light shimmering around her white-blonde hair and gleaming off her cream silk shirt, she appeared to Dani like an angel, resembling an icon she had seen in one of the churches visited with her mother on their explorations.

"My dear, this is Dani, the new secretary's daughter. I've brought her up to meet Berta. I thought she was with you."

"She's here somewhere." The consul's wife rose and moved toward them. Dani saw, with a jolt of surprise, that she was wearing trousers: wide linen pants in a pale peach tone. Dani had never seen a woman wearing pants before. Her shock was rapidly replaced by admiration. How comfortable they looked and how practical for climbing trees and other games. Not that this elegant lady would ever climb a tree. Dani blushed at her thoughts, and was grateful when a voice coming from a shadowy end of the room diverted their attention.

"I'm here!" A small girl crawled out from behind a sofa. She had tied a blanket over her shoulders in a cape and knotted a wide red ribbon—it looked as if it had come from a chocolate box—around her head. She held a doll by its yellow hair.

"And who are you today, sweetheart?" the consul asked, his voice softening.

"The miller's daughter who gets to be queen."

"Ah, Rumpelstiltskin! Do you know that story, Dani?" Dani shook her head. "Well, Berta can explain it to you, and perhaps you can take turns being the miller's daughter and Rumpelstiltskin. I have to get back to work. Margriet?"

His wife's attention had wandered back to her book.

"Yes, of course. They can play here as long as they're quiet, or in the garden, or in the nursery. Marta will be back soon from the market, and she can see to them." Margriet spoke rather distractedly, and the consul frowned at her for a moment before heading to the door.

"I'll see you at lunchtime then. You girls have fun." After he left, Dani and Berta stood looking at each other in awkward silence. The consul's wife sighed.

"So, Dani, you are…seven?"

"Yes, *M-Mevrouw* Vandercam," Nellie had schooled Dani on the correct way to address the consul's wife in Dutch, but nervousness made her stumble over the syllables.

"Oh, please don't call me that! I prefer that you call me 'Madame.' It's much easier to say, and I prefer it."

"Yes, Madame."

"Now run along and play. Berta can show you around."

Without speaking, and still dragging her doll by the hair, Berta led the way up to the nursery on the third floor. Dani gasped with pleasure at the sight of shelves crowded with books, a dollhouse, and a whole family of stuffed animals arranged around a miniature table set for a tea party. She couldn't resist trailing her hands over the books, and peering into the dollhouse windows. She had only been able to bring a tattered bear and a much-read volume of Hans Christian Andersen stories with her from Holland.

"Do you want to play Rum…Rusty…Riskin? The miller's daughter…?" Dani felt that, as she was older, she should break the ice.

"Rumpelstiltskin. It's in this book here." Berta extracted a book from the bottom shelf and opened it to show Dani a beautifully drawn illustration of a dwarfish man astride a wooden cooking spoon. "You can borrow it if you like."

A daily routine was thus established between the girls. Dani would follow Berta's lead in acting out scenarios derived from fairy stories and folk tales the consul shared with his imaginative daughter. Some, like Red Riding Hood and Sleeping Beauty, were already familiar to her. Others she would learn about in the books Berta showed her. Not able to read yet herself, Berta identified each story by its illustrations.

The girls shared a lively—sometimes lurid— imagination. Having the free run of the consulate and its garden, they were able to construct a dismal dungeon in the downstairs cloakroom and create an enchanted forest from a rhododendron hedge in the garden. They rotated leading roles, with dolls and teddy bears assuming the supporting parts. Hours passed in earnest make-believe. When Marta or Nellie sought them out to come to lunch, it would take some minutes before they heeded the call to return to the real world.

Berta adored her father. Their special hour was Berta's bedtime, when he would spin elaborate stories for her that combined elements of Nordic folk tales with Greek myths, and always had a beautiful, wise, and virtuous princess as their heroine. Dani, not present for this nightly ritual, heard the stories secondhand the next day, as the children incorporated them into their play. In the process, Dani fashioned the consul himself into a fairy-tale hero. So firmly was he lodged in her mind as a knight in shining armor that she was sometimes taken aback during the course of the day to come face to face with the man himself, rumpled, bespectacled, thinning hair, and all.

As the weeks went by and Dani's friendship with Berta deepened, her relationships with the adult members of the household also solidified. Ivan, the Cossack of Nellie and Dani's first visit, quickly became an ally. He grumbled constantly about how much work he had to do, but still found time to play the ogre at Berta's command. Although he mimed incomprehension when Margriet or Marta addressed him, somehow he was able to communicate with Berta without a common spoken language. He would lurch around the garden growling like a bear, and then submit to being tied to a tree with twine while the girls danced around him. The garden was his domain. Much of it was left untended, but he had carved out beds for vegetables near the kitchen door. He taught them the Russian names for the herbs and flowers that struggled to survive in the wilderness.

Ivan belonged to the house. Before the Russian Revolution, he had served on a grand estate near Minsk. When the prince, his master, lost both the estate and his Moscow mansion, Ivan followed him first into the White Russian army and then into exile in Latvia, which was newly independent. It was as close to Mother Russia as the prince could safely live. The prince's children entertained no such nostalgic yearnings and decamped to Paris. When the old man died, they sold the house, its contents, and, apparently, Ivan to the Netherlands government.

Besides opening the door to visitors and tending his vegetables—spurned by Margriet as peasant food—Ivan's main occupation seemed to be irritating Marta. Marta had been in service with Margriet's family for most of her life and felt keenly the superiority of her position as housekeeper-in-charge. However, she spoke no Lettish or Russian and showed no inclination to learn even the basics of either, so ordering Ivan about had no effect. She would become more and more frustrated as she pointed to the item she wanted moved, washed, cut up, or otherwise dealt with, articulating her commands in Dutch with increasing volume. He would grin foolishly and shake his head, a passable imitation of the village idiot, until she stomped off to complain to her mistress. The consul's wife would merely shrug her shoulders and relay the complaint to her husband. By the time the consul got around to good-naturedly explaining to Ivan in Russian what task Marta wanted him to complete, Marta had either done it herself or it was no longer needed. Berta and Dani found these exchanges hilarious. Of course, they did nothing to help Marta and Ivan reach international understanding.

As Marta had been Margriet's nursemaid when the consul's wife was a child, it had been assumed, by the consul at least, that she would reprise this role with Berta. But Marta insisted she could not serve as housekeeper, cook, and lady's maid to Madame as well as look after a child, much less two children. For a few days, she grudgingly carried up the girls' lunch tray to the nursery, but after the third time she spent twenty minutes looking for them, she abandoned the effort. Now, the children usually ate sandwiches with Nellie in her office, while Marta served the consul and his wife more formally in the dining room. Not knowing what she had done to inspire Marta's disapproving frown and pursed lips, Dani tried to avoid her whenever possible.

That first glimpse of Madame as a gilded icon colored Dani's feelings toward her: she worshipped her and feared her in equal parts. Not that she spent much time in Madame's company. On occasion, as the summer ripened, the consul's wife took the girls on outings to the park. Once, they went to the zoo, but Madame found the heat and the smell unbearable, and they quickly left. Dani was not sorry; the animals looked pathetic and listless in their undersized cages. Their following gaze seemed to reproach her for her freedom to leave while they were doomed to do nothing but yawn and stretch and search their fur for fleas. On the way back, they went to ride the carousel. The afternoon was improving until Berta dropped her ice-cream down her frock. Berta took matters into her own hands by jumping into the fountain to rinse off her dress. While the passing strollers smiled good-naturedly at the sight of a little girl wringing out her skirt, her mother, furious, turned away as if Berta was nothing to do with her.

Dani was shocked by Madame's indifference to her daughter. Used to noisy demonstrations of affection from the adults in her life, she struggled to understand Madame's aloofness. However as Berta seemed unfazed by it, Dani grew to accept it as part of Margriet's ethereal superiority.

Chapter 10

As a child from a well-to-do home, Margriet had taken music lessons, but the dreaded word "practice" killed any hope she would master an instrument. Anything that enforced thirty daily minutes of staying in one place was impossible for her. She loved to dance, so her mother had enrolled her in ballet, but she only endured the boring and repetitive barre exercises for the reward her teacher offered of "free dance" at the end of each session. Then, Margriet would drive the other students to the perimeter of the studio with her whirling leaps. A more sympathetic teacher might have found a way to tame the child's talent, but Madame Farikova, a White Russian émigrée who claimed tsarist connections, was exhausted by her wildness. She reported to Margriet's mother that her daughter "lacked the self-discipline necessary for progress in ballet," so classes ended.

But dancing did not. Margriet would take the opportunity of her oldest brother's absence at boarding school to sneak into his room to play his collection of records. She waited until her parents went out to crank up the phonograph, while faithful Marta kept watch for their return. Her favorite—a piece of ragtime jazz—became worn and scratched with use, yet she continued to play it, running over to nudge the needle when it got stuck.

One evening, Marta was preoccupied in the kitchen and failed to notice the sound of the front door opening and closing. As the music finished and Margriet completed her dramatic final spin, she came face to face with her mother standing in the open doorway to the bedroom, an expression of horror on her face.

"Shameless! Gyrating like that in your underwear!"—Margriet disliked the restriction of clothes when she danced—"And that awful American music! Get dressed at once and come downstairs."

The immediate punishment—banished to her room with no supper—was not as hard to bear as the confinement of records and player under lock and key in her parents' bedroom.

Dancing had brought Margriet and Richard together. His first diplomatic appointment at the Dutch embassy in Budapest involved attendance at cultural events, and he developed an interest in Hungarian folklore and dances. The intellectual appeal of the music turned into something more visceral when, during a summer leave back in Holland, he saw Margriet invent her own dance moves.

At twenty-eight years old, he had dutifully squired female cousins and friends' sisters to the performances and parties that made up Amsterdam's social season, but he had resisted the long-term alliances urged by well-meaning family members. On a warm day in July, he accompanied a bunch of university friends to a picnic on the beach at Zandvoort. As the summer dusk lengthened into night, they lit a driftwood fire. Someone had brought a portable gramophone to the gathering and persuaded Richard to contribute records carried back from Budapest. Margriet was one of several young girls caught up in the thrill of an adult party, laughing at nothing, tossing their hair about self-consciously, and drinking too much champagne. He had not noticed her until the dancing began. Margriet's movements captured something primal. Her dancing had nothing in common with the choreographed steps of the Hungarian National Folkdance Troupe, but in Richard's view better reflected the emphatic rhythms of the music's Romany roots. He was entranced.

Her verve and *joie de vivre* carried them through the first years of marriage. Delighted to be free of her mother's critical eye, Margriet developed style and confidence that, combined with her beauty, made her a star in the Hungarian capital's diplomatic circle. Richard bathed in her reflected glory, gaining advancement his lack of experience and self-effacing personality hardly warranted.

The first seeds of discord sprouted with the couple's differing reactions to Margriet's pregnancy in 1934.

"Darling, I'm so happy!" Richard paused, taking in Margriet's pout. "Aren't you? We'll be a real family at last. It's what I've always wanted."

"What *you* wanted! You don't have to have the thing. Getting fat and ugly, and missing out on all the fun parties. Women *die* in childbirth, you know. I don't want children, at least, not yet."

Richard's mouth dropped open.

"You never told me that. I assumed you felt like me, like everyone—children are a blessing." He realized as he said the words they sounded pompous.

Margriet flared up in rage, her voice piercing.

"*You* assumed! Why do you think I've not got pregnant before now? Because I've been careful not to!

The one bloody time I forgot... Well, you're going to have to hire someone to take care of it, because I'm not going to."

Richard hoped that after the first difficult trimester was out of the way, Margriet would change her attitude, but her resistance toward the coming baby and by extension to Richard only increased when he told her about his next assignment, to Yugoslavia.

"Ljubljana isn't even the capital city. And Yugoslavia? It's just a made-up place, no culture." Margriet slouched on the sofa, staring at the bump thickening her waistline as if she could frown it away.

"I'll be consul, head of mission. At my age, that's exceptional. It's a big promotion." Richard hated the wheedling tone he now used in conversations with Margriet. He suspected the posting owed as much to his wife's sparkling presence as his own dogged performance. They sat together in uncomfortable silence until he noticed tears tracking down Margriet's cheeks.

"Oh, Margriet, my love, it'll be all right."

She held up a hand to fend him off.

"No, you don't know that! I'm frightened, Richard. I don't want to have a baby in some out-of-the way place, where I don't know anyone and I don't even speak the language. What language do they even speak in Ljub— Ljubljana anyway?"

In the end they agreed that, after their home leave at Christmas, Margriet would remain in Holland at her mother's house, and the baby would be born in Holland. Richard would leave for Yugoslavia alone to take up his new consular position. He wondered if he could pull it off without her.

****

"Berta, please don't shuffle your feet like that. You're kicking up sand and ruining your shoes."

When Margriet decided to take Berta and Dani on an excursion to the zoo, she had not realized how hot the weather was. She imagined something like the zoological gardens in the Plantage Park in Amsterdam: leafy avenues and smartly dressed locals taking the air. But Riga was not Amsterdam. The heat and the smell from the animals was unbearable, and visitors—smartly dressed or not—were few. They quickly left.

"Let's go home through the park. We can stop for an ice cream at the café." The little girls grinned at each other but said nothing. Margriet sighed. She was used to Berta's long silences but had hoped Dani's presence might draw her daughter out. Dani was always polite, her "pleases" and "thank yous" a good example for Berta, but in Margriet's presence, at least, she had little more to say.

The park was more of a parade ground: a wide expanse of sandy gravel, but the benches around the edge were shaded by trees. People, more than at the zoo, were mostly young and gaily dressed. There was a carousel, too, which diverted the children's attention from ice cream. They lined up for a ride. The heat beating down and the jangly organ tune repeating from the central mechanism made Margriet's head throb with pain. She paid the fee and situated the girls on side-by-side ponies, then retreated to a bench in the shade. Two little girls still waiting in line started dancing to the carousel organ. They held hands and spun around, the colors of their skirts merging into a rainbow. Margriet found herself sobbing; when had she last danced like that, free and careless in the sunshine? She couldn't remember.

The carousel slowed. She dashed the tears from her cheeks and sniffed hard before approaching Berta and Dani, who were flushed and excited from the ride.

"Come on, you can have an ice cream now." She strode ahead, head up and face hidden from the girls.

The ice cream vendor ignored Margriet's request in slow, clear German for dishes and spoons—willfully?—and dispensed small mountains of ice cream in wafer cones. Drips were already running down the wafers onto the girls' hands as they walked over to a table.

"Do pay attention, girls—You're going to get all sticky. Eat them quickly before they melt." Ugh, it was like watching animals at the trough: little pink tongues darting in and out chasing the sweet dribbles around the soggy cone. Dani was making fast work of hers. Had she never had such a treat before? Maybe she didn't get fed properly at home. With a working mother, she was doubtless neglected. Margriet was doing a generous thing, having her come to the consulate every day. At least she ate a good lunch there.

"Oh, no, Berta! Look what a mess you've made!"

The softening ice cream had fallen off the cone onto Berta's lap, and from there slid to the ground.

"No! Don't try to pick it up. Throw the cone into the wastebasket over there. You too, Dani." Dani looked up in dismay; she still had ice cream left. "I don't care if you haven't finished. You're both making a terrible mess. Throw them away now!"

The girls obeyed, only Berta's scowl protesting the injustice. Margriet swiped at the sodden patch on the front of Berta's dress with a tiny, lace-edged handkerchief.

"This will stain if it's not washed in cold water

immediately. Come with me." Margriet headed over to the fountain in the middle of the open space, intending to dip her hankie in the water. Dani and Berta ran ahead. Before Margriet could reach them, Berta climbed over the low stone lip and plumped herself down in the six inches or so collected in the basin around the fountain. Dani started laughing, and Berta joined in. Passersby turned to look, smiling at the tableau of a child enjoying a cool dip on a hot day.

"You—you bad child!" Margriet screeched at her daughter. Berta stood up and started wringing out her skirt, still giggling. Margriet gripped Dani's arm and pulled her away to prevent the older girl joining Berta in the fountain. "Get out at once!" Margriet detected a smirk as Berta obeyed with irritating slowness. Exasperated beyond endurance, she lifted her hand to strike the child but froze, aware of the knots of people watching. A memory of her own mother, hand raised in the same pose, flashed into her mind. But Margriet was never hit in public, only behind closed doors. Shaking with anger, she lowered her hand and stalked off toward the park entrance, not looking back to see if the children were following.

They did follow, still shaking with a mixture of laughter and nervous excitement. They found Margriet waiting for them outside the park, and, calmer now, they walked home in silence. Marta opened the door when the three arrived at the consulate. She stretched out a hand to her mistress.

"Oh, dearie, you look all done in. It's the heat. Why don't you go up to your room and I'll draw you a nice cool bath. There's time for a nap before dinner." Noticing the girls for the first time, Marta frowned.

"What have you two been up to then? Look out! You're dripping all over my clean floor. Off out to the back garden, both of you, and leave Madame in peace."

"Thank you, Marta," Margriet said in a weak voice. "And then could you bring me up a gin martini? I need a really big one."

Chapter 11

Nervous about her ability to perform in an employment role she had never undertaken before, Nellie worked hard to fit in with *Meneer* Vandercam's erratic work habits. About to leave for the University library to pick up materials for the consul's folklore research, she would be called back to type a dispatch to the Foreign Ministry in the Hague. Before she could complete that task, the consul might urgently seek her help to find a missing document amongst the piles of books and papers in his office. Nellie enjoyed the variety of the work and gained confidence in her ability to handle its unpredictable demands. In turn, the consul gained confidence in her and entrusted her with increasing levels of responsibility.

On one particular day in July, the consul hosted the regular meeting of a group of foreign representatives in Riga, and she was called in to take notes. As Nellie walked home with Dani through the evening warmth, she anticipated describing the events to her family over dinner. She could hardly wait until they sat down and she could launch into her story, glad that tonight there was no eclectic gathering of students and artists around the table.

"There were several diplomats there," she reported. "Someone from the German embassy, the British Consul—six or seven all together. It was difficult to find chairs for them all, in that mess! I was a bit embarrassed, but the consul didn't care. He was in a furious mood. He wanted to discuss what he calls the 'Russian threat.' He believes the Russians are scheming to take back the Baltic states."

Simon Kutner leaned forward, nodding and frowning. He relished these evening debriefs since Nellie had started at the consulate. Although he had secured the requested library pass for Richard Vandercam, he had not yet met him. He felt sure they would have much to talk about. Ekaterina, Sarah, and Piotr were less enthralled but happy to see Nellie so animated.

"Everyone just seemed to be wringing their hands. 'What can we do?' 'Isn't it awful?' but the consul wanted something concrete, perhaps a pledge of support for an independent Latvia. Then the German diplomat spoke." Nellie put on an exaggerated German accent that made Dani laugh. "'The Baltic is within the Russian sphere of influence, just as Austria, Alsace, the Sudetenland, and *other* areas are within Germany's. We do not care to rush to the defense of these Balts!' And then he looked directly at me, knowing I was Latvian. 'They are an inferior race, anyway.'"

Sarah gasped, but her mother shrugged.

"Perhaps he suspects you're Jewish, too." Kat made a disgusted sound. "Nazis!"

Nellie waved her to silence and continued. "Then the consul stood up. He said, 'The Latvians, Estonians, and Lithuanians have a right to their independence, just as Germany has a right to hers. This theory of spheres of influence is exactly what led to the carnage of the Great War, an outcome I think Germany would wish not to repeat. As for 'inferior race,' perhaps you have forgotten that the Baltic states owe much of their culture and traditions to the Teutonic Knights who settled the area seven hundred years ago. Any student of European history can tell you there is no 'inferior race'—or superior one, for that matter. We are all the beneficiaries of centuries of intermingling."

"Bravo!" cried Simon, as if it was his daughter's speech he was cheering. Again, Nellie held up a restraining hand.

"Then the German stood up too. I thought he was going to challenge the consul to a duel, but after a moment, he just turned on his heel and marched out. I felt so proud of *Meneer* Vandercam, and after the meeting, I told him so!" She beamed around the table. She had surprised herself in addressing her employer with such uncharacteristic forwardness, but he had responded by taking her hand in both of his and shaking it as if she were a partner, not an underling.

Nellie did not describe the rest of the conversation after the German diplomat left. None of the other diplomats congratulated *Meneer* Vandercam as she had expected. There was an uncomfortable silence, and then the British consul spoke up.

"Richard, my dear friend, was that wise? Our governments are working hard to accomplish a compromise that will protect Poland. We don't want to undermine their efforts."

The consul's face reddened and he seemed about to explode.

"So we are to say nothing? What's the point of meeting if only to provide a platform for that man's outdated theories on race!"

The other men calmed him down, agreeing with his

position but urging more caution in expressing it. The meeting broke up without any joint statement on the Russian question. But Nellie was left shaken. When the German had looked so coldly at her she had felt a visceral fear. She saw that fear echoed in the well-spoken, dark-suited men around the table: it was not Russia but Germany that threatened them. All but the consul. He had spoken out bravely, but as she looked at her gathered family, she wondered whether others might be forced to pay the price for his audacity. She remembered the hateful scrawl across the door of the printing house: Jews Out!

The next day, her amusement was tinged with dismay when she found the little girls in the garden playing "meetings," taking turns to play the heroic consul, who stood up for the beautiful princess, and his wicked German adversary.

Chapter 12

July became August, and by the middle of the month, the weather turned sultry. Leaves hung limply on the trees in the park. Traffic fumes and the smell of sweaty bodies seemed locked down by a ceiling of heavy cloud. Those that could escaped to summer cottages on the Baltic coast, thirty kilometers away. Those that couldn't, like the Kutners, flung open their apartment windows and complained about the heat.

On Saturday, Nellie allowed herself the luxury of sleeping in, followed by a long cool bath. Piotr was teaching a student in the living room, so the rest of the family was gathered in the kitchen when Nellie entered, still in her robe with a towel wound around her wet hair. Dani stood on tiptoe at the sink with Grankat, helping wash the dishes and enjoying the feel of soapy water over her hands and arms. Simon sat hidden behind his newspaper, shaking it in irritation each time the same hesitant musical phrase drifted in from the living room. Sarah leaned against the wall next to the open window, smoking a cigarette in short angry puffs, deflecting the smoke out of the side of her mouth.

The remnants of breakfast were scattered on the table. Nellie sat down and poured herself a cup of cold coffee. No one spoke. She looked from sister to mother, eyebrows raised in enquiry. Kat shrugged, Sarah turned to look out over the park, and Simon's paper rattled.

"What's going on?" Her question hung in the humid air for a moment. Then Sarah jerked back toward the room.

"They've cancelled the orchestra tour! Something about 'the international situation'!" She curled her lips around the words in disdain. "It's so unfair! We've prepared all year, worked so hard! Krakow, Warsaw, Dresden—some of the best concert halls in Europe, and I'll never get the chance again!"

"No, don't say that. They'll probably reschedule in the spring." Sarah dismissed her mother's appeasing comment with a roll of her eyes.

"Well, the situation *is* very dangerous," Nellie began tentatively. "The consul says—"

"*The consul says! The consul says!*" Sarah sing-songed the words in a childish voice. "I'm sick of hearing about your consul. He's just a grubby little bureaucrat from an insignificant little country. And he's *married!* Perhaps you ought to remember that!"

Nellie's mouth opened but no words emerged. In the shocked silence, only Dani seemed capable of movement. She took a step toward her mother, hands dripping and eyes wide.

"Mama?"

Sarah abruptly ground out her cigarette in the soil of the window box and stalked out of the room, avoiding everyone's eyes. The student repeated the same four bars, and Simon Kutner folded his paper with a snap.

"Dani," he said, "I think it's time we took a stroll down to the patisserie to see if they have any of those almond cakes Grankat likes so much."

After they left, Kat sat in the seat the professor had vacated.

"Sarah didn't mean anything—"

"Of course, she did!" retorted Nellie. "She meant to imply that something's going on between me and *Meneer* Vandercam, but Mama, she's wrong! Nothing's going on!"

Kat nodded, brushing some crumbs off the tablecloth into her hand and depositing them onto a saucer. Nellie watched her mother's hands smoothing the cloth and released a deep sigh.

"I *do* like working for the consul—the work's interesting, and I like *him,* I admit it. He's kind and appreciative, but always professional. I'm sure he'd never think of...of what Sarah hinted at." She sought her mother's eye, looking for a response, but the older woman continued to focus on picking up crumbs. "*Do* I talk about him a lot, Mama?"

"Well, maybe," Kat acknowledged with a smile, "but, as you say, the work is interesting. Perhaps you need to see things from Sarah's point of view." Nellie started to protest, but her mother raised a finger to silence her. "Since you moved to Holland eight years ago, she's been the only child, with all the attention focused on her. Maybe we spoiled her a little—she's so talented, admitted to the Conservatoire at sixteen, a place in the National Orchestra at twenty—that's unheard of."

Nellie nodded. Sarah's talent had always set her apart, given her the starring role in the family. Nellie had been more than content to be the quiet older sister, often unnoticed amongst the admirers who attended the Kutner *soirées.* They contrasted in looks too: Nellie, petite with dark unruly hair like her father, and Sarah tall, her long straight hair the color of chestnuts. The four-year age difference meant they had never been rivals in the old days. Why was she so spiteful now?

Her mother continued. "Sarah's immature in many ways. Yes, she's married, but she's still living at home, with me to cook her meals and her father to remind her to take an umbrella when it rains. Then you arrive, already a mother with a lifetime of experience—yes, I know, some of it tragic—and you walk into an exciting job with an inside view of current events. She's jealous, *cara*! She thought the orchestra tour would even things up and she would be the one to travel abroad and see the world—and then the tour is cancelled." Kat reached out to stroke Nellie's cheek. "Life goes on, *cara*. Hitler and Stalin play their games, make treaties, break them, but we must keep on living our lives, taking care of each other, making the best of it. Don't let bad feeling come between you and Sarah."

****

Nellie sat on her makeshift bed in her father's study, brushing out her damp hair, and considered this new concept. *Sarah jealous of me!* Except for her mother humming a melody from *Cosi Fan Tutte* in the kitchen— even Ekaterina's humming could penetrate walls—the apartment was quiet. The professor was still out somewhere with Dani, and Sarah and Piotr had left as soon as he finished teaching to meet up with friends heading to the woods to find some shade, and no doubt to continue their complaints about the cancellation of the tour.

Sarah *was* a child, Nellie thought. A beautiful, talented child. Her single-minded devotion to music, encouraged by Ekaterina, had precluded a broader education. Even her marriage to Piotr, a fellow symphony orchestra musician with the same professional preoccupations, had served to insulate her from the harsher realities that threatened Europe. When Nellie met Piotr for the first time on her arrival from Holland, he impressed her with his gentleness. He hovered on the edge of their impassioned dinner table conversations, rarely offering an opinion, even when the talk turned to music. Nellie knew he was a native Russian speaker, from a Lutheran farming community near the Estonian border. His family had been bewildered by his early demonstrations of musical ability. Their bafflement turned to ridicule, until, at sixteen, he escaped the drudgery of the farm to come to Riga. The Kutners had provided him with a home, a connection to the classical music world, and, ultimately, a bride. A decade on, he had no contact with his family.

Nellie pondered their marriage of opposites: Sarah's fiery temper and obsessive nature contrasted with Piotr's easygoing temperament. He had been more successful than she in attracting and retaining students, patiently nursing even the talentless through easy pieces they could show off to their parents, while Sarah's demands for perfection drove the young aspirants away in tears. Nellie wondered which of them would have the strength to meet the trials the consul was convinced were coming to their country. At present, they both seemed oblivious to Latvia's position squeezed between two military powers intent on domination. But she reminded herself that she too had ignored the threat when she decided to bring her daughter home to Riga. Sarah and Piotr were typical in discounting the danger. Only through working side by side with the consul had Nellie become aware of the larger picture. He had freely discussed his inside knowledge and his predictions with her.

She suspected he did not share all this intelligence with the elegant Margriet. In her limited interactions with Nellie, Madame seemed more interested in fashion and flower-arranging than politics.

Chapter 13

At least the day had started satisfactorily. Margriet went out early with Marta to the covered market near the river, where she bought armfuls of gladioli, white blossoms with a frill of pale violet. She arranged them in front of one of the ornate mirrors in the large reception room on the second floor, so that the reflection doubled their number. The flowers arrested the eye as one entered the room, distracting from the dark heavy furniture that came with the house and which no amount of rearranging could minimize. She had tried to lighten the space with tasseled pillows and creamy silk throws—to make it modern and comfortable like the rooms pictured in the society magazines she ordered from Paris and London— but even flowers could not disguise that this was a stodgy, old-fashioned room in a city lacking the culture and refinement of other European capitals.

Margriet changed before lunch into a dress the exact shade of the edge of the gladioli petals. It was tailored in a silky fabric that draped nicely over her boyish figure, making her look sophisticated and more womanly. She favored pastel shades; anything stronger tended to overwhelm her pale skin and fair hair. When Richard came up from his office, he failed to notice either the dress or the flowers. She was hardly surprised. He seemed to notice little these days except newspaper headlines about troop movements and international conferences. He insisted on having the radio on during lunch, which he knew she hated, especially when it was tuned to the BBC.

"Couldn't we at least listen to music? This gloomy talk is so depressing."

Richard slowly brought his attention back from the news bulletin. "Umm...yes, yes. I suppose so. It's finishing now anyway."

But even after he turned the radio off, the conversation limped. She tried to interest him in her visit to the market.

"It's amazing what these Balts will eat. Some of the displays on the butchers' stalls quite turned my stomach. Marta, of course, disapproves of everything, and walks around the market with an expression on her face as if she smelled something bad."

Richard didn't immediately respond, and Margriet's thoughts wandered. Marta was a sweetheart to have accompanied them to Latvia at all, and she was doing sterling service as housekeeper and lady's maid. She came because she so adored Margriet and had done so since first coming up to Amsterdam from the country to be Margriet's nursemaid. Marta had made no attempt to learn Lettish. Who could blame her? It was such a difficult language. It amused Margriet to think of the miscommunications occurring in the kitchen between Marta and Ivan, the Russian factotum who had served in the house since earlier days before it had become the Dutch Consulate. Richard—stubbornly, she thought— refused to be entertained by her anecdote about the market. He took everything so literally these days—no sense of humor.

"I could ask Mrs. Loesseps to teach Marta a few

useful phrases, I suppose," Richard said, after a pause.

"Don't bother. Marta would hate it, and I'm sure Mrs. Loesseps has more important things to do with her time."

Richard finished his lunch and moved to the sideboard to pour two cups of coffee.

"Are you taking your coffee downstairs?" she asked. He nodded.

The ground floor housed the consul's office, on the right of the marble-tiled entrance hall. The secretary's office was the other side of the hall. Both these rooms had double pocket doors that usually stood wide open, so that Richard and his secretary could call across rather than getting up and entering the other's office. This habit irritated Margriet, even if she only confronted it when she came out to the top of the stairs or went down to speak to Marta and Ivan in the kitchen at the back of the house. It was too casual, disrespectful of her husband's position. Nellie Loesseps should get up and go into Richard's office when he needed her, not yell across the hall like some fishwife.

She focused on the two cups that Richard was carrying toward the door. So the second cup was not for her but for his secretary. She suppressed a pang of jealousy. No, she told herself, it was just socially inappropriate for him to serve his underling coffee; she would not take it as a personal slight.

"Shall I send Berta and Dani up to you?" Richard asked. The children lunched with Dani's mother in her office. That had not been Margriet's plan when she had agreed to Nellie Loesseps bringing her little girl to work with her. She had thought that Marta would take lunch up to the children in the nursery on the third floor.

However, Marta, although she had doted on Margriet when *she* was a child, seemed reluctant to resume the role of nursemaid for Berta. Berta worshipped the Loesseps girl, who, in turn, hung onto her mother's skirts like a limpet. So the nursery went largely unused, while the girls had the freedom of the house, spending most of their time downstairs with Nellie or out in the garden with Ivan.

"Yes, I suppose so." Margriet thought it proper to spend a part of each day with Berta. She had adored being a mother when Berta was a baby, even though the birth itself had been difficult. She loved holding the baby's face up against her cheek to feel her soft warmth and breathe in her milky, powdery smell. Of course, she had Marta to help her with the less agreeable tasks, and her mother was alive then, always a fountain of advice: "Don't run to her every time she cries. You'll spoil her! Babies should be fed on a schedule. Otherwise they'll never learn!"

As Berta grew, she became more difficult to love. She had the unnerving habit of staring at people with luminous, almost accusatory eyes. Berta was slow to talk, as if withholding herself from the world, and more particularly from her mother. When she did start to talk, she spoke slowly, deliberately, not in the babbling stream that Margriet had expected. It was as if Berta thought her words out first, judging her audience before she spoke. At least, Margriet felt judged. When she found out Richard's secretary had a daughter a little older than Berta, she was delighted. In the guise of extending a favor to a member of the staff, she permitted Dani to come and play each day with Berta, thus relieving her—and Marta—of the burden of entertaining the child.

However, it was disconcerting that Berta now seemed to prefer Nellie's company to her own mother's.

Margriet had not gone with Richard when he received a posting to Ljubljana: she was pregnant, and she was certain that this backwater Yugoslavian town could not offer the services a new mother might need. Then her own mother became ill, another excuse not to join him. She wondered now if that had been a mistake, had been the reason why her marriage had wilted into its present flaccid state. Three years spent mostly apart, and then the Riga posting. Her mother was dead by then, and Berta was older. There was no reason to stay behind in Holland.

But Riga was not like that first posting. Budapest had been a fairy tale. They were newly married. The city, although reduced from the glories of its pre-Great War days, was still lively with concerts and plays. They went to receptions and dinners almost every night. She was young and beautiful, one of the stars of the diplomatic circle. And Richard, too, had glowed with the sheen of an up-and-coming player, someone to take note of. But that early promise was never fulfilled. Budapest was a first-rank European capital. After that, Ljubljana was a slap in the face, although Richard never complained. And then Riga, the back of beyond.

The girls ran into the room, hand in hand.

"Oh, the flowers!" Dani gasped. This was the reaction Margriet had hoped for from Richard. How exasperating that a seven-year-old girl should notice what her husband had failed to see.

At three o'clock, Margriet sent Berta up for her nap and reached for her journal. This was her favorite part of the day. In her journal, following a habit of her mother's,

Margriet recorded every social event they attended: what food was served, who was there, what she wore. She used this book to plan the occasions she and Richard hosted. Overcoming his reluctance, she insisted on entertaining formally once a month. If it was left to him, she'd never meet anyone except dusty old professors and so-called intellectuals with no sense of humor or style.

Last month, they'd held a cocktail party. The whole Riga diplomatic corps had attended. She remembered with satisfaction the effect she had created, in a summery white frock, her hair dressed simply, no jewelry, just a fresh flower corsage. Of course, the other women showed no imagination. To them, cocktails meant garish satin, and piling on jewelry and makeup. Even without her advantages of youth and a slender figure, she made them look like frumps.

Now she was designing a dinner for twelve. What would she give them? Strawberries and asparagus were over. Caviar was just too boring—everyone served that here. She'd seen tomatoes and peppers in the market that morning. You could always get good fish in Riga. So perhaps a Mediterranean theme? Bouillabaisse to start, peaches in brandy for dessert, and for a main course...? A worrying thought interrupted her musings: the lunchtime news bulletin. She wished now she had paid more attention. She would have to ask Richard to review the seating plan carefully. It wouldn't do to place the German ambassador next to the British *chargé d'affaires* if they were about to go to war! Well, she wouldn't invite the Englishman at all. His wife was a bore, and Margriet's German was better than her English anyway. Although it would be a shame if the international situation prevented that charming French diplomat attending. He was so good-looking…

She flicked through magazines for ideas on table settings and flower arrangements, so immersed that she hardly noticed when Berta and Dani returned. Thank goodness they knew to play quietly when she was busy. The event was coming together nicely in her mind. If only she had more help than Marta and Ivan. She cringed at the thought of the struggle ahead to get Ivan into a proper footman's suit, and to pacify Marta when she took offense at some imagined insult to her cooking. But these were exactly the challenges she was made for. If Richard's next posting was not in a major western capital, no one could blame her!

As if summoned by her thoughts, Richard burst into the room. He looked quite wild. He hadn't even put his jacket on, and instead of apologizing for the intrusion, he barely acknowledged her. Nellie Loesseps followed close on his heels with what looked like a smirk on her flushed face. She had no right to come into Margriet's sitting room. She should understand that just because the daughter was allowed in here to play with Berta, it didn't mean the mother was welcome upstairs. Margriet suspected that the woman was not just unwittingly inappropriate, she was deliberately taunting her, trying to demonstrate that, unlike his wife, she was intimately involved in Richard's work, in what mattered most in his life. Margriet's simmering irritation boiled into a sudden white-hot rage. This was intolerable, and Margriet was going to put a stop to it right now.

Chapter 14

The day the war started began like any other during that summer. Nellie walked hand in hand with Dani across the park to the consulate. Dani had saved some crusts from her breakfast toast, and they stopped for a few minutes to feed the ducks. Nellie sat on a bench, raising her face to the sun, eyes closed.

"We'd better enjoy this. Winter will be on us before you know it." She had warned Dani that winters in Latvia would be much colder and darker than winters in Holland, but the little girl could not imagine it.

They arrived at the consulate a little before ten o'clock. Although the consul had issued Nellie a key, an unspoken protocol demanded that she use the cast iron bell pull to the left of the heavy oak doors and wait for Ivan to open them. The problem: Ivan was becoming increasingly deaf and had difficulty hearing the bell from the kitchen at the back of the house. Or he might be out in the garden tending the potatoes, cabbages, and other vegetables he grew where, in the mansion's glory days, flowers had bloomed in profusion. Often the consul himself greeted them. On this morning, the reverberation of the bell had hardly ceased before he flung the door wide open.

"Nellie! The Germans are advancing! The Polish army is falling back to Warsaw! Oh—" The consul broke off when he saw Dani. "I'm sorry. Good morning to you both. Dani, Berta is waiting for you in the kitchen. Madame has gone to the market with Marta." He let go his grip of Nellie's hands, which he had seized with his first words, and patted Dani's cheek. "Have fun today." He stood aside to allow them to enter.

Ivan shambled through the baize-covered door that separated the front of the house from the servants' quarters at the back.

"The bell rang…" Ivan grumbled in Russian.

"Yes, I've got it." The consul replied in the same language. "Take Dani through, please. We must start work." Nellie hurried after him into his office, turning at the door to give a little shooing wave to her daughter.

Dani found Berta in the kitchen, pushing a spoon around in a bowl of bread and milk.

"Ivan says we can help him in the garden today," Berta said, her face brightening at the sight of her friend. It was amazing that Berta and Ivan communicated so well, given they had no common language. Ivan adored the solemn little girl who was so frequently left in his care while her mother and Marta managed the affairs of the house.

Under Ivan's direction, the girls passed the morning in the garden delving beneath the potato plants to find tubers nestled in the dirt like new-laid eggs. By noon, when Nellie came looking for them, the girls were as grimy as coal miners at the end of a shift. After she dusted them down and supervised a thorough handwashing, they followed her to her office where they ate sandwiches prepared and served grudgingly by Marta.

At lunch, Nellie was distracted. She usually talked with the children about their morning activities, but today she was silent and thoughtful. The girls caught her mood and ate quietly. Eventually, Nellie gave her head a little shake as if to clear it, and smiled.

"Well, we *are* very serious today. Perhaps it's because summer is ending. Soon Dani will be starting school and she won't be able to come and play every day. No, Berta, don't be sad. I'll bring her whenever I can, and perhaps your mama will let you come to our place occasionally. Would you like to learn to play the piano? My sister can teach you. I'll talk to your mama about it."

Berta nodded. With adults she was usually silent, although she would chatter like a little bird with Dani.

After lunch, following a routine established in the first days of Nellie's employment, Berta and Dani went up to the grand salon on the second floor to spend some time with Madame. On entering the room, Dani noticed the flowers on the table between the windows, and observed that Madame's dress was the exact same shade of violet as the edge of the flowers. She resolved that when she grew up and had her own home, she too would match her dress to the color of her flower arrangements. Madame's elegance awed her. Dani sometimes tried to imitate the way she moved, as if she had a book balanced on her head, but it was more difficult than it looked.

The girls played until Madame suggested that Berta go up for her nap. At four years old, Berta still slept for an hour each afternoon. Dani, almost three years older, sat on the stairs outside Berta's darkened bedroom and read one of her friend's many books.

On this day, she found her attention wandering from the beautifully illustrated tales of princesses and paupers. She felt an odd uneasiness that had begun when the consul grabbed her mother's hands at the entrance that morning. Their garden play had pushed the feeling away, but it had re-emerged during lunch with her mother's silence. Now she listened hard for any sound rising up the stairs from the offices two floors below. Something was wrong, she was sure of it. She crept down toward the second floor, only to retreat when Marta lumbered up the stairs and disappeared into the salon. Marta came out a minute later laden with the coffee tray and began a laborious descent, shuffling sideways down the wide stone steps.

After a while, Dani heard voices—her mother's and the consul's—drifting up from below. She inched down the stairs again and peeped over the balustrade outside the salon door in time to see her mother cross the black-and-white marble of the lobby, enter the consul's office, and shut the door behind her.

When Berta woke, the girls descended to the salon again. Soon, Berta and Dani were engaged in one of their games of make-believe, hidden behind the immense sofa at one end of the room. The sofa stood out a little way from the wall, and its curving back afforded a meter-wide tunnel to which they had brought Berta's dolls and various other paraphernalia to create their pretend household. Dani was the king, coming home tired after a busy day slaying dragons. Berta was the queen, whose job it was to cater to Dani's whims while keeping the dolls from misbehaving. They were deep into this game, conducted in whispers, when the door to the salon opened and the consul rushed in, with Nellie trailing behind. The girls peered out from their hiding place, amazed at this unaccustomed incursion into Madame's sanctum.

"Margriet, the radio! There's going to be an

announcement!" The consul made straight for the walnut cabinet that housed the wireless set.

"Richard, I wish you wouldn't bring your business affairs up here." Madame, very pale, had risen to her feet, and was looking straight at Nellie as she said this. Nellie, still in the doorway, stared back at the consul's wife. Her cheeks were as scarlet as Madame's were white. Her mouth hung half-open but she made no sound. The silence lasted for a couple of beats. To Dani, it seemed an eternity.

"Don't be ridiculous. I think we're at war." The consul was bent over the knobs of the wireless. He had not seen the two women lock eyes. "Ah, here it is. Listen."

"This is the Dutch Broadcasting Service talking to you from Hilversum. Today, September 3, 1939, at 3 p.m. Greenwich Mean Time, Britain, France and Belgium declared war on Germany. Prime Minister Dirk Van de Geer has announced that the Netherlands will remain neutral in this conflict." The tinny voice droned on amid waves of static, but the consul talked over it.

"How *can* we stay neutral? Does that fool Van de Geer think that will save us from a German invasion? I'm sure the Queen doesn't agree with this!" He looked around at his wife and secretary, but they were frozen in place and did not respond.

"You do see, don't you, that the Germans will not be satisfied with just Poland. They'll keep coming east through the Baltic states to Russia, as well as west into France and Belgium. They won't leave Holland out of it, whether we're neutral or not."

The consul's wife finally spoke.

"If the government decides Holland is to remain

neutral, you have nothing to say about it." She dropped her voice to a hiss. "And *never* call me ridiculous again!" She swept from the room, the phantom book still balanced on her perfect chignon.

"What on earth...?" The consul was confused, and looked toward Nellie for an explanation. She failed to give him one, but turned toward the children, still half-hidden behind the sofa.

"Come on, Dani. Time to go home." Dani struggled out and ran to clasp her mother round the waist.

"I'm sorry, Dani. I didn't mean to frighten you." The consul said in a softer tone. "The war is far away. It won't hurt you and your mama."

But it was not the war with Germany that frightened Dani but the war she had seen Madame declare against her mother; her pale eyes had pierced the air between them like a thrust of steel.

Part Three: Berta's Story

Chapter 15

"Pigs!" Grandmother Vandercam hissed the words with such venom that Berta froze. The grip on her hand tightened, and she was dragged forward past the elegant double-fronted canal house on Herengracht. Later, Berta understood that this was the family home where her father grew up. The green-uniformed soldiers guarding the entrance indicated that the building had been requisitioned by the Germans.

Berta's memories of the war were crystalized into moments like this, mountain peaks emerging from the clouds, then enlarged and made vivid with information she read or had been told. Not much of the latter: neither her grandmother nor her father seemed eager to answer her questions.

"Did I live there, Oma?"

"Just for a while, after you came back from Latvia."

"Was Mama there with me?"

"Sshh, dear. We have to hurry."

She could not remember ever being inside that house, and her memories of her mother were nebulous, formed by photographs. She knew what she looked like—serene and beautiful, glowing like an angel in the framed photograph that stood on the mantel in the house where the three of them now lived on a side street in the

Jordaan district. But try as she might, she could not recall her mama's voice, what she smelled like, or how it felt to touch that silky-smooth hair.

Another mountain peak memory was her papa crying. Oma had sent her up to the attic room where Richard Vandercam spent his time. She was to summon him for supper. The soup consisted of potatoes again, spiced with whatever her grandmother could find in the jars and bottles left by the previous occupants. Having lived with servants throughout her life until the Occupation, Oma had no cooking expertise. Still, they needed to eat, and she thought it important to maintain a civilized routine with linen napkins and crystal glasses, even if the glasses contained only water.

Berta climbed the steep flight of stairs to stand at her father's door. She heard a strange snuffling, whining noise, like an animal in pain. She nudged the door open. Richard was sitting on the bed, his head thrown back and eyes squeezed shut, cheeks glistening with tears. He was oblivious to his daughter's presence. Seconds passed while she searched for words to comfort him. He spent so much time hidden away here with his books that she scarcely knew him. At last she crept forward and sat next to him on the bed, leaning against his shoulder.

"It's all right, Papa. She's in Heaven now."

Richard jerked around, staring at her with wild, reddened eyes.

"She's dead?" His voice cracked. Then, as if waking from a nightmare, he took a deep breath. "Yes, of course. I'm sorry, my darling. Sometimes it's just so hard to remember..." He took out a handkerchief, blew his nose, and wiped his face. Then he leant over and kissed the top of Berta's head.

"Let's go see what Oma has cooked up for us, shall we?"

But mostly the sameness of every day under the Occupation deadened Berta's recall of specific events. Her grandmother marched her to school every morning. Coached not to volunteer information, Berta daydreamed her way through lessons. Even if she knew the right answer, she kept her eyes on her desk and her hand down. When schoolmates asked her questions about her family or where she lived, she mumbled a one-word response. Consequently, she made no close friends and received few invitations to other girls' houses or to participate in after-school activities. This did not set her apart from the other students, since even the youngest children were taught to be careful about revealing too much. Someone's father might be important in the NSB (the Dutch Nazi party) or, on the other hand, a family might be hiding Jews or others subject to deportation orders. They all maintained a polite wariness, even the teachers.

She never left home unless accompanied by her grandmother or, more rarely, her father. If they came across German soldiers on patrol or conducting a sweep, they ducked into a side street or crossed the road. Sometimes it was impossible to sidestep contact. Some of the soldiers were friendly, attempting a greeting in mangled Dutch, even offering a piece of candy. Following instructions, Berta smiled, said thank you, and, as soon as she returned home, threw the candy in the trash.

For year after dreary year, the only things that changed were the decreasing number of men in the streets, and the diminishing amounts of food to eat or fuel to warm the house. Berta's tenth birthday fell in

February 1945, during the Hunger Winter. The Dutch government in exile had ordered a rail strike to impede delivery of armaments to the German army fighting off the Allied advance in the south of the country. In retaliation, the Germans cut off all supplies to the part of Holland they still occupied. She could count every one of her ribs, and her limbs looked like sticks, but she had grown twelve centimeters taller than she'd been the previous year, and none of her skirts reached her knees, even with the hem let down. She stood shivering in her underwear while her grandmother made final alterations to a dress she had unearthed from a closet of abandoned clothes.

Removing the last pins from between her lips, Oma sighed.

"I hate to do this, take something without asking, but I can't let you out of the house looking indecent. When the Rosens return home, we'll pay them for the dress, and everything else. We'll make it up to them." She spoke with a show of confidence, but she knew the Rosens, previous inhabitants of their current home, might never return. She had seen the long columns of Jewish deportees walking from the theater where they were held to the central train station, and heard the rumors about the work camps in the east to which they were taken.

The ground floor of their little dwelling had housed Mr. Rosen's tailoring business. The name "I. Rosen" in gold letters could still be seen through the white paint splashed onto the name board above the shop window. Brown paper covered the window now, and when they entered from the street, they had to feel their way through a shadowy space peopled by dressmaking dummies to the stairs that led to the living quarters above. The

Germans—or perhaps neighbors—had snatched any bolts of uncut cloth before the Vandercams moved in, but most of the Rosens' personal possessions upstairs remained intact. Oma diligently polished the furniture and swept the rugs. She wrapped their fine china in tissue and hung lavender in the clothes closets to deter moths. When forced to "borrow" some provision from their larder, she left a note describing the item used.

The dress she was working on belonged to the Rosens' teenage daughter. A photograph of the family group—father, mother, and a dark-haired, smiling girl—used to stand next to the portrait of Berta's mother on the mantelpiece, until Oma put it away in a drawer. She had found Berta gazing at it too often. The Rosen girl—her name was Rachel—fascinated Berta. She had never met her, but she seemed familiar. After all, Berta slept in her bed, read her books, and sat at her desk to do her homework. Some nights when she couldn't sleep, she felt her presence in the room with her.

Rachel's dress was beautifully made—no doubt by her father, the tailor—the seams so meticulously finished that it could be worn inside out without anyone noticing. Made of fine wool in black-and-white houndstooth check, with red piping on the cuffs and collar, it remained Berta's favorite for years. She kept it in remembrance of Rachel Rosen even after it no longer fit her.

All through that terrible winter and into the spring of 1945, the citizens of Amsterdam waited for liberation. The Allied advance had stalled north of Rotterdam, and even though defeat was inevitable, the Germans clung on in the city and the northwest provinces. Then, suddenly, at the beginning of May, they were gone. At first, people walked the streets in a daze, barely daring to believe that after five years of occupation they were free again. Then Dutch flags, unearthed from attics and cellars, started flying from every building, and spontaneous street parties broke out.

In the midst of the euphoria, Berta's grandmother took to her bed. A rattling cough, remnant of a bout of bronchitis months before, worsened. Her fever rose, and the doctor diagnosed pneumonia. Richard stayed by her bedside day and night. His mother had stood in line for food rations for hours, and struggled to cope with cooking and housekeeping chores previously delegated to servants. Barricaded in the attic with his books, he had avoided the harsher realities of the Occupation and relied on his mother to look after his daughter. Now, guilt gripped him.

Berta crept in and out, trying to be helpful, but she hovered by the door, frightened by the change in her grandmother's appearance. The skin on Oma's face and hands was papery thin and pale, the cheekbones and chin newly prominent. Her eyes were closed. Only the moist wheeze of her breath told the watchers that she was still alive. About ten o'clock, when the city had at last fallen silent, she opened her eyes.

"Richard?"

"I'm here, Mama," he whispered, and leaned in toward her.

"Don't...waste your life."

Berta thought those were the words, but she couldn't be sure, her grandmother's voice was so weak. About an hour later, after Richard had at last persuaded Berta to go to bed, the old lady died without saying anything else.

She had shepherded Richard and Berta through the

war when they were not equipped—Berta because of her youth, Richard because of his depression—to take care of themselves. With the Liberation, she could release her burden. Richard needed to step forward now, shake off whatever darkness had paralyzed him, and resume his role as head of their diminished household.

And he did. As the summer progressed and Amsterdam sorted itself out, Richard renewed his pre-war contacts, leading to the offer of a teaching position in the History Department at the University of Amsterdam. Father and daughter did not move back into the family house on Herengracht. Richard said it was much too big for the two of them. True, but Berta believed he also wanted to bury unhappy memories associated with the place. He secured an apartment in a modern building in East Amsterdam near the campus, and, except for his books and a few treasured pieces of furniture rescued from Herengracht, they made a fresh start there.

****

September sunlight flooded through the bay windows of the second-floor apartment. Berta was enjoying a breakfast of waffles and applesauce, unheard of luxuries a few months before, when her father proposed an outing.

"I want to go to Rotterdam to see if I can find some people I knew before the war."

"But wasn't Rotterdam bombed? Will they still be there?" Berta was reluctant to spend one of her last days of idleness before classes started on a stuffy train going to see a bomb site.

"The place is outside Rotterdam, in the country, next to a canal, as I remember." Something in his voice made

Berta examine his face. He had a sad, faraway look in his eyes, a look she associated with the time they lived in the Jordaan, when he barely spoke for days on end. "You don't remember your little friend Dani, do you?" Berta shook her head. She had never heard the name before. "Or Nellie, her mother?" Richard stared out of the window, lost in his memories.

"No," Berta said, a little sharper than she intended. She couldn't afford to let her Papa drift back into the past. He looked at her then and smiled. "Well, I just want to make sure they're all right. After we left Latvia, everything was so chaotic—the Occupation, your mother…" His voice trailed off and he turned toward the window again. This was Berta's opportunity to ask the questions her grandmother had evaded: exactly how and when did her mother die? But she remained silent, afraid of disturbing the fragile optimism that surrounded their new life.

The train journey was pleasant. The flat farmland crisscrossed by canals seemed untouched by the war. Sunlight glinted off the water, and cows stood like cutouts against the intense green of the fields. Only as the train neared the station in Rotterdam did they see the devastation that bombing had caused—the Germans in 1940, then the Allies last winter: buildings sheared in two, revealing an interior wall like a stage set, boarded-up shop windows, and a surviving church spire with the body of the building reduced to rubble.

Richard remained silent as they drove out of the city in a taxi. The driver was equally taciturn. Berta studied him while her father scanned the fields and cottages along the road. The man's shoulder blades stood out like wings beneath the faded cotton of his shirt. Although she guessed his age at about thirty, the hands on the wheel were scarred and calloused, the knuckles swollen like an old man's.

"Was there much fighting here?" Richard asked, breaking his silence as they bumped over the cobbles. The road ran parallel to a canal, separated from the waterway by a dyke.

The driver shrugged. "I wasn't here."

Richard nodded. Berta pulled his sleeve and questioned him with her eyes. He hushed her with a gesture. After a pause, the driver resumed.

"Got back a month ago."

"From Germany?"

He nodded. "The Ruhr. Two years working twelve hours a day in a coal mine. I survived." Seeming to regret this admission, he clamped his jaw shut and leaned toward the windshield, closing off further enquiry.

They pulled up outside a whitewashed cottage. The shutters were fastened shut, and the small front garden was overgrown.

"I don't think there's anyone here, Papa," Berta said, following him out of the taxi. He ignored her, pushing open the gate and striding up the path. He rapped so vigorously, flakes of faded blue paint flew off the front door. Berta turned a pleading look toward the taxi, worried it would drive off and leave them outside this abandoned house. The driver looked back at her without expression.

"I'll try around the back."

Before she could restrain him, her father hurried off, with Berta in pursuit. The back garden was as unruly as the front. Richard bent his head against a crack at the side of a shuttered window.

"Can you see anything?"

He grunted and moved to the back door, crouching again to find a space through which he could look inside.

"Papa, there's no one here," Berta said again. This time he nodded and came to her side. They walked together back to the car.

"Let's try next door."

The driver nodded, and they moved off slowly to the next cottage, maybe a hundred meters along the road. A woman opened the door in response to Richard's knocking, positioning herself in the gap. She was young and heavily pregnant.

"Yes?" Her tone was unfriendly.

"I'm looking for the Loesseps family? They live next door." Richard nodded in the direction they had come from.

The woman shrugged.

"An old couple and their granddaughter?" He persisted.

"Yeah, I haven't been here long. Don't know the neighbors. I heard they died."

"What? All of them?" Richard's voice rose high in panic. The woman stepped back and started to close the door. Realizing that he was scaring her, he spoke in a lower tone. "Is there someone else here who might know—" He gestured behind her.

"No!" Then she seemed to relent. "You could ask in the village. The woman who keeps the shop. She knows everyone's business," she added with a touch of bitterness. Before Richard could thank her, the door slammed shut.

The taxi driver made no complaint about prolonging the search. The village consisted of no more than a half-dozen dwellings, one of which was distinguished as the shop by boxes of produce displayed in front. A woman stood up from arranging some cabbages as they approached.

"Yes, lovely couple." She was more forthcoming than the pregnant neighbor. "The old man went first, beginning of winter, I think. Then the old lady died a couple of months later, after the Allies took over. Chaos, it was. I don't think there was even a funeral. Anyway, the place has just been left empty. Shame, really, with all these deportees coming home, looking for homes. And the folks that were bombed out from the city—"

Richard interrupted.

"What about the granddaughter?"

"Taken in by relatives, I heard."

"Who? One of the Loesseps' children?"

"No. They only had the one son, and he died before the war. Married a foreigner, I heard, but I never met her."

"She didn't come for the little girl?" Again, that rising note of anxiety. Berta gripped his hand to remind him of her presence, of the here-and-now, but he took no notice. "Dark curly hair, not very tall."

"No, it wasn't the mother. Other relatives. Don't know who." The woman bent to her cabbages again, tiring of the questioning. He still continued.

"Who else might know what happened?"

"Look," she straightened up, putting her hands on her hips. "There's nothing else to know. The old couple kept themselves to themselves, like we all did. They died. A lot of people died last winter. Someone took the girl in, someone not from around here. I don't know who, and if I don't know, no one does. End of story."

At last, he allowed Berta to lead him back to the taxi. On the journey to the station in Rotterdam and on the train home, he was distracted, staring out of the window and frowning at his thoughts. Berta knew he was unreachable in this state and asked no questions. She could only hope that when they resumed their life in Amsterdam, he would let go of this search.

Chapter 16

As time spooled out, and the shadow of the Occupation—although always present—lightened, Berta grew more confident, both in herself and in her father. She was encouraged in this confidence when she saw him relax in the company of his colleagues at faculty social events she attended. His special area—European folklore—placed him on the border of the History and Literature Departments. It was not a prestigious or glamorous topic which might inspire academic jealousies, and his gentle, self-deprecating manner quickly found him a circle of companions with whom to play chess or go to concerts. Students who selected his classes, thinking it an easier option than Nineteenth-Century Military History or the Agrarian Revolution, were drawn in by his enthusiasm and approachability, and ended up as devoted admirers, even if the subject turned out to be more demanding than they'd anticipated.

However, the habit of protecting her father from upsetting references—for example, to her mother's death—was ingrained. She resisted the urge to ask questions about the past and instead wove elaborate fantasies about Margriet, inventing mother-and-daughter conversations and imagining tender family scenes. If she had known about the files in her father's office at the University containing correspondence with the International Red Cross, Simon Wiesenthal's

Documentation Center in Austria, and other refugee organizations, she would have worried that he was sinking again into depression.

Richard Vandercam had not stopped looking for Nellie. Hundreds of thousands of refugees from the east followed the initial wave of returning deportees. Hundreds of thousands more had disappeared without leaving a trace. The story of what had happened in Eastern Europe during the war emerged at a glacial pace over the next months and years. Richard requested lists of displaced persons from every aid organization he could identify, and combed through them for Latvians. It was almost impossible to get accurate information about those who had not made it out from the territories now occupied by the Soviet army. The Russians made propaganda use of the Nazi atrocities but maintained a grim silence over the mass arrests and expulsions, torture, and firing squads carried out under the banner of Communism.

Richard conducted his efforts through his office at the University, reasoning that an academic letterhead might elicit a more complete response than an impassioned personal plea. But the urge to keep the research at a distance from his home life and hidden from Berta was also driven by an underlying sense of shame: he had left Nellie in Latvia in 1940. If only he had tried harder when he first arrived back in Holland to locate and evacuate her while he was still nominally employed by the Foreign Ministry. He had been anxious then about provoking inquiries into the visa scheme they had operated out of the consulate; it would have aroused the wrath of the German occupiers. Now, piecing together what might have happened to a single individual after five years of successive waves of violence seemed hopeless. And yet he persisted.

Ignorant of his fruitless efforts to find Nellie, Berta felt free to explore her own friendships with adolescent peers. The *gymnasium* she now attended was close to campus and numbered several faculty offspring amongst the students. The academic level as well as the students' level of sophistication were much higher than at the elementary school she had gone to in the Jordaan district. Berta hovered on the outskirts of various social groups until she found her niche.

Anika and Stefan Buls had spent the war years in Montreal—their mother was Canadian. Because they had escaped the privations of the Occupation, many of their classmates viewed them with a certain disdain. It might have been their status as outsiders that drew Berta to them. Anika was her age, fourteen, but physically more mature, already wearing a bra and sporting a jaunty ponytail rather than the schoolgirl braids that most girls, including Berta, wore. Her brother Stefan, two years older, seemed to relish his differences. He despised the rough sports that preoccupied his peers, preferring to spend his Saturday afternoons at the cinema rather than on the soccer field. His dark hair was longer than the norm, and he dressed in blue jeans and oversized black sweaters rather than the tweed jacket and peg-topped trousers that were *de rigueur* for Dutch teenage boys aping their elders.

The Buls family lived in a large house in the Plantage, a leafy neighborhood surrounding the oldest park in Amsterdam, with a zoo and botanical gardens. Professor Buls taught economics at the University and was frequently away advising governments on how to rebuild after wartime devastation. His wife's life was completely taken up with the youngest Buls, twin boys born in Canada, now three years old and united in an alliance to drive their mother to distraction. The teenagers had taken over the attic floor of the house, a haven where Berta spent many after-school hours listening to Stefan's collection of American jazz records and to Anika's descriptions of life in Montreal.

Elsa, another friend, often joined them. Her father had been killed during the Occupation, and her mother earned a scant living teaching art classes. Elsa, pale skin, light eyes, and white-blonde hair, had inherited her mother's talent. She sat now sketching the tray on which stood a jug of iced coffee and glasses. Rays of afternoon light fell through the single dormer window, picking up dust motes in the air and illuminating the tray like a spotlight. The summer heat collected in the attic space, but the four of them refused to complain. This was *their* space, furnished with a shabby sofa, exiled from the sitting room below, a rocking chair, its cane seat sagging toward the floor, and miscellaneous boxes shrouded in sheets. Stefan's prized gramophone occupied a rickety card table placed under the window.

"I don't understand why your father brought you back to Holland. Montreal sounds so wonderful—the food, the culture, the freedom..." Elsa's eyes darted between her sketch and her subject. "Everything here's so...gray."

"I'd go back in a heartbeat," Anika said. "Do you mind if I pour?" She indicated the jug. "Otherwise it'll get warm."

Elsa nodded her assent and put aside her pencil.

"What about you, Stefan?"

Berta leaned forward, eager to hear Stefan's response. She was the quiet one in the group—"our little owl," Stefan called her—reluctant to ask personal questions but curious about her friends' lives, contrasting them with her more limited experience.

"Canada's not so great. Montreal's quite conservative, you know. And the winters!" He pretended to shiver. "I think Father felt guilty about running away from the war, and he wanted to come back home to help with the reconstruction. He has some theories about uniting Western Europe into one economic zone, with one currency and free movement of goods and labor."

"What? Including West Germany? That'll never happen!" Elsa had told them her father was shot by the Germans. She was uncertain of the exact circumstances, but in her mind he had assumed the stature of a hero of the Resistance, and the enemy was never to be forgiven.

Berta sipped her coffee. She would have liked more sugar in it, and perhaps a dash of milk, but deferred to the others' more refined taste.

"What about your father, Berta?" Stefan asked. "What did he do during the war?"

"Hmm? Well, he was a diplomat, the Dutch consul in Latvia, but when the Germans took over, he was dismissed. And then…" She hesitated. How to describe his years of isolation in the Jordaan house? "Well, he stayed inside, mostly. I think he was grieving: my mother died in 1940. My grandmother looked after me." She knew her explanation sounded inadequate, but she lacked the bravado to fabricate a story that might depict her father's seclusion as some kind of courageous stand against the Occupier.

The others were silent as they contemplated her

statement. Then Elsa spoke, her voice softened with sympathy.

"She must have been very young, your mother. And you were only five. What was she like? Was she beautiful?"

"Yes!" Berta was glad she knew this from photographs at least. "Very beautiful. Blonde, like you."

"How did she die?" Stefan asked.

Berta looked down into her glass. She felt color rising to her cheeks. Her failure to remember her mother seemed shameful, as if she had let her mother down in some way. When Elsa spoke of her dead father, not just his bravery but the everyday details of life with him, Berta sensed a reproach. Why was her memory such a blank?

"I don't know. I just know she died when we returned from Latvia in 1940—that was my father's last posting." She took a deep breath. "To be honest, I really don't remember her, and I don't know how she died."

"But haven't you asked your father about it? If he loved her so much, you'd think he'd want to talk about her." This was Anika, frowning as she tried to grasp the situation.

"No. I don't want to upset him." This was true, but not the whole story. There had been so many times when it would have been natural for her father to make a reference to Margriet—nothing deep, just a casual comment, such as, "That was your mother's favorite color," or "I went there with Margriet in '34," but he never did. Berta came to accept his silence on the subject as inevitable. In the absence of concrete information, she wanted to protect her fantasies about her mother.

"Well, I think you have a right to know about her, or

at least how she died. She's *your* mother, as well as his wife." Elsa had never met Professor Vandercam and was puzzled by Berta's reticence. After a pause, she dropped her voice into a conspiratorial whisper. "Perhaps he's hiding something. Maybe he took advantage of the chaos to do away with her!"

Berta gasped.

"That's not true! How can you—"

"Shut up, Elsa!" Stefan cut in. "Stop making a big drama out of everything!"

An uncomfortable silence ensued. Berta fought back sudden tears. She wanted to defend her father, even though she knew Elsa wasn't serious in her accusation. She wanted to tell them they didn't understand how kind and gentle her father was, but she couldn't find any words to explain, and knew if she tried, she would end up floundering.

Stefan moved over to the sofa to sit at Berta's side. Anika emptied the last of the iced coffee into her glass. Conversation resumed in a stilted fashion. After a few minutes, Elsa said she had to get home, and left.

Stefan put a Benny Goodman record on at low volume.

"Elsa's an idiot, but you know it *is* strange your father won't talk about your mother. After all, it's been eight years since she died. Perhaps the wound has healed. He may be ready to speak about her now."

Anika nodded in agreement with her brother.

"I suppose so," Berta murmured. "But it has to be the right moment. He's so much happier than he used to be. I don't want to make him sad again."

"Aren't you leaving soon for your trip? Perhaps, when it's just the two of you, relaxing away from home, there'll be an opportunity to talk about her."

The following week, Berta was to accompany her father to the Languedoc region of France, where Richard would conduct field research into local folklore. Berta was excited to see a different landscape than the flat Dutch countryside, taste different food, and try out her schoolroom French. After a couple of days in Perpignan, where Richard had an introduction at the university, they would strike out into the foothills of the Pyrenees, staying in village inns and hiking or begging rides on farm carts to get from place to place. Berta knew her father anticipated the expedition with equal pleasure. Cut off by the Iron Curtain from Eastern Europe and his previous areas of study, Languedoc offered Richard a fresh beginning. Perhaps their trip also offered an opportunity to broach the subject of her mother's death. Berta was a teenager now; she couldn't continue to make up childish stories to fill the gaps in her knowledge.

"Yes, you're right. I *will* ask him about her," Berta said, resolved to end the silence between herself and her father.

But, a little later, as she said goodbye to her friends and mounted her bicycle for the short ride home, she wondered whether she would find the courage to disturb the serene surface of their relationship with questions about the mysteries of the past.

Chapter 17

Everything about the Languedoc region enchanted Berta: the colors, the heat, the food. The fragrance of lavender that remained on her hand after she ran her fingers through the bush. The walnut-brown faces of the farmers' wives behind their market stalls. The music of cicadas at night. Even the taut feel of sunburned skin on her shoulders.

In these exotic surroundings where no one knew her, she felt liberated from self-consciousness. When she and her father first arrived in Perpignan, she hesitated to try out her schoolgirl French, but she soon discovered that the years of repetitive drills, chanting verb conjugations and memorizing vocabulary, had served a purpose: she had an ear for the language. No one corrected her; on the contrary, the innkeepers, waiters, and bus drivers on whom she practiced her well-rehearsed phrases praised her efforts and found her "*charmante!*" In four weeks of wandering between hilltop villages and dusty small-town libraries, accompanying her father as he tracked down the guardians of centuries-old traditions, she lost her shyness.

Richard called her his amanuensis. Uncertain exactly what the word meant, she embraced her assignment to take notes as he conducted his interviews. In the evening, once they had washed away the dust of the day and were waiting to be called to the table at their *auberge*, they would compare their transcripts and talk about the individuals they had met that day: the ancient *abbé,* his rusty black cassock redolent of incense; the amateur folklorist who had sung to them—in a trembling tenor—a ballad from the time of the Crusades. Berta felt closer to her father than ever before.

The expedition freed Richard too. He was embarking on a new field of study: the Cathars, a thirteenth-century sect that rejected the corruption and materialism of the Catholic hierarchy. The Cathars were brutally suppressed by the armies of the established church, their strongholds in the Pyrenees besieged, and when the starving inhabitants surrendered, they were burned at the stake. Although very little of Cathar culture had been recorded, Richard remained hopeful that somewhere deep in the mountains a trove of stories and songs survived, passed on through generations of peasants isolated from modern life. This area of research was a complete departure from Eastern European folklore; its novelty energized him, and sharing the journey with Berta heightened his delight. This summer, he would merely chart the outline of his investigation. He planned successive trips to delve deeper.

In a couple of days they would start their homeward journey back to Perpignan to catch the train. As a reward for their labors, and an opportunity to review and annotate his notes before memories faded, Richard had booked them into a small hotel on the harbor at Collioure, a fishing village thirty kilometers north of the Spanish border. Even in August, there were few visitors. On the surface, the war had not touched this corner of France. No Germans had been stationed here; no Allied Army had pushed through to liberate the populace. When locals spoke of "the war" they might mean the Spanish Civil War, concluded before the hostilities that embroiled the rest of Europe began. Collioure was in Catalan country. The refugees who fled north after Franco's victory in Spain had found a welcome here. They spoke the same language, ate the same food, and, once they spread out into the surrounding countryside, they grew the same crops on the rocky terraces that climbed up from the Mediterranean. Masked by a grave courtesy, the Catalans—both French and Spanish—maintained a suspicious eye on the few tourists now beginning to penetrate into their territory.

Richard and Berta were the only diners left on the terrace of the hotel. Moths hurled themselves at the lights suspended over their heads. Scraps of conversation from the regulars at the bar inside competed with the lap of water against the sea wall, as a three-quarter moon climbed up the sky, unrolling a path of silver across the harbor. Berta sighed with contentment, and her father smiled back at her.

Several times on their trip, she had thought about Stefan's advice to start a conversation about the past, the events and people in her early life that she could not recall, but something had stopped her, either an external distraction or her own failure of nerve. She had even rehearsed how to approach the subject. *This was the moment*, Berta thought.

"Tell me about Latvia." Berta kept her voice soft, her eyes on her father and her body motionless.

Richard looked into his glass of cognac and swirled it around before responding.

"Those were terrible times." He paused. "Latvia was squeezed between the Germans and the Russians; the country was invaded three times. Such suffering!"

With an effort, Berta suppressed her impatience.

"I didn't mean the war. I meant before, when we were living there: what was it like? Where did we live? What did we do?"

Richard let his breath out slowly.

"Well, we lived in the Dutch Consulate, a big house built of stone, with high ceilings and old-fashioned furniture. The offices were on the ground floor, which opened straight onto the street, and the living quarters were upstairs." As the memories came, he gathered speed. "There was a large, walled garden behind the house, a bit overgrown. You used to love playing there—" He broke off and took a swallow of his drink, coughing a little.

"And Mama? What did she do?" Berta imagined her mother chasing her around the wild garden, both of them giggling. Her father's answer was disappointing.

"Your mother organized the entertaining, dinners for officials and such. And she supervised the staff."

"Oh. Did she like it there?"

Richard smiled at her sadly.

"No, I don't think she liked Riga that much. She would have preferred Paris or New York, something livelier. In the end, she just wanted to go back to Amsterdam."

Berta digested this in silence. Her mother had got her wish: she had come back to Amsterdam, and then she had died. Why? She had to know.

"What did she die of, Papa? Did she catch some disease on the train home? Grandmother said the journey was awful. Or did the Germans—"

"I don't know. I wasn't there." Richard's voice cut

flatly across her rising tide of questions. Berta stiffened. Her father's words echoed around in her head, drowning out the hum of chatter from the bar, the splash of wavelets in the harbor. He wasn't there when her mother died. It made no sense.

"What do you mean?" she whispered.

"As soon as we got back to Amsterdam, I had to leave again. I had to take a little girl—a Dutch child who had been living in Latvia—to her grandparents. I left you and your mother with Oma. When I returned a few days later, your mother was already... Your grandmother took care of everything."

Berta stared at him, waiting for more, willing him to explain. Eventually, he dragged his eyes back from the horizon and met her gaze.

"She died in her sleep, that's all I know. Your grandmother took care of..." Realizing he was repeating himself, Richard stopped. He tossed off the rest of the cognac, and looked over his shoulder into the bar to catch the proprietor's eye to signal for the bill. "Do you want to go up first? I'm going to take a stroll before bed."

A little later, after she had changed into her nightdress and washed her hands and face, Berta crossed to the window and nudged open the shutter. Their rooms were at the front of the hotel, looking out over the harbor. The air was warm and still. The lights on the terrace had been extinguished, and the moon now reigned supreme. Leaning out, Berta could discern the headlands on either side of the bay, reaching out to form a darker profile against the indigo sky. Her father's shirt showed as a gray patch at the end of the jetty. He was looking down into the water, shoulders hunched and hands shoved in his trouser pockets.

He wasn't there. Was that the reason he avoided any mention of her mother or her death? Guilt? Her father believed he *should* have been there. Berta's instinct was to agree. Having brought them across war-ravaged Europe to enemy-occupied Holland, he shouldn't have abandoned them, even into the care of his own mother. Perhaps if he'd been there he could have somehow prevented her mother's death. Then she thought back to the trip they took to Rotterdam three years ago, just after the war. Papa was looking for a little girl who had been living with her grandparents. The grandparents were dead, but the girl had survived the war and gone to live with other relatives. *She* must have been the child from Latvia he brought back to Holland, the reason he was absent when her mother died. He was fulfilling his duty as a diplomat. But Berta felt a nagging impression that there was something else, not guilt or duty but some other narrative underlying the bald facts he had disclosed. She peered out at her father's back, willing him to turn and spot her, give a wave, and head back to the hotel. *Look, ask me anything you want. I'm sorry I've made such a mystery of everything. I was just trying to protect you, but you're almost grown up now, so…*

Her father did not turn around. She knew with gloomy certainty that a door had closed, and she would be unable to pry it open. Her father would continue to bury his memories inside. She needed to be content with the present and look forward into the future. She had to give up questions about the past.

He wasn't there.

Chapter 18

The letter came a few days before her eighteenth birthday.

After school, she had gone home with Anika to study. The school leaving examinations were months away, but the pressure was already mounting among the senior class. All her teachers and classmates expected Berta to go on to the University to take a place in the Modern Languages department. Her high grades and studious habits, not her father's faculty position, ensured this. For Anika, academics were not so easy. Hence the daily sessions up in the Buls' attic.

Stefan offered to walk her home. He still lived with the family although he was a second-year student of political science at the University. As they approached the entrance to Berta's apartment building, Stefan grabbed her hand.

"Why don't you apply to McGill, and come to Canada with me?" He was to transfer to the prestigious Montreal university in the fall.

Berta laughed.

"You're not serious! I couldn't leave Papa." She turned to look at him closely. "You *are* serious. What is it? Are you nervous about going to Montreal? You know the place, and you have family there."

Stefan shrugged and looked away. Berta sensed the reason for his unease. They had been a couple for a while, but, besides themselves, only Anika knew the truth. Other than holding hands and chaste goodnight kisses, their relationship was platonic. Stefan was not attracted to girls. In a new environment, without Berta to cover for him, he would be exposed and vulnerable.

When Stefan did not reply, Berta did not press the issue. She busied herself with opening the mailbox and sorting through the contents.

"Hey, look at this." The envelope, addressed to her, was good quality stationery; the return address in elegant script read *Willem Kemp, Advocaat.* She held it out to Stefan. "What do you think it's about?"

"Open it, silly!" Stefan adopted a stagey foreign accent. "Perhaps you will learn something to your advantage!"

Berta extracted the single page letter, and stood close to Stefan as they read it together:

In the matter of the De Vos Family Trust:

I have the honor of serving as trustee of the above-named trust, established under the will of Gertrud De Vos, deceased.

Please present yourself with a form of identification at my offices on Tuesday, 17 February, 1953 at 10 a.m. to be informed of the provisions of the trust and the conditions for its dissolution.

Willem Kemp.

"Who's Gertrud De Vos?" asked Stefan.

"No idea, but my mother's family name was De Vos, so a distant relative, I guess."

"Maybe you're an heiress—rich beyond your wildest dreams!"

"Ha! Not likely. I've never had any contact with my mother's family. I thought they were all dead." Berta refolded the letter and replaced it in the envelope. Although she pretended disinterest, her mind was alive with questions—questions she had taught herself to suppress. Perhaps this lawyer had some answers.

****

Berta did not share Willem Kemp's letter with her father. The omission was not deliberate—at least at first. On the day the letter arrived, Richard did not return home until after Berta was in bed asleep. He had gone straight from the University to a performance of *Lohengrin* at the opera. The next morning, he was humming the Wedding March when he came into the kitchen for breakfast. Berta was already seated with a bowl of muesli in front of her.

"I overslept. Wagner does go on a bit. Is there coffee?" Richard bent to kiss Berta's cheek. She pointed to the coffeepot on the stove and steeled herself to broach the subject of the lawyer's letter.

Richard glanced at his watch. "Never mind. I'll get something on the way. I have an early seminar. See you tonight."

With a wave, he was gone.

As Berta sat for another fifteen minutes over a cup of coffee, her frustration hardened into a knot of anger. Why was it so difficult to touch upon anything that reached into the past? Her father guarded his secrets like a miser. But it was *her* history too. Papa was selfish to hoard his memories. Well, if he kept secrets, she would have secrets too. She would not tell him about the appointment with the lawyer. She might learn nothing from *Advocaat* Kemp. Or he might reveal a mine of information about her mother. Depending on the outcome, she would discuss the appointment with her father *after* it happened.

With this resolved, she started to plan. Tuesday, February 17th was her birthday, but also a normal school day. Papa no doubt would make a celebratory breakfast before he left for work and she left for school. She would have time to double back and change into more adult clothes appropriate to a meeting with a lawyer. She checked the Kemp office address: close to the Rijksmuseum, a single tram ride away. Now she had to keep her growing excitement in check over the intervening weekend. If Papa questioned why she seemed nervous, she could say she was looking forward to her birthday.

Tuesday dawned cold but dry. Her father became damp-eyed as he presented her with a slim rectangular box. Berta opened it to find a gold chain with an oval locket dangling from it.

"Papa, it's lovely!" She unclasped it with anticipation, but both interior faces of the locket were empty.

"I thought I'd let you choose: perhaps a photo of Stefan?" Richard spoke shyly. He liked Stefan and was pleased about his daughter's friendship, but it was against his nature to press her for details. "Open the card."

The card was decorated with a design of pink roses and inscribed with a saccharine poem "to my daughter." But Berta's attention was on the folded paper inside.

"Oh, thank you! A check for one hundred guilder!" She laughed. She had never had this much money.

"I thought we could go together on Saturday and open a bank account for you. It's time you had some financial independence." Richard looked at his watch. "We should get going. Tonight, I'd like to take you out to dinner—if you have no other plans. Do you want to invite Stefan?"

For a few minutes, Berta had forgotten about the appointment with the lawyer. Now she thought that this evening she might have something of substance to talk to her father about.

"No, Papa. Let it just be us two."

Richard beamed, pleased with his daughter's preference.

As soon as her father disappeared around the corner of their street, Berta turned and let herself back into the apartment. She thought the dark green dress she had bought for Christmas would work. Made of fine wool, it was cut simply, with a boatneck and a narrow black leather belt. She exchanged socks for nylon stockings and put on her only pair of high heels. She wished she had borrowed some makeup from Anika, but then considered that without Anika's expertise in applying it, she might end up looking clownish. She wasted ten minutes trying to fashion her long brown hair into a French pleat, then gave up and tied it at the nape with a ribbon matching her dress.

She arrived at Willem Kemp's office a minute before ten. The nameplate at the door announced several professional offices, but Kemp, on the ground floor, was the only lawyer. She entered the reception area and walked toward a woman seated behind a desk.

"I have an appointment with *Meneer* Kemp. I'm Berta Vandercam."

The receptionist rose and came around the desk, gesturing for Berta's coat. Berta was glad to relinquish it. Having no other, she had worn her everyday school raincoat, too short to cover the skirt of her dress. As she was ushered through to the lawyer's office, she remembered that the required form of identification—her passport—was in the raincoat pocket. The door closed behind her, and she stood uncertain whether to retreat or go forward.

The office was paneled in dark wood, interspersed with floor-to-ceiling bookshelves containing leather-backed tomes. Heavy drapes tied to the side with silk ropes let in weak shafts of winter sunlight. Behind a director's desk sat a large middle-aged man with a florid complexion. Willem Kemp rose slowly to his feet. He was dressed with old-fashioned formality, black suit and white shirt with wing-tip collar. Another man was sitting in the visitor's chair. He rose too, revealing a slighter build than the lawyer. He wore a gray suit too lightweight for the season. His neatly trimmed hair and beard were blond-turning-to-gray, his eyes as pale as his suit.

"Miss Vandercam? Berta Vandercam?"

Berta nodded. Kemp indicated another chair, and Berta moved carefully over to it and sat. The men followed suit.

"I am Willem Kemp. I, and my father before me, have represented the De Vos family for over fifty years." He paused and looked at Berta sharply. "You know who I mean?"

Berta cleared her throat.

"I... er... My mother's family name was De Vos."

The other man interrupted.

"Kemp, you're frightening her!" He smiled at Berta. "Let's start with introductions. Hello, Berta. I'm your Uncle Martin. Very pleased to meet you."

The lawyer seemed offended at being upstaged, but

Berta did not notice. She gaped at the man in the gray suit, unable to form a response. Uncle Martin. Her mother had a brother! She felt completely unprepared for this.

"Hrumph. Well, yes, Martin is another beneficiary of the trust, and he's here—"

"To meet my niece!"

Kemp seemed to feel control of the meeting slipping away. His face reddened further.

"As I was saying, I represent the De Vos family, including the De Vos trust established under the will of Gertrud De Vos, Martin's mother, and...er...your grandmother." He spoke fast now to forestall any further interruption. Berta struggled to keep up. "Grandmother" elicited an image of Oma, white hair piled high, patrician profile, the grand old lady who had steered Berta and her father through the war, her father's mother. The lawyer continued to speak.

"The beneficiaries of the trust are—were—her daughter, Margriet, and her sons, Martin and Gilbert. And their offspring."

Sons? Berta looked to Martin for an explanation.

"Gilbert lives in the south, in Limburg. He inherited our father's estate there, and he manages it with his sons." Martin's voice was precise, with a faint accent Berta could not place.

More sons. Cousins. She had a whole extended family, just like other people!

"The trust terminates on the eighteenth birthday of the youngest child of Gertrud's three children." Kemp raised his eyes from the papers in front of him. He and Martin looked at Berta.

After a pause, she felt compelled to say, "Me."

"Exactly." Kemp gathered speed again. "After termination, the corpus of the trust is to be divided amongst the surviving beneficiaries with any deceased beneficiary's share going to the deceased's offspring. Martin has no known offspring—"

"I have *no* offspring, known or unknown."

"Quite. Martin will execute a release attesting to that fact and renouncing any further claim on the trust beyond his own share of the corpus. Gilbert has signed a similar statement on behalf of himself and his sons…" Kemp fumbled through the papers in front of him, searching unsuccessfully for their names. "Anyway, all that remains is for you to acknowledge the terms of the trust and its dissolution." More fumbling. The lawyer separated two documents, which he placed on the side of the desk facing Martin and Berta. With his pen, he indicated where Martin should sign. Martin scrawled a signature without reading the document, then handed the pen to Berta. He looked amused.

"Aren't you going to ask how much is coming to you?"

Berta was startled at the question. Her thoughts were spinning around the fact of her newly discovered family. She had not considered the money. Kemp took over again.

"You will receive one-third of the trust corpus, your sixth and your mother's share, which reverted to the trust after her death. It's all there in the trust termination statement."

Berta stared at the jumble of words on the page. The dense legal language defeated her. After a few moments, she signed on the line above her name and handed the document back to Kemp. He produced a manila folder.

"This contains an account of your share of the trust assets currently being held in your name at the Amsterdamsche Bank. The bank officer's business card is in the folder. I suggest you make an appointment with him as soon as possible."

Inside the folder, several stapled pages listed companies on the left and guilder amounts on the right. Berta recognized the names of major European manufacturers, banks, and conglomerates. She turned the pages to the last, where the total value of holdings was double-underlined: 113,408 guilders. She gasped. It was an unimaginable sum of money. She flashed back to her birthday present: one hundred guilders might buy a small, second-hand car. A hundred times that amount would buy…?

Kemp's voice brought her back into the room.

"So, if you have no questions, that concludes our business." He stood up.

****

Berta drifted in a daze toward the tram stop.

"Hold on!"

Martin De Vos came up beside her and took her arm.

"Don't think you can just disappear. I'm taking you to lunch, and I'm going to find out where you've been hiding all these years."

Berta stopped walking and turned to her uncle. He was about the same height as she. She calculated he must be almost fifty, but he looked younger, aided by a tan that made him look exotic in the winter streets of Amsterdam. His mouth had a twist, as if he was trying to suppress a smile, and his eyes twinkled. Berta realized with a rush of pleasure that this was her chance to find out about her mother.

"I'd love to have lunch. But I haven't been hiding. I've lived in Amsterdam since I was five years old."

"To be honest, it's me that has been hiding. I moved to Paris in '36, and I come back to Amsterdam as little as possible." He gave a mock shiver. "How can you stand it?"

Berta was wise enough to recognize that Martin did not require an answer. He continued to chatter as he guided her toward the restaurant. He was an architect and traveled frequently for his work. He had an apartment on the Ile de la Cité, and a studio in Antibes. Had she been to Paris? Did she like French food? He hoped so because this was the only decent restaurant in Amsterdam.

He opened the door and followed her into a dimly lit dining room. In spite of his claimed aversion to the city, he was apparently known in this establishment. A waiter showed them to a corner table and began an intense conversation in French about the menu.

"Shall I order for you?" Martin asked.

Berta thought it was time she asserted herself. She addressed the server in French.

"The *sôle bonne femme* sounds delicious. May I have *pommes mousseline* with it?"

Martin laughed with delight.

"Superb accent! Do I detect a hint of the *Midi*?"

"My father and I spend every summer in Languedoc. It's for his research."

"Ah." The wine arrived and Martin poured her a glass without asking. "Now, go on. You want to know why we've never contacted you before this."

"I never knew my mother had brothers, that I have cousins. My father never said…"

"No, and I think I know why." He sighed. "We never

understood why they married. Margriet was quite the party girl, and Richard was so dull and serious. But then I moved to Paris and lost touch. After Mother died, I had no reason to come back to Holland, and anyway Margriet was off in foreign parts. Then the war." He sipped his wine, considering his words. "Gilbert chose the wrong side. He joined the NSB, and when the Germans occupied Amsterdam, they appointed him to some important position. He enjoyed the power. It was an opportunity to even scores."

"You mean with Papa? Why?" Berta could not imagine her mild-mannered father making enemies.

"I think he felt Richard looked down on him. Gilbert's no intellectual, boasts of being a simple country farmer, although after the war he really didn't have much choice. Amsterdam became extremely uncomfortable for him and all the others who collaborated with the Nazis. He escaped to Limburg and the family estate. He stays down there all the time now. But it was more than just resenting Richard's brains. He was protective of Margriet."

The waiter arrived with their food. During the pause, Berta absorbed this information, working out how it fit with her father's withdrawal during the Occupation. When they had been served, Martin resumed.

"Gilbert blames Richard for Margriet's death."

"What?" The baldness of Martin's statement shocked Berta. "Why?"

Martin shrugged.

"Margriet was unhappy in Riga. She wrote to us, more often to Gilbert than me. I knew she was bored, and I think the differences between her personality and Richard's were beginning to show. She wasn't interested in politics, and he wasn't interested in parties. Gilbert told me—this was years later—that she suspected Richard was having an affair. I thought it was most unlikely, but Gilbert adored Margriet and disliked Richard from the start, so…"

Martin began to eat his fish, while Berta just stared at her plate. He seemed unconcerned that he was delivering shock after shock to an unsophisticated young girl. He assumed everyone was as detached and urbane as he. A life lived for style and culture had not equipped him with empathy. To him, Berta was charming, a curiosity, and the situation he found himself in was intriguing. He was already rehearsing the anecdotes he would share with his Parisian friends.

Eventually, Berta spoke quietly and emphatically.

"That is ridiculous. Papa wasn't even in Amsterdam when Mama died. He was devastated by her death. And he has never shown any interest in other women. You don't know him."

Martin shrugged.

"You're right, of course. I'm just telling you what Gilbert thinks. That's why he never showed any interest in you, why he wouldn't come today to meet you. Now, let's talk about something more pleasant. What are you going to do with all that lovely money?"

Berta shrugged. She had no idea. Martin leant back and surveyed her through narrowed eyes.

"You have Margriet's build: tall and slim," he said. "I suppose you get your coloring and facial features from your father's side."

Berta knew this was not a compliment: her mother had been beautiful. Berta was not. In her own estimation, she was ordinary, with light brown hair, regular features, gray eyes. But she was not interested in visual comparisons.

"Tell me what Mama was like growing up."

"Hmm." Martin emptied the wine bottle into his glass and drank before responding. "I didn't actually see a lot of her. I'm six years older, so I was away most of the time at school and university. She was a pretty little thing, full of fun. Our parents were rich, but it was new money; they weren't quite "top drawer" so they entertained a lot—barons and judges, government ministers and the like—trying to acquire class by association. I remember one time, a reception Margriet was too young to attend—she was about ten—but Gilbert and I were scrubbed and suited, told to be on our best behavior, not to get drunk. Anyway, Margriet dressed herself in a party frock and crept downstairs. Before Mother could intervene, she approached this old general, all moustache and medals, and asked him if he wanted to watch her dance. Mother was livid, but the general thought Margriet was charming." Martin smiled at the memory.

"And did she dance?" Berta prompted.

"Oh, yes. She twirled and sashayed, brought the party to a standstill. Everyone applauded. But she paid for it later."

"What do you mean?"

"Locked in her room with no food," Martin paused. "Mother did not tolerate disobedience."

Berta tried to imagine her mother's childhood— lavish parties and cruel punishments, and the nerve to perform in front of a room full of important guests. It contrasted so markedly from the narrow, protected world in which she had grown up. She couldn't imagine flaunting the rules and showing off as her mother had done.

Martin continued.

"Maybe that's why she married so young—to escape Mother. Richard came along at just the right time."

Berta pressed for more stories, but after the second bottle was opened, Martin's responses became vague and wandered off into reminiscences of his pre-war days in Paris.

Chapter 19

After she left Martin, and without a second thought, Berta abandoned her plan to return to school for afternoon classes. She let herself into the apartment and walked through to her bedroom. Kicking off her shoes, she fell back onto the bed, allowing the images and phrases of her meeting with Kemp and more especially the lunch with Martin to swirl around in her brain. A Parisian architect, a Limburger farmer, grown-up cousins whose names she still didn't know. And, at last, some memories of her mother, even if they were secondhand. She drifted into sleep, picturing her mother as a child, dancing in her party dress.

Berta woke to the sound of her father's key in the front door. She sat up and swung her feet to the floor. Her head was pounding and her mouth tasted sour and dry. She closed her eyes and waited for her stomach to stop churning. When she looked up, Richard was framed in the bedroom doorway.

"Hello, dear. I see you've already changed for our evening out." His beaming smile faded as he took in his daughter's scowl and disheveled hair. "What is it? What's the matter?"

"Why didn't you tell me I had uncles and cousins— a real family?"

Richard recoiled as if he had been struck. He followed Berta as she pushed past him to the kitchen. She filled a glass from the tap and drank it down. Richard was still struggling to find a response.

"Your uncle Gilbert is not a good person—"

She cut him off, her voice shrill and loud.

"I know, Gilbert was a Nazi during the war. But the war's over, Papa. It's been over for eight years. Now he's just a Limburger farmer with two grownup sons. And Martin's an architect in Paris. Completely respectable. Why wasn't I allowed to know about them?" She had never spoken to her father in this tone before.

"Martin's still alive? He disappeared years ago—"

"Of course he's still alive! He's younger than you. And he just moved to Paris, not to Mars!"

"How do you know all this?"

"I had lunch with Martin today." She couldn't help feeling triumphant at her father's shocked expression. "That was after a meeting with the family lawyer." She swept past him again to retrieve the manila folder left in the entrance hall. "Another thing you didn't tell me about—Mama's trust fund." She pushed the folder into his hands and stood, hands on hips, as he opened it and read Kemp's letter, then flipped through the trust fund account.

"I didn't know..." He looked up at his daughter's face. "I mean, I knew your mother had a share in the family trust, but I assumed it reverted to the fund when she died. I didn't realize..." Again, words failed him.

Berta remembered Gilbert's claim that her father had been having an affair, and that her mother's despair over this contributed to her death. She was on the point of repeating the accusation but held back. After all, Martin had quickly distanced himself from Gilbert's theory. Looking at Richard now, the bravado of an affair

155

seemed improbable: he was diminished, shoulders bowed, eyes watery behind his glasses. A trace of pity penetrated the anger that propelled her.

Her voice softer, she asked, "Why, Papa, why?"

"I was just trying to protect you."

Her rage flared again.

"No! You were just protecting yourself! You felt guilty because you made Mama unhappy, and her brothers knew it. You couldn't face them."

For several seconds, they stood staring at each other in tense silence. Then Richard turned and walked slowly into his bedroom, shutting the door behind him.

****

As anticipated, Berta scored well in her school leaving exams in June. But she did not take up the place offered at the University. When she and her father left Amsterdam in July for his annual research trip, she remained in Paris while he continued his journey south to Languedoc. She stayed with Martin in his apartment on the Ile de la Cité. Martin accompanied her to art galleries and the theater, but mostly she was left to explore the city on her own. At a reception for some visiting architects, Martin introduced her to an acquaintance, an editor of books on architecture and design. He in turn connected her with his publishing house, and when her father returned to Paris on his way home in September, she announced her new position. She had accepted an entry-level job with a prominent publishing firm in Paris.

Relations between father and daughter had calmed to mutual civility, with awkward subjects avoided. Richard understood he had lost parental authority, but he had never been heavy-handed in his child-rearing, preferring to trust in Berta's good sense and natural caution. He had been nervous at leaving Berta with Martin, but their meeting had gone smoothly, Martin's courteous refinement avoiding any embarrassment that might have intruded. If Richard was distraught at Berta's decision to start a new life in Paris, he disguised it, fussing about the practical details of accommodation and transport.

Finances were not a worry. Although her new position paid very little, she had her newfound wealth to cushion her. Initially, she stayed with Martin while she searched for a place of her own. She settled on a three-room apartment on the top floor of a nineteenth-century building in the Marais, walking distance from the vast wholesale marketplace of Les Halles, and with a view over the rooftops to Notre Dame's twin Gothic towers.

"The fourth *arrondissement* is not a fashionable area now," Martin observed. "But the building has good bones, and I predict in a decade people will be killing each other to get a place here. You're making a good investment."

She paid cash, astonishing the owner and depleting her inheritance by a third. She was careful about furnishing the apartment, scouring the flea markets at Place de Clichy and Clignancourt for pieces she could haul up three flights and refurbish to fit the style of a place with sloping ceilings and uneven floors. A particular joy was the tiny south-facing terrace abutting the kitchen. Before the cooler weather set in, Berta had filled it with pots of herbs.

She described her life in glowing terms in letters to Anika, a struggling Social Sciences student at Amsterdam University, and Stefan, now in Montreal.

"I can't wait to have you visit me here. It's so cozy and close to everything. There's a café downstairs where I can grab a croissant on my way to work. The neighbors have lived here for ages. They're so sweet; they fuss over me like I was their daughter. I'm beginning to make friends outside of work. There's a jazz club around the corner with the most fantastic musicians. Django Reinhardt played there last year! Lots of students from the Sorbonne go, and I've got to know a few." She did not reveal that one, Gilles, a medical student from Toulouse, was a particular friend.

The confidence she projected in her letters was a shield she constructed to still the occasional misgivings about the wisdom of her move to Paris. The apartment was her haven, but every time she left its sanctuary she became *l'étrangère*, the foreigner. Her accent, her clothes, her long straight hair marked her out amongst the *chic* Parisian women, with their little black costumes and pixie cuts. They even smelled different: a mixture of Chanel No. 5 and Gauloise cigarettes. Friends, especially female friends, were not so easy to make as she pretended. But she was determined to survive; she would not slink back to Amsterdam defeated.

To allay her doubts, she threw herself into her job at Jacquard Presse. Her title was "editorial assistant," which translated to "gofer." She arranged hotels and dinners for visiting authors, couriered galleys to and from the printer, and typed cover letters. Gradually, her quiet reliability earned her the respect of a few senior editors, even though to most she was invisible. Her small successes gave her confidence. She enjoyed many aspects of the publishing world: the smell of a freshly bound preview copy on its way to *Le Figaro*; an editor's excited yelp when he (and they were all men) found new talent in the slush pile. There were some prima donnas amongst the editors, agents, and authors, but she learned to avoid them, even while studying their style and self-assurance.

At Christmas, she returned home for a week. Amsterdam seemed dull and provincial, her father older and paler. She wondered if he was ill, but he denied it, and she could find no evidence in the bathroom medicine cabinet. He asked polite questions about the apartment and her job. She answered with a cheerful portrayal of her life, short on details but designed to allay any suspicion that she was regretting her move. She spent time with Anika—Stefan would stay in Montreal until the next summer—and sympathized with her over her demanding study schedule. They went together to a New Year's Eve party where Berta recognized several of her former classmates.

"Where's Elsa? Is she coming?" Berta scanned the room for Elsa's white-blonde hair. Standing nearby, two boys who overheard Berta's question smirked. Anika drew her away into a corner.

"Elsa's having a baby," she whispered.

"What? Why didn't you tell me?" Berta was pulled between pity for Elsa and irritation at the secrecy that seemed to dog her. Why couldn't people just be honest?

"No one's supposed to know, but of course everyone does. She's gone to stay at a place on the coast until the baby's born. It'll be adopted."

"Have you been to see her?" Berta demanded.

Anika was downcast.

"I wanted to, but Mother said it was best to stay away. Elsa won't say who the father is. Obviously, he

159

refused to marry her. It's such a shame."

"But I don't understand. Elsa's an intelligent girl. Surely, she knew to take precautions."

Anika looked shocked.

"Take precautions? What do you mean? She should never have let him do it! If she'd stayed a virgin, she wouldn't have ruined her life!"

Berta turned away, suppressing an angry outburst. She was suddenly aware of the gulf between her and Anika, between her and all the other old friends in the room. They were still living by an old-fashioned code, narrow-minded and conservative: Elsa's pregnancy was Elsa's fault, and she would carry the stain of it forever. After four months of living independently in Paris, that code no longer controlled Berta.

She wondered what Anika would say if she told her that a month ago, she had deliberately invited Gilles up to her apartment and into her bed. She had planned every detail of the evening, including getting fitted for a diaphragm, which she was amused to discover was called "a Dutch cap" in English. She was under no illusion that she and Gilles were in love or that they would marry. She knew that in June, when he finished classroom studies, he would return to Toulouse for his clinical internship. Gilles was attractive and fun to be with. He was a considerate lover who understood his role in introducing her to the pleasure of sex, and virginity was a burden she was eager to shed.

No, she would not tell Anika about Gilles.

Chapter 20

An early heatwave held the city captive. Every window in the apartment was flung wide to catch a breath of air. They lay hip to hip on the bed, sweat glazing their limbs.

Berta was taller than Jean-Paul. When they were out together, he liked her to wear flats, but after lovemaking, he called her his beautiful beanpole, and traced the superior length of her thighbone with a lazy finger. He came to Paris almost every week, and almost every week a long lunch turned into an afternoon of pleasure in her apartment. She told Genevieve, her assistant—since she was an editor now and had her own gofer—that she had a meeting and would not be back that day. The assistant nodded, eyes downcast, but Berta felt her smirking as soon as she turned her back.

Jean-Paul and Berta had met two years before at a gallery opening. He was not an art connoisseur; he ran a manufacturing company in Rouen owned by his wife's family. But he had received an invitation to the *vernissage* through a business associate, and, having nothing better to do before he caught the late train home, he had accepted. As soon as he entered, Berta caught and held his eyes.

In the seventeen years since she had arrived in Paris, Berta had become beautiful. She carried herself with the assurance of a mature woman. Honey streaks lightened her mouse-brown hair. She favored simple sheath dresses, ending—in the fashion of the day—three inches above her knee. If it was cool, she threw on a Chanel jacket (bought half-price at a sample sale). If it was wet, she wore a classic Burberry raincoat. In winter, chestnut riding boots, and in all seasons, the hint of a golden tan, thanks to Uncle Martin and the loan of his Antibes studio. There had been other lovers since Gilles, the medical student. None had lasted more than a season, and with most she had parted friends. Work was her focus. She thought the affair with Jean-Paul had lasted longer than the others because their weekly trysts fitted into her schedule.

Jean-Paul lit a cigarette, and Berta, irritated by the smoke, got up and walked naked to the open windows.

"Shall I make a reservation for dinner?" she asked, looking out over the rooftops. Notre Dame shimmered in the heat but everything beyond was grayed out by smog.

"Sure. I don't have to go back until tomorrow," Jean-Paul blew a steady stream of smoke at the ceiling and smiled with contentment, thinking of the night to come.

"When are you leaving for the Riviera?"

Berta's question made him frown. On July 1, the annual exodus would begin. He, his wife, and their sulky teenage son would join most of France on clogged roads aiming south—in his case, to his wife's family villa in the hills above Cannes.

"Thursday," he replied. "It's even hotter there than here. Don't know why I bother."

Berta didn't respond. It was part of their compact that his family life should continue undisturbed by their affair. A month every summer on the Côte d'Azur was expected, as were a week's skiing in the Alps every February and spending Christmas and *Réveillon* at home in Rouen. Berta suspected that his wife knew he had a mistress in Paris, but they never discussed it. It would have been in bad taste, and bad taste, in Jean-Paul's world, was the ultimate sin. Still looking out over Paris, Berta's jaw tightened. Was it the heat making her testy? Or the nagging feeling that she deserved better than the occasional, if ardent, attention of a man ten years older than she, with a complete existence in which she played no part?

Her reflections were interrupted by the telephone ringing. Probably Genevieve calling her bluff by phoning her at home with some trumped-up office emergency.

"Let it ring," Jean-Paul beckoned her back to bed.

"No, it might be something important." She wrapped herself in a sheet and headed into the living room, glad of the distraction.

"*Âllo, oui?*"

"Berta, your assistant said I might catch you at home," Her father's voice, and the switch to Dutch surprised her.

"Papa! Where are you?" she asked once she had recovered. "I didn't expect to hear from you until next week." She infused her voice with pleasure, conscious of Jean-Paul in the next room. He didn't speak Dutch, and some contrary spirit in her enjoyed his frustrated eavesdropping. But the happiness she felt talking to Richard was real. She had on occasion regretted her abrupt move to Paris so many years before. Her youthful impatience with her father's reticence on family history had mellowed. She had encountered others of his generation who for whatever reason avoided talking about their experiences during the war, and she came to place him in the same category, assuming again the protective role she had played as a child.

"I'm here, in Paris. I had to come earlier than I planned. I need a letter of introduction from a colleague at the Sorbonne. He leaves for a lecture tour in Japan tomorrow evening. And he's my only way into this marvelous newly discovered archive in an old house near—"

"That's wonderful," She cut him off, glancing through the doorway at the disheveled bed, John-Paul's calf and foot visible. "But the apartment's a mess, and—"

"No, that's fine. I've reserved a hotel room for tonight and I'm leaving for Languedoc tomorrow. I just thought we could get together for dinner. I'm at the *Gare du Nord*. Is there a restaurant near your place where we could meet, say, in an hour? Is seven too early for dinner?"

Berta glanced at the clock: already six p.m. She considered the situation. She had not told Jean-Paul much about her background, allowing him to build a picture of a boring middle-class upbringing, from which Paris—and, by implication, he—had rescued her. It would be interesting to have him meet her father. The devil that the heatwave implanted in her took satisfaction in the thought that Jean-Paul might be at a disadvantage in an encounter where his assumptions were undermined.

"Seven's great. I'll be bringing a friend, if that's all right. We'd planned to dine at Bertrand's anyway." She gave him directions to the restaurant and rang off.

"Come on. You can shower first. We're meeting my father for dinner in an hour." She entered the bedroom with a false breeziness, bending to pick up discarded clothing and avoiding Jean-Paul's eye.

He groaned.

"No-oo. Do I *have* to spend our last evening listening to you gargling incomprehensible Dutch with your father?"

"Papa speaks fluent French. He was a diplomat before the war."

That silenced Jean-Paul for the moment. He sighed and strutted off to the bathroom.

****

Richard was already seated when Berta and Jean-Paul entered the restaurant. As they made their way across the room, Berta was swept with a rush of affection for the aging man who rose to his feet, flushed and damp, a little out of his element in this fashionable bistro.

Introductions made, they sat as the proprietor and waiter fussed with menus and recommendations. Berta watched, detached, as Jean-Paul performed the gourmet, mulling over the choice of wine. She was reminded of that long-ago lunch with Martin in Amsterdam. Now it was her father who was forced into the role of the naïve visitor, supposed to be impressed by the other man's sophistication.

"So, Berta tells me you are a professor of folktales?" The waiter had taken their order and departed.

"Well, I'm a professor of history, but my specialty is medieval European folklore." Richard smiled across at his daughter, wishing they could be alone. He thought she looked nervous, too thin.

"And what brings you to Paris in this dreadful

heatwave?"

"I'm seeing an old friend at the Sorbonne tomorrow. He's leaving for a lecture tour, so I brought forward my travel plans." Why didn't Berta say something, anything, to interrupt this cross-examination? Richard looked around the room, hoping for their food to arrive as a distraction.

"Another professor of folktales—sorry, folklore?" Jean-Paul asked with a grin.

"No, Marc is a philosopher. Marc Debuchard? He's a member of the *Académie Française.* Perhaps you've heard of him?"

Score a point for Papa, Berta thought, holding her face expressionless. The *Académie* was France's pre-eminent council on all matters concerning the French language. Richard's colleague was one of only forty members, elected for life and known as *les immortels.*

"Ah, the wine!" Jean-Paul struggled to reassert his control.

Conversation continued in fits and starts, Berta contributing little. After they agreed that the food was superb and the wine delicious, Richard asked politely about Jean-Paul's business.

"I have a manufacturing concern in Rouen. We make electrical systems for aircraft. New technology, very exciting." Berta noted that he did not mention the firm belonged to his wife and her brothers.

"Oh, did you start the business?" Richard's question seemed innocent, but Berta sensed a sharpening of interest in her father's eyes.

"No, it was founded fifty years ago. I, er, joined after the war." *When you married into it,* Berta thought. But her father was pursuing another track.

"Ah, the war. Terrible times."

Jean-Paul smiled.

"Not for everyone. The Germans took the factory over and invested heavily in new machinery. It wouldn't be so successful today if the *Boche* hadn't used it as a research center for their weapons guidance systems. The V-2 was partially developed there."

"Using slave labor." It was a bleak statement, not a question. Berta realized that her father knew more about Jean-Paul's business than she did.

"Before my time," Jean-Paul replied abruptly.

Berta broke the silence that followed with some questions to Richard about life in Amsterdam, the courses he'd been teaching, people she remembered at the University. Plates were cleared, and the waiter proffered dessert menus.

"Not for me, I'm afraid," Jean-Paul said, looking at his watch. "I have to rush to catch the last train. It's been a pleasure meeting you, Professor." He stood and shook hands as Richard struggled to his feet. *What happened to staying the night?* Berta thought, beginning to rise as well and planning to say a more intimate goodbye on the sidewalk outside, but Jean-Paul rested his hands on her shoulders. "No, you stay and catch up with your father."

Richard sat again, and father and daughter watched as Jean-Paul threaded his way through the tables toward the door. He stopped to press some bills into the proprietor's hand, indicating their table with a jerk of the head. He left the restaurant without a backward glance.

Berta turned back to Richard.

"He's married," she blurted, unsure if she wanted to excuse Jean-Paul or condemn him.

Richard gave a small smile and a quick shake of the

head, dismissing the importance of her statement and perhaps the man himself. Then he leaned forward, serious again.

"Are you all right, Berta, my love? I mean, are you happy?"

Berta could not respond. Inexplicably, her throat closed up and tears spilled from her eyes. Richard reached across the table to cover her hand with his own while she regained control.

"Sorry," she mumbled. "It must be the heat. I'm fine now."

"Look, why don't you come south with me. It'll be like the old days, travelling around together—only now I rent a car! Surely you can take a couple of weeks off?"

It was tempting—escape the city, immerse herself in ancient monasteries and quiet libraries, plumbing the memories of octogenarian scholars in slow, gentle interviews. The undemanding company of her father at the end of the day...

"I can't. Oh, I'd love to, Papa, really I would! But I have two books coming out in September, and there's so much to do—cover design, copyright permissions, not to mention one author who's still making textual revisions. But when you come back through Paris at the end of the summer, I promise I'll make some time. Perhaps we could take a few days in the country and I could help you organize your notes?"

Richard's face mirrored the disappointment she felt. It could not be helped. Intent on proving herself competent to the other editors, she had taken on too much.

****

When her father returned north the first week of

September, Berta was still putting out fires, coddling hysterical writers, organizing and reorganizing publicity tours, and fighting with lawyers over foreign rights. Rather than a few days off in the country, she didn't even have time to share a meal with Richard.

"As soon as things calm down," she assured him, "I'll take a week off to come visit you."

It was October before the chaos subsided. Berta stood at her office window, watching the wind whip the leaves off the plane trees that lined the boulevard below. A gust lifted a page of a newspaper almost up to her level. She craned to read the headline. Perhaps there was a message there for her. Laughing at her fancifulness, she turned back to her office. A tidy desk, a quiet phone: luxuries she relished.

She had not heard from Jean-Paul again after the dinner with her father, although his family vacation was long over. She felt disconcerted that he had not broken off the affair with more ceremony; she had expected a bouquet of roses accompanied by a rueful note. Perhaps he was not the gallant sophisticate she had imagined him to be. But on the whole, she felt relief. Possibly they had both been mistaken in the other, each pretending happiness in a relationship beset with unspoken subjects.

Genevieve stuck her head around the door.

"There's a woman on the phone. Terrible accent. I think she must be Dutch."

Her assistant regarded all non-French speakers with a supercilious attitude; being born abroad was a moral failing, or at least a serious misfortune.

"Does she have a name?" Only Berta's impeccable French saved her—most of the time—from Genevieve's contempt.

"Hooten, Grooten, something like that."

Lotte Van Grouten, her father's secretary. A dark apprehension overcame her.

She picked up the receiver.

"Hello? Lotte?" To begin with, all she could hear was ragged breathing. Then, between sobs, the words poured out.

"Berta, I'm so sorry, your father... I went into his office with the mail, and there he was. I thought he was taking a nap—he had his head on the desk—but he's never done that before and it was midmorning—or he had leaned down to pick up something he'd dropped. His heart, they said. I called the ambulance at once, but..." Here she broke down completely.

Papa's dead? Not possible! With exaggerated care, she laid the receiver on her desk and moved over to the window. The wind had driven the newspaper page into the street, and passing vehicles had shredded it into a pulpy illegible mess.

Only then did she start to cry.

Chapter 21

It seemed as if the whole university attended the funeral. A few faces were familiar from long ago or from her annual visits at Christmas, but most were unknown to her.

"Such a fine man…"

"A wonderful teacher…"

"So generous… The best friend… Gone too soon…"

They grasped her hand or hugged her close. Colleagues, current and former students, the couple that owned the bakery on the corner, the janitor from the History Department building: the mourners filled the University Chapel for the brief service. Berta was glad she had declined to speak; there were several who could eulogize her father more eloquently than she. She sat in the front row wedged between Lotte Van Grouten, her father's secretary, and Claudia Martinelli, the housekeeper who had cooked and cleaned and mothered Richard for the last fifteen years. The two older women wept into their handkerchiefs, Berta squashed between them, fighting the urge to struggle into the aisle and run away. She was a fraud, a neglectful daughter whose last interaction with her father had been to push him away, to prioritize some project she could now barely remember above spending time together. Guilt kept her dry-eyed, and her face impassive. After the last prayers were said, she led the congregation back out into the daylight to take her place in the receiving line.

"He will be sorely missed..."

"I don't know what we'll do without him..."

The procession wound on. Berta found it increasingly difficult to murmur the appropriate acknowledgments. She wondered how many of them were thinking—behind their earnest condolences—that she had abandoned her father. The line from King Lear ran around her head: "How sharper than a serpent's tooth it is to have a thankless child!" In the center of all this collegial affection, had Richard always felt alone, forsaken by his daughter?

With a feeling of relief, Berta recognized Anika at the end of the string of mourners.

"Oh, I'm so glad you came!" Berta enveloped her smaller friend in a long hug.

"Of course!" Anika leaned back to examine Berta's face. "How are you holding up?"

Berta let out a shuddering sigh.

"I'm a mess. I should have been here. We were supposed to have taken a vacation together. And now I'll never—"

"You know that's ridiculous, Berta," Anika interrupted, frowning. "You loved your father and he knew it. You can't blame yourself for leading your own life. It's what he wanted for you."

Berta took a breath. She didn't quite believe Anika, but it felt good to hear it, all the same.

"Will you come back to the apartment with me?" Berta pleaded. "Claudia's prepared sandwiches and sherry. It would be so nice to have someone to talk to. I hardly know any of these people. I don't belong here."

"And now you're being silly again. This is your home! You were born here. You grew up here." Anika threw a sidelong glance at Berta's sharply tailored black suit. "Just because you've got a fancy French *couturier* doesn't mean you aren't a little Dutch girl underneath."

Berta laughed, then glanced around guiltily, but the mourners had all moved on to the reception. She tucked Anika's hand under her arm and they headed out of the University precincts.

"Thank you. To be honest, I don't know if I belong in Paris either. All those years of trying to fit in, of striving to succeed, and then this happens. I ask myself, was it worth it?"

"Then move home! You have the apartment, and Amsterdam's changed since you lived here. It's not stuffy and provincial anymore. There's good theater, restaurants, art galleries—everything Paris has."

"Hmm. Something to think about." But for Berta, Amsterdam becoming another Paris was not an attractive idea. "Now I want to hear all about you, and Stefan too."

****

Berta was grateful that Lotte and Claudia had assumed the role of hostesses, passing from group to group with trays of food and replenishing glasses: two fiftyish women, one plump and fair, the other spare and dark. Berta speculated whether one or both had fancied herself the next Mrs. Vandercam—in their different functions they were both clearly devoted to Richard. She wondered how he had navigated that situation, if it had arisen. With grace and kindness, she was sure. She thought back to the scurrilous story Martin had related at their first meeting, about her father having "another woman." Given the decades of faithful celibacy, that story appeared even more laughable now. She had received a sympathy note from Martin, apologizing for not attending the funeral due to "prior commitments." She had hardly expected him to come; it would have been a lapse of good taste, and Martin never lacked taste.

After shaking more hands and accepting more expressions of condolence, she settled into a corner with Anika. Anika had married, immediately upon graduation from the University, a handsome classmate with more charm than brains. She suffered a series of miscarriages before giving birth to her daughter Lizbeth, now eight years old. Within days of Lizbeth's birth, Anika had discovered her husband was having an affair and that it was not the first time he had strayed. They divorced and he faded quickly from Anika and Lizbeth's lives. These days, she taught history at the *gymnasium*, and lived five minutes from her parents in the Plantage district.

"After the twins moved out, Mother was overjoyed to have Lizbeth to look after. It's perfect. She goes to my parents' house after school, and we often eat dinner there too. I'm very happy." Berta wondered if there was a note of challenge in her statement. Their lives had taken such divergent paths. Perhaps Anika envied her—the glamour of Paris, her independence from family responsibilities. Now she was campaigning for Berta to return to Amsterdam. Soon she'd be fixing her up with dates, suggesting she ought to have a baby before it was too late, thus validating the course of her own life by encouraging Berta to copy it. No, now Berta was being cynical. Her friend was happy and just wanted her to be happy too.

After breaking off to talk to a former student, Berta returned to Anika.

"And Stefan? I was in New York last year but never managed to get to Montreal to see him."

"He's moved to Ottawa, working for a senior Member of Parliament, drafting policies, writing speeches. Very well thought of, apparently." Anika glowed with pride for her brother.

"Perhaps he'll run for election himself. I know he'd be great."

Anika frowned.

"Well..." She leaned closer. "He's living with someone, another man. They've been together for several years. I've met him. His name's Raoul. But if Stefan ran for office, it would all come out...I mean, about being a homosexual." She was whispering now. "He'd never get elected."

Berta felt a pang of irritation at Anika's primness and replied a little louder than necessary. "Really? Anyway, I'm so happy he's found someone to love. I do hope they'll come and see me when they come to Europe. Can you give me Stefan's new address?"

The guests were departing. Berta and Anika stood up and started to gather plates and glasses, to take them into the kitchen. Lotte was putting leftovers into the refrigerator.

"There. You'll have plenty of food to tide you over while you're here. You are staying a while, I hope?"

Berta nodded. "I'm not sure how long. I haven't made any decisions yet about the apartment, whether to sell or rent it—"

"Or live in it yourself!" Anika finished for her with a smile. Berta said nothing. She was too exhausted to explain that she felt adrift, no more at home here than she did in Paris.

"It's just that I need to clear out the professor's office. The department wants to put a junior lecturer in there." Lotte's face betrayed her displeasure at the prospect. She continued, "I can handle the books. You'll probably want to donate them to the University library. And his published papers and lecture notes—I think they're technically property of the department anyway. But he has other files too, and pictures and things. I'd really appreciate your help in sorting through it and telling me what to throw away and what you want to keep."

Berta didn't relish going through the accumulated record of her father's academic career, but she couldn't let poor Lotte do it alone.

"Of course. I'll come tomorrow morning. And thank you, Lotte, for everything you've done for me. And for him."

Lotte's face collapsed into grief, and she hugged Berta hard.

****

Entering her father's office the next day felt like stepping back in time. Berta had not been here since she left Amsterdam in 1953. Richard would have been entitled to move into a larger space as his seniority in the History Department increased, but he had opted to remain. The shelves were more crowded with books, and some of the framed photographs on the wall were new to her, but the desk, the rug, and the visitor's armchair were the same, if now a little shabby.

Lotte followed her in. The two women stood side by side staring across the desk at the empty chair. After a moment, Lotte gave a sigh, and started to explain the probable disposition of the office's contents. Berta listened while running her fingers along the rows of books and opening and closing file drawers.

"...and that just leaves the desk. Did you bring the professor's keys?"

Berta fished them out of her pocket and handed them to Lotte, who sorted through them until she located a small, old-fashioned key.

"I think this is the one that opens the desk drawers. I only did the regular filing in those cabinets." She indicated the steel file cabinets Berta had already examined. "I think he kept personal files in the desk. I'll leave you to it while I go and find some boxes for all the other things, all right?"

After Lotte left, Berta moved behind the desk and sat in her father's chair. Richard's presence felt stronger here than in the apartment. She leaned against the chair's worn leather back, her head resting where his head would have rested: they were the same height. She breathed in the familiar smell of old books. She would have liked to close her eyes and just sit for a while, but she knew she had to get to work.

She unlocked the deep drawer on the left first. When she saw the contents, a rush of pleasure overtook her— her father's notebooks containing field notes from his summer research. Ranged from his earliest trips to Languedoc at the back of the drawer to the past summer's expedition at the front, the notebooks all had a similar marbled cardboard cover, each labeled in Richard's meticulous handwriting with the date. Berta pulled out the oldest: July–August, 1949. As she paged through it, memories flooded back. She could smell the thyme and lavender on the rocky hillsides, feel the damp cool of a church crypt. She laughed out loud to find her own girlish handwriting on a few pages. She seized the next few in sequence, 1950, '51, '52, all the summers she had spent with her father, following him around from abbey to library to crumbling old chateau where an ancient document or a moldy collection of artifacts might be lodged. Interleafed between the pages were a few black-and-white photographs. She looked in vain for herself or Richard, but remembered her father's stricture that the camera was not for holiday snaps but to record places and people essential to their research.

She pulled out a few of the later journals at random. These notes did not sing to her as the earlier ones when she had been present, but she delighted in Richard's precise observations, occasionally mixed with an excited report of some unexpected discovery. His voice was in her head as she read his words, as well as a clear memory of the region. She regretted that she hadn't been back there; her trips to the south of France had been to the Côte d'Azur, where Uncle Martin had his second home. Arty, sophisticated Antibes was a world away from wild and sparsely populated Languedoc. The realization was sudden and visceral: Languedoc was where she belonged, not Paris or Amsterdam.

A thought began to take shape. She still had money from her inheritance, and if she sold the apartments in Paris and Amsterdam, she'd have enough money to live simply in Languedoc for years. Maybe she could write a book; the notebooks contained a wealth of raw material. It wouldn't be an academic tome but more like a memoir or a travel book. Her mind raced with possibilities. She felt a weight lifting off her heart. *Thank you, Papa. You've rescued me.*

When Lotte returned with empty boxes, she found

Berta's earlier listlessness had been replaced by animation.

"I'm going to take all these field research notebooks with me. They're marvelous! I want to use them as the basis for a project about Papa. No one will object to me taking them, will they?"

"No, I'm sure not. And that's a lovely idea. Here, let me help you pack them up." Lotte started to fill one of the boxes. "Are you all done with the desk, then?"

"Oh, sorry. I got engrossed in the journals and haven't gone through the other drawer yet." Berta handed the rest of the notebooks over to Lotte.

"Never mind, you take your time. I'll go get you a cup of coffee."

As Lotte left the office, Berta fitted the key into the lock of the right-hand desk drawer. This drawer contained a dozen or so hanging files, each dark green file containing a manila folder filled with what appeared to be correspondence. Her thoughts still full of plans for the future, she opened the first folder and glanced at the top document, a letter in English, addressed to "Dear Consul Vandercam." Puzzled, she checked the date at the top of the page: May 10, 1971, less than six months ago. Richard had not borne the title of consul for thirty years, not since 1940 and the start of the war. The sender's address was in Tel Aviv, Israel. She concentrated on translating the content of the letter.

"*I am sorry that it has taken me so long to write to thank you for what you did for me in 1940. I only recently discovered your identity and address from Yad Vashem, the Holocaust Remembrance Center here in Israel. I immigrated to Israel in 1960, after living in New York. I met my wife in New York, and we now have two boys.*

179

But what I want to tell you is what happened after you gave me the life-saving papers that allowed me to leave Riga and go to Sweden. I waited in Stockholm for six weeks trying to find a way to get to America, or England, or anywhere the Nazis would not find me. Finally, I found work as a stoker on a freighter going to Portugal. It was a very frightening voyage, especially when the boat docked in Hamburg. I stayed hidden where the coal was stored. In Lisbon, I was lucky to get passage to Miami on a Panamanian ship, but the USA authorities would not admit me, so I ended up in Curaçao after all! After the war, I was admitted to the USA as a refugee.

My father, uncles, aunts, and cousins all died in the camps. I count it a blessing that my mother died when I was a child and did not have to suffer as they did. Thank you from myself and my family to you and your colleague. You saved my life. I hope you will accept the invitation to come to Jerusalem to be honored as you deserve.

With lifelong gratitude,
Jacob Levitt

Written at the bottom of the letter, in Dutch and in her father's handwriting: *Responded May 15, 1971.*

The next letter in the folder was also in English, this time from a London address and dated the previous December. Again, it told of an escape from Latvia in 1940 and expressed profound gratitude to "the Consul and his colleague." Berta quickly scanned the rest of the pile. There must have been twenty or more letters, most in English but some in German or what she thought was Polish. They came from Israel, the United States, England, one from Zurich, one from Hong Kong. Berta sat back, stunned. Her father had never hinted that he'd helped refugees during his time in Latvia. He was always reluctant to speak about the war, but for all those years, she had believed his evasiveness concerned his guilt over her mother's death and the resulting animosity of her family.

Lotte came in with a mug of coffee.

"Do you know anything about these?" Berta pointed at the pile of letters. Out of shock, Berta spoke sharply, and Lotte flinched.

"No! I just open your father's mail. I don't read it. He dealt with all his personal correspondence himself. Anyway…" She came close again to peer at the letters. "I don't read English."

"I'm sorry, Lotte, but I had no idea…" She pulled the folder out of the next hanging file and opened it. This contained letters from various refugee resettlement or Jewish organizations: the United Nations High Commissioner for Refugees, HIAS, a Jewish temple in Paris, and at least three from Yad Vashem, the center referenced in one of the letters in the first folder. These seemed to be invitations to events or award ceremonies, or requests for interviews. Flicking back through them, Berta saw they had been written over the last three years. On each, Richard had noted "Declined" and a date.

Lotte had come around the desk and was looking over Berta's shoulder.

"I don't understand. What do they all mean?"

"I don't understand either, Lotte, but it looks like Papa helped save a lot of Jewish refugees during the war, while he was the Dutch consul in Latvia." Her voice dropped, as if she was speaking to herself. "How did we not know this?"

The next folder contained letters too, this time mostly in Dutch, from journalists and newspaper reporters, a TV station. There were business cards and phone message slips too.

"Oh, I know about some of these," exclaimed Lotte. "This one—" She picked up the card of Jan Boren with *De Tijd*. "He called and called, but the Professor refused to speak to him. These others too. He said they must have muddled him up with another Vandercam, that what he did wasn't newsworthy."

"I can't understand why he wanted it all kept secret. I'm so proud of him. I think people should know about this. I'm going to contact Jan Boren and all the others. Look! Even the United Nations wanted to honor him!" Caught between laughing and crying, Berta stood up and wrapped the older woman in her arms. Did this explain her father's reticence to speak about his service in Latvia? Not guilt about her mother's unhappiness there, but the outcome of his natural modesty and reluctance to draw attention to himself? Her father was a war hero! Excitement at her discovery struggled with sorrow that his courage had not been celebrated in his lifetime. She imagined how he might have ducked his head and blushed as accolades were piled upon him, but she was determined to make his contribution known to the world.

There was nothing in the next hanging files. Berta slid the drawer shut with her foot, and piled the manila folders she had extracted on top of her father's notebooks in the cardboard box Lotte had found. She left the office with a sense of purpose, and a vitality she had not felt for years.

What she did not notice was another file at the back of the drawer. It had fallen off the runners from which the others were suspended and lay on its side hidden from view. The material it contained—lists and letters—predated the correspondence Berta had found by more than a decade. It documented Richard's unsuccessful search for any trace of Nellie Loesseps, his secretary for just under a year at the Netherlands Consulate in Riga, the colleague referred to in the survivors' letters.

Part Four: *1939-40*

Chapter 22

For a while nothing changed. The farmers still trundled their carts heaped with produce into the market. The neighbors Nellie met on the stairs still complained about the approach of winter. No war planes strafed the park; no tanks rumbled through the narrow streets of the old town. Classes resumed at the university, and Ekaterina proclaimed her relief that Simon was no longer under her feet all day. Sarah, busy preparing for a series of concerts in Riga to replace the cancelled international tour, made no further snide references to Nellie's relationship with Richard Vandercam.

Only when Nellie was closeted with the consul in his office, poring over news reports or preparing dispatches to send to the Dutch Foreign Ministry, did the war feel real. The wireless was moved from the salon into the consul's office, creating an even clearer break between upstairs—Margriet's domain—and the downstairs offices. The workday now revolved around broadcasts from the BBC World Service, and the consul usually lunched at his desk or joined Nellie for sandwiches at hers. He sent Nellie out to purchase a large-scale map of Europe and mounted it on one wall. With different colored pins, they together marked the advance of the German army into Poland and the corresponding Russian troop maneuvers in the east.

Standing side by side with the consul in front of the map, Nellie thought of Sarah's inference that she was having an affair with her boss. She remembered the piercing look Margriet had shot at her when she entered the salon on the day war was declared. And the comment about "business affairs." Nellie was suddenly conscious of the consul's physical nearness, and her cheeks became hot. She was *not* in love with him. She admired him, respected him, was grateful for the trust he placed in her —that was all that existed between them…wasn't it?

"Does your mother still sing professionally?"

Nellie was startled out of her reflections by the consul's question.

"Ah—um—yes, but just for private parties, not on stage." She turned away from the map, aware she was blushing. The consul followed her back to his desk and resumed his seat while Nellie fussed with a pile of papers, keeping her head down.

"My wife insists we continue to entertain, even though the diplomatic corps is quite reduced now. She has an idea about holding a musical *soirée,* and she heard your mother's name somewhere—her professional name, that is. I don't think she knew about your connection. Anyway, it would be a great honor and a pleasure if she could be persuaded to sing for us. Your father and you will come too, of course. Would you ask her?"

Nellie felt certain that any invitation from Margriet would not have included her or her father, but she responded calmly enough.

"Certainly *Meneer* Vandercam, I'll ask her tonight."

"Thank you. I particularly look forward to meeting

your father. I'd like to know more about Latvia's political history. There are such clear parallels between the situation we're facing now and the end of the Great War."

Glad to be on safer conversational ground, Nellie listened as the consul revisited the rumors circulating about a pact made between Hitler and Stalin. Germany had agreed to cede all designs on the Baltic states in exchange for Russia's acquiescence to Germany's invasion of Poland. The consul feared a Soviet takeover of Latvia was imminent. He went on to talk about earlier events, although Nellie was already aware of them. Her father had described to her the Bolshevik invasion of early 1919 and the atrocities that followed. The Communists had attempted to wipe out the bourgeoisie in the cities with mass arrests, torture of prisoners, and executions. The countryside had fared no better: forced collectivization of land led to food shortages, then widespread disease. Before the country was liberated later that year by a ragtag army of Nationalists, Baltic-Germans, and White Russians, many thousands died. Everything now pointed to a repeat of that chaotic episode. The Russians had already moved into Vilnius, Lithuania's ancient capital on the nation's eastern edge, forcing the national government to relocate away from the Soviet border to Kaunas, in the middle of the country.

Nellie walked home in a daze, the political and military threats now fused in her mind with a more obscure personal anxiety. She watched as people crowded onto the trams or hurried along the sidewalk bent over against a blustery wind. How could they carry on as if nothing had happened? And how could she solicit her parents' participation in a gathering that she suspected would end in embarrassment? She knew Ekaterina would be unable to resist corseting herself into a black satin recital gown; she loved to perform. Simon would be eager to brush shoulders with diplomats and share his insights with them. She wondered if her own reluctance stemmed from a fear that once her two worlds—work and home—collided, the fiction of professional detachment might collapse, and the agitation she experienced that afternoon in front of the map of Europe would be revealed to all.

Dani was waiting for her inside the front door of the apartment. The little girl frowned at her mother's distracted air. Nellie bent down to give her daughter a hug. When she stood back up, she had rearranged her face into a warm smile.

"So, what new words did you learn at school today?"

Nellie took Dani's hand and led her to the sofa for their daily ritual. School had been challenging for the little girl at first. Although she could understand Latvian reasonably well, and some Russian, she was hesitant to speak; Dutch was still her first language. The children and even her teacher had mocked her silence. But cautiously, over the early weeks of term, she made a couple of friends, other girls who were different in some way. One girl had a lisp that rendered her even more reluctant to raise her hand in class than Dani. Her other friend was the daughter of the school's janitor and lived in the basement of the building next to the furnace room. The three misfits carved a safe place on the margins of the classroom community. Dani studied hard, which eventually endeared her to the teacher, if not to the mainstream of pupils, and her written work always received good grades.

Dani often asked her mother about Berta and the consulate. Nellie realized that, in Dani's mind, the past summer had taken on a fairy-tale light, the glow of some charmed time when life was simple and surrounded by beauty. The consulate replaced Dani's memories of her life in Rotterdam. She had difficulty remembering her father's face now. Although she still demanded bedtime stories about him and their previous life in Holland, she paid more attention to the details she pressed her mother to disclose about Ivan's battles with Marta, the dresses the consul's wife wore, and, of course, Berta, left to play make-believe games on her own. Nellie, who now saw little of Berta, Ivan, and Marta, and avoided Margriet whenever possible, obliged with tales spun out of her own imagination.

****

Nellie decided to wait until her father came home to tell her parents about the musical *soirée*, but Simon Kutner's news drove any thought of the invitation out of her head. Dani was already in bed and dinner cleared away before he returned. Nellie went to greet him in the entrance hall.

"Pavel's disappeared." The professor shrugged off his outdoor clothes.

"What do you mean?" Nellie hung up his hat and coat, then hurried after her father into the living room.

"I went to deliver a draft of an article to *The Free Press*. The place was locked up, not a soul there. Then I went to Pavel's apartment—same thing. The Soviets have taken him, I'm sure."

Pavel was a frequent visitor to the apartment, and Simon's favorite intellectual sparring partner. He was a large untidy man, shirttails hanging out, the remnants of his last meal decorating his lapels and walrus moustache. He had never married, which was one reason he came so often to the Kutners', arriving strategically at the dinner hour, a bottle of vodka protruding from his coat pocket. He flirted outrageously with Ekaterina, which she loved. They would make elaborate plans to run away together—all in her husband's hearing, and for his benefit.

"Go on then. Send me a postcard from Paris. Better still, send me Sartre's latest book—it'll be ages before it's available here." Simon Kutner played along with their games during the meal, but then the talk would turn serious, and the men were left to put the world to rights as the level in the vodka bottle went down. Pavel had some kind of attachment to the University, but his real vocation was as publisher and editor of, and main contributor to, *The Free Press*, a small circulation weekly with a reputation for high ideas. In recent years, the Latvian government had clamped down on the freedoms that had flourished after independence in 1919. *The Free Press* had survived mainly because Pavel accepted contributions reflecting a wide range of ideologies, from the centrists and the Christian Conservatives as well as from socialists and anarchists. Or perhaps its circulation was just too small to attract the authoritarian government's attention until now. Stalin's "pact with the Devil"—the German-Soviet Non-Aggression Pact—had destroyed Pavel's lingering faith in the Revolution. He had written a blistering editorial after rumors of the treaty emerged. Although Stalin was not directly named, Pavel's allusions to the Baltic states as "pawns on Satan's chessboard" had been transparent.

Now, the professor stood at the window, peering out

between the curtains into the winter darkness.

"What are you looking at?" Nellie asked.

"Oh, nothing, nothing…"

"Perhaps Pavel has just gone away for a few days."

"Yes, that must be it." He didn't sound very certain, but he turned from the window with a smile.

Ekaterina urged her husband to retell his visits to the newspaper's shuttered offices and Pavel's empty apartment to Sarah and Piotr when they came back from the cinema. As the discussion went on, the professor dropped the pretense that Pavel had simply taken a pleasure trip. It was, after all, the beginning of winter.

"Where will they have taken him?" Piotr asked.

"It depends who 'they' are. If it's Ulmanis's thugs, he'll still be here." The professor referred to Latvia's self-appointed president, who was slowly but systematically dismantling the country's liberal institutions. "In the basement of the Justice Department perhaps. If the Soviet secret police kidnapped him, then he may already be in Russia. The question is, how are we going to find out?"

"*You* are not going to do anything." Ekaterina placed her hands over his. "You are too closely associated with Pavel. If you poke around, asking questions, they'll take you too. We need you here." For once, her intensity seemed appropriate. The others nodded in agreement.

"We must do *something*!" Simon's face was taut with anguish.

"I'll ask the consul. He can ask questions without putting himself in danger—diplomatic immunity: it still works, even with the Soviets." In the midst of their anxiety about Pavel, Nellie couldn't help a guilty flicker of pleasure at speaking of her boss.

"Oh, thank you, child. Yes, the consul will be able to find out something."

Later, when Nellie went over to the window to kiss her father goodnight, he pulled the curtain aside.

"Do you see that car over there by the park entrance? There's someone in it."

"Papa, you must be mistaken. Who would sit in a parked car on a freezing night like this?"

"Watch. You can see the red light of his cigarette when he inhales… There! The car's been in the same place since I got home from Pavel's apartment."

They stood together looking out through the gap in the drapes.

"I'll talk to the consul tomorrow. Don't tell the others about the car. It may be nothing."

Nellie sounded no more convincing than when she suggested Pavel had just gone away for a break.

Chapter 23

November turned to December. The musical evening was postponed, and then abandoned, to Ekaterina's chagrin and Nellie's secret relief.

"Maybe they found out we're Jewish," observed Kat as she folded her recital gown between sheets of tissue paper and replaced it in its box.

"No, I'm sure the—" Nellie bit off her words. She had been about to say she was sure the consul would not be so bigoted, but what did she know, really? That she and her family were Jews had never come up in conversations with him. "Anyway, Madame's left for Stockholm to do some shopping. She's taken Berta and Marta with her." Nellie believed Margriet had called off the concert when she found out that Nellie was the great Ekaterina Sokolova's daughter. Now Nellie considered whether her mother had hit on another reason Madame had cancelled the event.

She thought of Madame's new friend, the Nazi. The German diplomat who had disparaged the Balts at that summer meeting had been replaced by a younger man in military uniform. Tall and slim, with dark hair and high cheekbones, *Hauptsturmführer* Hans Weber was becoming a frequent visitor at the consulate. He would bound past Ivan as soon as the door opened and take the stairs two at a time, to be received by Margriet in the salon. The ancient building's sturdy construction did not allow sound to penetrate to the lower floor, but when Madame, arm-in-arm with her guest, descended to show him out, Nellie heard her tinkling laugh.

If the door to Richard Vandercam's office was open, *Hauptsturmführer* Weber would shout a greeting.

"*Herr* Vandercam! You work so hard! What is there to do, now your colleagues have all gone home?" The British and French legations had been recalled during the autumn.

Before the consul could respond, Margriet would interject.

"Oh, he's probably researching folktales. It's his passion. Don't disturb him." And then she would whisk him out with some *sotto voce* comment that sent the German away chuckling.

Nellie kept her head down during these exchanges, but out of the corner of her eye she noticed the silver insignia on Weber's collar: two lightning bolts that showed he was *Schutzstaffel*, or SS, an elite group within the military, the most fervent Nazis, and the most loyal to Hitler.

"Shall we invite him to dinner?"

"What?" Nellie was paying no attention to her mother's voice until the question broke into her thoughts.

"Well, the poor man's all alone in that mausoleum. I thought we could have him over for a Hanukah feast. I'm sure I can dig up a menorah and a dreidel from somewhere."

"Mama! No!" It took a moment to realize Ekaterina was teasing. The Kutners did not celebrate Hanukah—or Christmas either, for that matter—except as an excuse for a party with copious amounts of food, wine, and music. Not that there would be such festivities this year.

Foreign foodstuffs had virtually disappeared from the shops, and there was some talk of fuel rationing. "I mean, he's much too busy, and anyway, he has Ivan to look after him."

But Nellie's quick deflection was false: there was little consular work these days, as Dutch citizens and businesses retreated from European outposts and consolidated in the Netherlands in anticipation of hostilities. The consul insisted Nellie cut back her workday to allow her to walk home in daylight, and the consulate closed completely for two weeks over the holidays while the consul joined his wife and daughter in Stockholm.

By the time the Vandercams returned and Nellie resumed work in January, other changes were evident. Soldiers with the red star of the Soviet army prominent on their caps guarded the radio station, the parliament, and other important buildings. "Peacekeepers," the government called them, but rather than instilling any sense of peace, their presence increased tension in the city.

The consul had met nothing but frustration in his inquiries about Pavel's unexplained disappearance. His closest contact at the Ministry of Justice denied that the Latvian government had anything to do with the missing journalist. When the consul pressed him, the government lawyer admitted that Pavel's politics may have offended "certain of our neighbors," but beyond that he would only shrug. The consul apologized that he had no relationship with the new military types that occupied the Soviet legation, but nevertheless he persevered with his inquiries there, only to be rebuffed. The rumors that others with liberal views had also vanished led Simon

Kutner to the certainty that the Soviets were behind Pavel's disappearance, as part of an attempt to gain a stranglehold on the Baltic states while Germany was busy "pacifying" Poland.

The parked car maintained sporadic surveillance outside the apartment. Professor Kutner also noticed the occasional attendance of a small dark man in an ill-fitting suit at his lectures. The watchers made no attempt to hide their activities. Under this scrutiny, Simon became a changed man. He had always called himself a humanist. In spite of his study of history, he believed in the basic goodness of mankind. His politics reflected that belief. If only people were free—free from the oppression of capitalism, or occupying foreign powers—their better natures would be revealed. Now, he was quieter, and the few opinions he did express were almost tentative, as if he had lost confidence in the convictions of a lifetime. He continued his teaching load at the University, but no one came by in the evenings anymore to argue over politics, art, or philosophy. He had warned them off, fearful their association might subject them to unwelcome attention from the authorities.

****

Nellie's route home took her past Dani's school at dismissal time now that her work hours were shortened. They completed the journey across the park together in the gloom of the winter afternoon. Snow, which in December had briefly transformed Riga into a charming monochrome print, was now trampled and heaped into soot-streaked mounds. Any new snow that fell was sleety and wet and did little more than add an icy glaze to what had fallen earlier in the year. In a few weeks it would be April, and these dirty remnants would melt away completely, revealing the dark earth. A slight reddish haze would surround the shrubs and trees where swollen places on each twig heralded new growth. Nellie did not anticipate the change of seasons with any pleasure. She felt as if her world was poised on a precipice, and spring would pitch it over into the void.

"Nellie! Quick! The rabbi's just arrived!"

With her opera-trained voice, Ekaterina was the master of the stage whisper. Her announcement reverberated across the landing where Nellie and Dani were propped like marionettes on either side of the entrance to the apartment, struggling to take off their slush-caked boots. Nellie glanced at their neighbors' door. She imagined Mrs. Zabovski on the other side, bent toward the keyhole, listening.

"Hush, Mama. Let's get inside."

A visit from a rabbi was unexpected, as the Kutners set foot in a synagogue only when close friendship required them to attend a wedding or other ceremony. Nellie didn't know the rabbi's name, or at which of the several Riga synagogues he presided. He was a short man, dressed in a rusty black overcoat and the traditional flat-crowned, wide-brimmed hat, with a beard so bushy as to look theatrical. His skin, what could be seen of it behind the beard, was very white, almost luminescent, and his eyes were hard black beads. He seemed never to blink. He brushed off Ekaterina's offer of tea and her attempt to take his hat and coat. He addressed himself entirely to Nellie's father, fixing him with those intense eyes, which made Dani, sitting forgotten on a chair in a corner of the living room, think of a bird of prey about to pounce.

"You've heard of what is happening to our people

in Poland?" he began without preamble.

"Yes, rumors, yes. I'm no longer in touch with anyone in Poland." Professor Kutner's reply was circumspect.

"Not rumors! Facts! They are rounding up Jews in the countryside and taking them to Warsaw. There, they are all confined to a small, walled-in section. The conditions are terrible. Disease, starvation, not to mention Gestapo raids. Old men, children—murdered!"

Simon looked increasingly uncomfortable. Of course, he had followed the rise of Hitler with dismay. He had been horrified at the increasingly harsh treatment of German Jews culminating in *Kristalnacht* in 1938. Colleagues, old friends who taught at German universities, were stripped of their positions. He knew some who had fled to England or America. But recently, he—everyone—had been so preoccupied with the threat from the east, the growing influence of Russia, and the suppression of what freedom was still left in Latvia, that the consequences of the German occupation of Poland on the Jews had not fully registered with him. Now he looked ashamed.

"I see. What can I do to help? Are you able to send money? We don't have much, but—"

The rabbi almost spat his disdain.

"Money does no good. The Germans take the money and then kill you for insulting them with a bribe." He paused, apparently finding it difficult to ask for what he needed from this lapsed Jew who had turned his back on the ancient traditions. An intellectual! His sneer was only partially covered by his beard. He breathed deeply, reminding himself that the root of his rage was not being forced to seek a favor from someone he despised but his inability to fight the Nazis.

"I understand your daughter works at the Dutch Consulate." Nellie was sitting directly at his right, but he ignored her, looking only at Simon.

"Yes, Nellie is the consul's secretary."

"And the consul is a good man? He might help us?" Again his remarks were directed at her father, but this was too much for Nellie.

"Yes, Richard Vandercam is a good man. If he can help, I'm sure he will. What do you have in mind?"

At her voice, the rabbi turned reluctantly to face her.

"Visas," he replied shortly, before turning back to her father. "Some young men, students at a yeshiva in Eastern Poland, have escaped. They are living with members of our community. They are convinced, and they have convinced me, that they are not safe here, that no Jew is safe here. They want to go to America to join people from their town who have emigrated to New York. The Americans will not grant them visas; they don't want any involvement in a European war. But perhaps the students could get to one of the Dutch islands in the Caribbean, and somehow get to America from there. If not, at least they will be safer than here."

"Nellie?" The professor looked inquiringly at her, forcing the rabbi to include her in the discussion.

"I don't know. Since I've been working at the consulate we've never issued a visa to Curaçao, Aruba— any of the Dutch West Indies. I don't think we even have a form for that. I can talk to the consul, see what he thinks." Nellie was pleased to think of bringing a project to Richard. It would show initiative, and that she had been paying attention when he spoke to her about the international situation.

The rabbi sighed. Was it with relief? Nellie began to see that she was his last hope, and he had been afraid of being thrown out, or laughed at, or just politely rejected. Now he turned to her and spoke in a more moderate tone.

"But the difficulty doesn't end with a visa. These students need to get to the West Indies. To do that, they have to get to a major port—not much shipping is going out of Riga. A port in a neutral country. I thought Sweden. More boats leave from there, especially as the spring advances. Sweden won't take Jewish refugees, but what if the young men are just in transit, with a visa to somewhere else?"

"How many are you talking about?" Nellie asked, now nervous that she had over-promised.

"Nine. They are all eighteen or nineteen years old, in good health. They have their Polish identification papers."

"I can't guarantee anything," Nellie hurried to respond. Then seeing the rabbi slump, she continued. "Can you get to the consulate tomorrow morning, about eleven? I could get you in to see the consul then. I think he'll want to work something out. It may take a while, though."

"I hope not too long. When the snow melts, the Germans will be on the move."

Before the rabbi left, Professor Kutner mentioned the surveillance, and that he suspected the Russians.

"I hope that your visit here doesn't mark you as a friend of the counter-revolutionary bourgeoisie."

For the first time, the rabbi smiled, albeit grimly.

"We Jews have a long history of being persecuted for one reason or another. Riga has been a brief interlude of tolerance in the larger scheme, but between the Nazis

and the Communists, I think that interlude is now over."
He turned and looked sadly at Nellie. Dani had come out
of her hiding place and was sitting within the circle of
her mother's arm on the sofa. "It won't matter to them if
you married a non-Jew, or that you're not observant.
Even your Christian friends won't be able to help you."
Nellie felt a chill run through her body.

"What a horrible little man!" Kat said, when she had
shut the door firmly behind him. She had been quiet
during his visit and was now making up for it, plumping
cushions and noisily collecting cups and glasses. "Don't
let him get you into trouble with the consul, Nellie. If
there's nothing you can do, there's nothing you can do. I
think it was very nice of you to offer to help, but the
consul may see it differently."

"Oh, I'm sure Richard will find a way to do
something. He's been aching at the futility of his
position, and he's furious that the Netherlands has
declared itself neutral. He'll want to get involved." Yes,
but what about *her* involvement? In her eagerness to
present an idea that might impress the consul, she had
overlooked the possible danger to herself and her family.
Her father's voice brought her back to the moment.

"Richard? Who is this Richard?" His tone was
teasing, but a frown betrayed his concern.

"Working every day together, 'Mr. Vandercam' and
'Mrs. Loesseps'—it's too formal." Nellie, blushing,
attempted a laugh.

"Oh, yes? And what does the lovely *Madame*
Vandercam think of that?"

"I don't ever see her. She's upstairs, and I'm
downstairs. We avoid each other." Nellie wondered what
Margriet would say about a scheme to help Polish

refugees. Perhaps more pertinently, what would Margriet's new friend, the SS officer Weber, think about it?

"Be careful, my dear. You don't need an enemy."

"I'm afraid it's too late. It's clear she doesn't like me. I wonder if she likes anyone, even her own child."

They had forgotten about Dani's presence. She kept very still so as not to remind them. This was more than she had learned before about what went on at the consulate since she had stopped being a daily visitor. Dani had thought many times about the exchange between Madame and her mother on the day the war started. Sometimes she was able to convince herself that Madame's comment meant nothing, that she had imagined the searing look that accompanied it, and the sudden heat it had elicited in Nellie's cheeks.

Dani also wondered how Berta was faring without a friend to play with. She had hoped that Madame, left with no alternative but to spend time with her daughter, might have become kinder to her. Nellie's comment suggested otherwise.

Chapter 24

After Nellie ushered the rabbi into Richard Vandercam's office the next morning at eleven, she turned to leave, but the consul gestured for her to stay. She took a seat at the side of the room and readied her notepad. The rabbi, who had again declined to surrender his hat and coat, glanced warily at her before launching into the Polish yeshiva students' story, and his idea that they could travel through Stockholm to the Dutch West Indies.

Richard listened intently, leaning forward and nodding at the description of conditions in Poland. "There is a small problem." He paused. "I'm not empowered to issue visas to the Dutch Caribbean possessions. Travelers can obtain a visa on arrival in those islands, a visa issued on the authority of the colonial governor."

The rabbi's shoulders sank.

"I said, 'a small problem.' I think we could find a way around it. The larger problem is the transit through Sweden. The Swedish government takes its neutrality very seriously and has refused to accept Jewish refugees. However, I know the Swedish representative in Riga. I suspect he may be frustrated with his government's stance. If I can persuade him that the students will move on quickly, he might issue transit visas. Leave it with me, and I'll see what I can do."

"But when can they leave? A spring offensive might bring shipping to a standstill. They don't have time!"

The rabbi's fervor pushed him to his feet. Richard rose too. Nellie looked from the rabbi's intense glare to the consul's placating smile. With another man, the rabbi's belligerence might elicit a hostile reaction, but Richard was not provoked. Calmly refusing to be pressed as to when he would have a result, the consul came around the desk to steer the rabbi out. He returned to his office with a spring in his step.

"Get the cypher box out, Nellie!"

Richard instructed Nellie to encrypt a telegraph to the Netherlands' ambassador to Lithuania, the Baltic state to the south. The position of ambassador in Latvia was vacant, so the consul was the Netherlands' sole diplomatic representative in the country. Although Richard did not formally report to the ambassador, the consul frequently sought guidance from him. Their communications were complicated by the fact that the Soviets had taken advantage of the German invasion of Poland to annex the Lithuanian capital, Vilnius, as well as sections of eastern Poland. The Dutch ambassador had followed the Lithuanian government to Kaunas, where a government-in-exile had been established.

Richard and Nellie labored together over the text, phrased in hypotheticals. "If certain non-Netherlands subjects wished to gain entry to a Dutch colonial possession, for example, Curaçao, what appropriate paperwork would need to be completed?" As Nellie was unfamiliar with the contraption that translated confidential messages into secret code, she needed more than an hour to create and send the communication. Meanwhile, Richard made some telephone calls to track down Pers Lindstrom, his Swedish counterpart in Riga. They arranged to meet in a busy coffee shop. There, they discussed the possibility of Sweden issuing transit visas for travelers seeking passage to the West Indies. As Richard had suspected, Lindstrom was impatient with his government's pusillanimous position, although he knew he could not change it. He could, however, provide limited permission for refugees to travel through Sweden to another destination.

Richard returned to the consulate to find Nellie decoding the reply from the Dutch ambassador in Lithuania. It was as ambiguous as the message it responded to. Once decoded, it merely read: "Visas are not generally required for travel to Dutch possessions in the Americas."

The consul telephoned his Swedish colleague. Having already explained the specifics in their face-to-face meeting, Richard carefully phrased his question in vague terms. Riga was becoming a hot house for spies, even at the telephone exchange.

"Pers, do you think an official notation that a visa is not required for admission to a specified Dutch possession would be enough for Sweden to grant a transit visa?"

"Perhaps, yes," the Swedish diplomat pondered. "But the traveler must leave Sweden within three weeks, whether to the specified Dutch colony or somewhere else."

"I don't think that will be a problem," Richard responded, thinking to himself that it didn't matter to the refugees where they went, as long as it was beyond Hitler's grasp.

And so the "Dutch West Indies Visa" was created.

The next day, the yeshiva students came to the consulate in groups of two or three in an attempt not to attract too much attention. They presented their dog-eared documents. Nellie attached to them the typed statement, "Visa not required for Curaçao," or, for variety, "St. Maarten" or "Aruba." Then the consul impressed the official Royal Dutch Seal and signed his name with a flourish, "on behalf of her Majesty Queen Wilhelmina of the Netherlands." Armed with this certification, the students went to the Swedish embassy, where Pers Lindstrom would issue them a three-week transit visa for Sweden.

It was after six o'clock when the last young man left the consulate. Nellie was putting her coat on when Richard came into her office bearing a ceramic flask and two shot glasses.

"*Oude jenever*. I've been saving this for the right occasion. It came from my father's cellar."

"I should be going home. It's late." Despite her words, Nellie threw her coat over a chair and took the proffered glass. The old gin tasted smoky, more like whisky than the clear, clean "young" gin that most people drank. Its warmth spread through her chest.

Richard had downed his drink and was pouring another. "Come on. Bottoms up! We did a good day's work today." Nellie couldn't help but smile at the consul's delight in the moment. Caught up in activity, she had not revisited her doubts about the dangers helping Jewish refugees might pose. Now she had a moment to breathe, they reemerged. Nevertheless, she raised her glass.

"All right. Here's to the Dutch West Indies Visa. Let's hope it works!" Nellie finished her drink in one gulp.

The consul's grin wavered. "Yes. And let's hope the Latvian government doesn't find out about it, or I'll be booted out of the country and you'll be out of a job."

"Won't it be worth it if those students escape?" Even as she said the words, Nellie felt a new panic clutch her heart. She couldn't imagine not working at the consulate, not seeing Richard every day. Her face must have betrayed her, because the consul stepped forward with a look of concern. He took the empty glass from her hand and put it on the desk.

"Nellie, you must know, I'm so glad you brought the rabbi here. It's given me a purpose, and I'll always be grateful..." He stood close enough that she could smell the gin on his breath. His eyes seemed to swim behind the rimless eyeglasses. She stood still, not breathing, holding his gaze. *He's going to kiss me.*

The moment passed. He turned away to cork the flask. She picked up her coat.

"Thank you, Nellie. I'll see you tomorrow."

****

The ferry between Riga and Stockholm was supposed to run weekly, but the service was irregular and depended on the number of passengers, the volume of freight, and the availability of coal to fire the ancient engines. While waiting for their departure, the excited yeshiva students spread the word about their escape stratagem to other refugees. Since the Germans had invaded Poland the previous September, many Polish Jews had fled to the Baltic states. Most headed for Vilnius, where there was a large and thriving Jewish community, but hundreds, perhaps as many as a thousand, ended up in Riga, and more were arriving daily, as Nazi atrocities mounted in the occupied areas.

Three days after the students obtained their visas, Nellie arrived at the consulate to find Ivan, arms folded over his chest and a dour expression on his face, barring the door to a group of two men, two women, and a boy of about Dani's age. They all wore good wool coats, the men in hats and the women with headscarves tied under their chins, but their faces—even the little boy's—were hollow-eyed with exhaustion. She squeezed past them and addressed Ivan in Russian.

"What's going on?"

"Poles," Ivan replied tersely without taking his eyes from the visitors. "They don't have appointments."

Nellie looked at the man closest to the door. "Sir, what do you want at the consulate?" She had little Polish so she spoke slowly in German. He turned to the others, and one of the women stepped forward.

"We wish to go to…" She hesitated looking around at her companions for help.

"Curaçao," another man supplied. Then they all started speaking at once in Polish and an unfamiliar sort of German Nellie thought was Yiddish. She scanned the street nervously for uniforms.

"It's all right, Ivan. They can wait inside. We don't want to attract notice."

Ivan stood reluctantly aside, and Nellie ushered the refugees into her office.

"Please, make yourselves comfortable. I'll go and find the consul." She gave what she hoped was a reassuring smile and backed out into the hall. Richard was hurrying down the stairs, the noise of the visitors' entrance having drawn his attention. Nellie preceded him into his office and closed the door.

"Polish refugees asking for visas to Curaçao. What should I tell them?"

The consul went to his desk, but he didn't sit down.

"These are just the first. There'll be others." He pursed his lips and stared blindly down at the papers in front of him.

"Yes, I'm sure there'll be others. What should I tell them?" Nellie repeated.

"What should we tell them? Hmm, I suppose I could issue more visas, but I'm not sure Pers will issue more transit permits. And if there are as many refugees as I suspect, the authorities might step in. You know there's no legal basis for what we're doing." Richard paced up and down. Nellie waited. The group she had just admitted to the consulate inspired her sympathy. She could easily imagine herself in their situation, fleeing with a child.

Richard nodded toward the closed door behind her. "Who are they? What are they like?"

"They're Jews." Nellie kept her voice calm, although she wanted to scream, *Jews, like me!* "Two men, two women, and a little boy. They look completely drained." She remained motionless, her face impassive, but willing the consul with all her might to make a decision, the right decision. It felt as if everything—*her* future, as well as that of the people waiting in her office—depended on what the consul said next.

"Well, I think if they want to go to Curaçao, we should help them, don't you?" He smiled at her and she nodded, thinking, *Yes, we should help them, whatever the risk*, before rushing back to her office to fetch the refugees.

Chapter 25

The weather had been miserable since the start of April, a cold driving rain that hit the windows like shrapnel. Better than snow, Margriet thought, as she pulled aside the drapes in her bedroom, but still hardly what one could call spring. She resolved to spend the day indoors being lazy. She had a new novel to read, and except for writing some letters and a couple of thank-you notes that could wait a day or so, she had no social duties. Richard had risen early as usual, leaving her to luxuriate under the covers for another hour until Marta brought up coffee and toast. Where was Marta? It was past nine o'clock and still no breakfast. No doubt she was embroiled in a dispute with Ivan and had forgotten the time.

Margriet dressed and went down to the kitchen to see what was delaying Marta's routine. As she passed through the entrance hall, she was irritated to find yet more bedraggled applicants, seated on the dining room chairs lining the walls. Richard had insisted Ivan carry the chairs downstairs to accommodate them. They had traipsed in mud from the street, and she was sure they were leaving wet patches on the upholstered seats. Peasants is how Margriet thought of them, although she knew better than to say the word aloud in front of Richard. Or the other word—not used in polite society— that came to mind. Not that she had anything against

Jews. When they were stationed in Budapest, there were quite a number in their circle. That charming banker and his elegant, ultra-thin wife who had danced with the Ballet Russe, for example. And the family lawyer back in Amsterdam had been Jewish, a frequent guest at her parents' dinner table. But these Jews were different. They looked pitiful, sitting there fingering their tattered papers, looking up when she descended the staircase, and then, when she refused to meet their eyes, turning back to murmur to their neighbor or resume an anxious review of the documents on their laps.

It had all started two weeks ago with the arrival of those students: pale unhealthy-looking fellows dressed in black, with long, greasy ringlets falling from under their hats.

"Visa applicants; refugees from Poland," Richard answered her questions distractedly.

"Yes, but why here? What on earth is their connection with the Netherlands? I don't think the Foreign Ministry would want to encourage them. We have enough Jews in Holland already."

Richard frowned. "This is consular business. I think I know my obligations better than you."

She retreated, stung. "Well, all I meant was, how were they referred here? Who introduced them?"

Richard's response was stiff. "Nellie Loesseps suggested they come to discuss the possibility of traveling to the Dutch West Indies. I believe they are staying with her rabbi."

That explained it! She always suspected the Loesseps woman had more influence than was healthy. A Jewess. And involving Richard in some scheme to smuggle refugees out of Latvia. This could not look good to his Foreign Ministry superiors back in the Hague. Or to their Latvian hosts. She knew enough about diplomacy to understand that Richard was overstepping his remit. No wonder his career seemed to be going nowhere. He could be so pompous at times, going on about civil liberties and human rights. What about her rights? Her rights to a loving husband who enjoyed spending time with her? But Richard had always preferred principles to practicalities. He had no idea of how hard it was to run a household and try to build a social life with no help from him. He didn't recognize how isolated she was, how difficult the adjustment to an alien culture had been.

She found it hard to remember a time when they had been close, when they had talked other than in polite and superficial exchanges. She acknowledged that they barely knew each other before their marriage, even though their families had moved in the same circles. Their courtship lasted a single golden summer of beach parties and country house weekends. She was a dazzling debutante, and back then he was easily dazzled. On three months' leave from a junior post at the Budapest embassy, he appeared more mature than the college boys who pursued her. He also contributed a touch of the exotic, with the gypsy music records he brought with him from Hungary. They played them all that summer. She and her girlfriends improvised wild barefoot dances to them, as dusk deepened into indigo night, and empty champagne bottles rolled off into the grass. Richard never joined in, but his eyes would follow her gyrations, and she enjoyed the feeling that they were burning right through her clothes, touching her naked body. She was not surprised when he proposed. Everyone was so pleased at the prospect of their union; it had a feeling of inevitability. And they *were* happy together, at least in Budapest. "Before Berta" was how she had come to think of it. That was also before Richard had become so absorbed in work, or at least those aspects of his work that excluded her; not the receptions and dinners where she could shine, but the tedious research in dusty libraries, and now with the tense political situation, the grubby meetings with contacts in coffee houses, and the pointless drafting of lengthy dispatches on military strengths and weaknesses.

Sometimes she thought she *did* understand his job better than he did. After all, his primary duty as consul was to look after the business interests of the few Dutch subjects scattered around Latvia. Then, if requested, to assist in greasing the wheels of international diplomacy by bringing people of influence together over drinks or a game of golf. This was how to ensure that Holland remained a rich and peaceful country, unentangled in the power plays of larger nations, its commerce undisturbed. But Richard always had to pick sides, take a position and judge who was right and who was wrong. After all the effort she had put into inviting the right people to her dinner parties, into charming them with her chatter, plying them with the best food and drink, now he was going to ruin it all by sticking his neck out for a gaggle of penniless Jews. Hadn't the German ambassador called them "the refuse of Europe"?

If only it had stopped with the students. Word had spread that the Dutch consulate was issuing visas, and the Swedish government had agreed to honor them by allowing transit through Swedish ports. Every morning, a line of applicants stood outside the front doors waiting for Ivan to open up. Then they clustered in the entrance hall, leaving dirty footprints on the black-and-white marble, chattering away in their guttural accents. Some even brought food to eat while they waited. She had to draw the line at that but was nervous about raising the subject again with Richard.

"Ivan, I'm relying on you." She made up for her lack of Russian by articulating loudly and clearly. "Please make sure that all eating and smoking is done outside in the street." Ivan had nodded enthusiastically. But his efforts to herd the overflow crowd outside had expanded the problem. From the salon windows, she saw passersby stop to gawp at the odd-looking characters picnicking on the doorstep, so she had to retract her order.

She closed the door to the kitchen quarters behind her, pushing the refugee problem out of her mind to concentrate on her search for Marta. Ivan and Berta were sitting at the kitchen table. They looked up at her, startled to see her there. How infuriating. She was the mistress of the house after all.

"Where's Marta?" She said to Ivan in a sharp voice. He winced at her question as if it hurt his ears.

"Marta?" Ivan cocked his head and knit his eyebrows.

"She's not here. Ivan gave me my breakfast." Berta, young as she was, intervened to play the peacemaker.

"I can see she's not here. Where *is* she?"

Berta and Ivan looked at each other, then back at her, shrugging like a pair of halfwits.

Exasperated, she returned through the hall, again ignoring the supplicant glances directed at her by the shabby crew waiting there, and ran up the stairs to the attic floor where Marta's room was located. Marta was lying on the bed, fully dressed but with a pained expression on her face.

"It's my back again. Every step is agony, and bending over is impossible." Marta was a champion complainer. She hated the weather in Latvia, the language, the food. She complained about Ivan constantly. Margriet felt she could be forgiven for having tuned out Marta's earlier complaints about her back pain. But this must be serious to keep her from her morning duties.

"You poor old thing! Shall I send Ivan up with some tea?"

"You'll do no such thing! That dirty old man in my bedroom! I should think not!"

Marta was steadfast in her adoration of her mistress. Why else would she have struggled to learn to cook the fancy French cuisine Margriet insisted on? Or steam-pressed three costumes, one after another, as Margriet wavered over which to wear? It wasn't all work, Margriet told herself. Marta had relished those late-night chats before Margriet was married, when she would come home from a party to find Marta nodding off in a chair, keeping the fire alight in her bedroom so Margriet could undress in the warmth. She would tell her who she danced with, who she had refused, and Marta would snigger at descriptions of the handmade dresses of the country cousins, and suck her breath through her teeth in disapproval at some flirt's behavior. In those sessions with Marta, she could play whatever role she fancied: the grand lady or the naughty little girl. She experimented, trying on feelings and opinions to see how they sounded. Marta's reaction was usually approving, but even when Margriet managed to shock her, all she would do was shake her head and say, "Well, I don't know what to say! You *are* a one."

Now Margriet told her, "Then I'll just sit here with you for a while, and we'll talk about old times." In spite of the difference in their social status, Margriet sometimes felt closer to Marta than to Richard or Berta. She could relax with Marta. She never felt the criticism that Richard's frowns implied, or Berta's hesitation when Margriet called her daughter to her. "Do you remember…" Margriet rambled on for a few minutes about long-ago escapades, rewarded by a gradual easing of Marta's expression.

Margriet stood up and, with her hands on her hips, looked down at her maid. Her thoughts turned to practical matters. She would have to send Ivan out to do the marketing, knowing he would return with all the wrong things—turnips instead of greens, sausage instead of steak—and some lame excuse about food shortages. She suppressed her irritation; it wasn't Marta's fault.

"All right then, I'll bring you up some tea and those nice butter cookies you like. You just take it easy today, and if you're no better tomorrow, I'll ask the German doctor to pop in and take a look at you."

Herr Doktor Felder. Such a charming man, and so good-looking in that clean-cut, clear-eyed German way. Hans Weber had recommended him when Margriet confided that she was having trouble sleeping. The doctor had been helpful, not only giving her the sleeping drug she needed but also the pick-me-up pills that counteracted the dopey feeling the medicine gave her the next morning.

Marta couldn't even get out of bed the next day. Margriet was seriously worried now. Even so, she couldn't help a small rush of pleasure at the thought of summoning the doctor. She reached for the telephone in the salon, only to find the line already in use. Nellie Loesseps was chattering away in Lettish or Yiddish or some other incomprehensible language. It was too much, having to share just one line for personal matters and consular business.

"I have a medical emergency. Please get off the line," she said crisply, then put the receiver down without waiting for a response.

****

She intercepted *Herr Doktor* Felder in the entrance hall before Ivan could consign him to limbo amongst the riffraff.

"Thank you so much for coming. Marta is so dear to me, I don't know what I'd do without her. She's been with my family for years. I know you understand."

"Of course! I'm only too happy to help. You have quite a lot on your hands, I can see." The doctor glanced back to the bedraggled crew waiting in the entrance hall as they ascended the staircase.

"Oh, that's consular business." She echoed Richard's words. "We are quite besieged. There's nothing my husband can do, apparently. Marta's on the third floor. I'd apologize for the climb, but I can see you're up for it!"

He responded with a smile to her flirtatious tone.

"I like to keep myself fit. You never know when you might be called on!"

Marta insisted Margriet stay through the examination, although she understood Felder's clear and concise German. Afterward, Margriet and the doctor withdrew to the salon to confer. The doctor refused an offer of coffee, citing other patients to see.

"Normally, I'd do more tests before I give a diagnosis, but I know you want to know what's wrong as soon as possible. I'm afraid it's bad news. Marta has a palpable mass on her kidneys. It's pressing on her spine, which is why she's experiencing severe back pain. She must also be having other symptoms which she may be hiding from you. Surgery is unlikely to be successful, and the facilities here are primitive for such a complicated procedure anyway. The best I can do is prescribe morphine for the pain."

"No! There must be something!" Margriet's voice rose in panic. "What if I took her back to Amsterdam? The doctors there know all the most advanced techniques—"

"Travel is impossible at this stage of the disease; it would kill her. Of course, if you'd like a second opinion…" Felder paused, looking down on Margriet, his earlier flirting replaced by a professional coolness. He didn't like having his judgment questioned, and this was just a servant, after all. Margriet was oblivious to his tone, absorbing what Dr. Felder was intimating: Marta was dying. He continued speaking, but his words barely penetrated the fog of her anxiety.

"…weeks, at most. I can arrange for her admission to the hospital later today, if you wish."

"No, she'll stay here. I'll look after her." Her response was instinctive, and more to do with her own need not to be separated from her lifelong companion than an understanding of how distressed Marta would be in a strange place where no one spoke her language.

The doctor smiled, wondering cynically how soon this elegant socialite would tire of emptying bedpans and changing sheets.

"I'll send my nurse to give…"—he had forgotten her name—"…the patient an injection of morphine, and you can discuss ongoing palliative care with her."

Left alone in the salon, Margriet paced the room. It seemed impossible that a bad back could turn out to be fatal. How could she cope without Marta? She was the constant in Margriet's life. Marta had cared for her when she was a baby, and been devoted to her ever since. Marta hadn't wanted to come to Latvia, but Margriet had persuaded her, arguing that she'd be miserable in Holland without her "baby" to fuss over. And was Latvia now to be the death of her? Margriet felt a sting of remorse, before telling herself that Marta would at least have the comfort of Margriet's constant presence to the end. But what comfort was there in this for Margriet? How was she supposed to go on without Marta?

Her own parents had spared little time for their young daughter; the older brothers took any attention left over after business or social obligations were fulfilled. Although Margriet had demonstrated appropriate grief at the time, her father's death when she was fourteen moved her little. If anything, it had achieved the welcome result of awakening her mother to Margriet's existence. She took on as her mission her daughter's instruction in what she perceived as the womanly arts. But by then the emotional distance between them was unbridgeable. While her mother provided a role model to Margriet, it was Marta who offered the only consistent and unconditional affection she had known.

Margriet had never felt so lonely.

Chapter 26

The intense activity at the consulate invigorated Nellie. She left the apartment early each morning, her eyes alight in anticipation of the work ahead. She returned late, often after dinner was already on the table. She neglected to eat while she told the gathered family about the people to whom they had issued visas that day.

"The husband and wife were both doctors. They had an adorable little girl. I would have liked to suggest she go upstairs and play with Berta while they waited, but Richard didn't want to bother his wife. Marta's ill. I don't know what's wrong with her, but it must be serious. She hasn't left her room for days." Although Marta had treated her with coolness, imitating Margriet's attitude, Nellie felt sorry for the aging servant who seemed so out of place in Latvia, especially now she was sick. "Madame is taking care of her. Ivan's doing the marketing and cooking, and looking after Berta, as well as opening the door to applicants. We had over thirty come through today. It can get quite loud." Nellie smiled, but then became somber.

"It's very sad. They've left everything—homes, businesses, family and friends. They're so scared of being taken to the camps. Apparently, the Germans are rounding up all the Jews—women and children too—and taking them west to do forced labor in Germany." She dropped her voice, with a glance at Dani. "They say they work them to death…"

Kat gasped. Simon clenched his jaw.

"Is it just Polish Jews that get visas?" Sarah asked. She and Piotr had moved into a place of their own in March, a tiny apartment left vacant by a friend of theirs, a cellist in the orchestra who had gone to England to enlist in the British forces. Nellie and Dani had abandoned the sofa bed in the professor's study and moved into Sarah and Piotr's old room. The couple came back at least once a week for dinner. They were almost as excited as Nellie by the visa scheme and plied her with questions each time they saw her.

"Only Polish Jews have applied. I suppose Latvians can still travel with just a regular passport."

"Hah! Not any longer!" Piotr flushed in anger. Usually an observer at the dinner table and content to leave political discussion to the others, he was now animated. "Oh, I expect we could go to Russia, if we were foolish enough to want to, but the rest of the world doesn't want any more refugees, especially if they're Jewish!"

"What do you mean?" Professor Kutner still found it hard to believe in the everyday cruelties that the war brought, even in those countries still supposedly at peace.

"My friend Talek told me about a boat loaded with Jews—refugees from Germany, Poland, and, yes, even some Latvians. They tried to land in America and were refused. They came back to Europe, and were refused again by France, Portugal—I don't know where they'll end up. He—Talek, I mean—tried to get on the Stockholm ferry last night. But they wouldn't let him on board without a Swedish visa."

"So Talek wants a Dutch West Indies visa to get a Swedish visa?" Nellie asked.

"Not just Talek," Piotr and Sarah looked at each other before Sarah continued. "We want to leave, too."

Her words dropped like a stone. After a second of shocked silence around the table, Kat began to protest, her voice rising. Sarah rushed on, drowning her mother out.

"We want to go to England! Piotr wants to fight the Germans!" Sarah reached over for her mother's hand, addressing her in an urgent tone.

"We have friends there—at least, one friend. We can't trust the Soviets to protect us. They're as bad as the Nazis, and anyway their army is no match for the Germans. Everyone says when the summer comes, the Germans will launch an offensive. It will be too late then to find a way out."

"But darling, your music! Your position with the orchestra. You can't give all that up." Ekaterina was proud that her younger daughter had inherited her gifts.

"There are orchestras in England, Mama. And what good is music if you're dead?"

"Now you're being hysterical. Germans love music! Even if they came to Latvia, they wouldn't break up a fine symphony orchestra!" Kat looked around the family, searching for support.

Sarah rolled her eyes and sighed in exasperation. Along with her musical talent, she had inherited a large measure of her mother's histrionics. "Nellie, you tell her! You know Piotr's right!"

"Mama, I told you about the pianist from Lodz, didn't I?" Nellie began. "He came to the consulate on his own. He escaped from a transport of Jews being shipped to labor camps. He said the SS captain in charge of the sweep admired his grand piano, told him to play something—" She hesitated, aware Dani was listening. She decided not to mention the unprovoked shooting of the pianist's father, an old man in a wheelchair. "But they took him for forced labor anyway. Being Jewish trumps being musical," she finished flatly.

Simon spoke for the first time since Sarah's announcement. "I think you should go. Everything here is unstable. The Soviets might take over completely; the Germans might invade. We have a choice—lie low and try to survive, or leave and try to find a better place. You youngsters should leave. Kat and I will stay and, God willing, survive."

Everyone was silent then, absorbing the professor's pronouncement, as well as his uncharacteristic reference to God. Nellie looked around the table, her eyes coming to rest on Dani. The child looked confused, and Nellie's heart swelled with love. Since their arrival in Riga a year before, Dani had shown such resilience. She had adapted to life in this apartment with its high ceilings and shabby furniture. Now that her memories of life in Holland had faded, Grandkat's impromptu arias and rich cooking, her grandfather's ink-stained fingers and mischievous grin, had become her anchors. Nellie could see the talk of leaving and starting out again in a new place alarmed Dani. She searched for something reassuring to say, but found no words—no honest words—that might settle Dani's fears about the future. Instead, as Sarah rushed to embrace her parents, tears on her cheeks—Nellie reached for her daughter's hand and drew her into a hug, hiding her own tears against Dani's hair.

****

What Nellie did not share with her family during her nightly narratives was how her relationship with Richard had deepened as they worked side by side to issue the lifesaving visas. Her earlier nervousness about the danger to herself and her family had been eclipsed by the exhilaration this intimacy generated.

The consul confided that he was still troubled by the unorthodox solution they had hit upon to aid the refugees' escape.

"I'm not worried that a colonial governor would refuse entry to a visa holder. By the time they get to Curaçao or one of the other Dutch islands, they'll be well beyond Hitler's grasp. It's all the steps in between." The last of the day's applicants had left, and they were sitting in Nellie's office, the flask of *oude genever* on the desk between them.

"I like Pers Lindstrom and I trust him, but he's probably acting beyond his remit too," Richard continued. "What if the Swedish authorities refuse to honor the transit visas and turn the refugees away? Or what if they're allowed to disembark in Sweden, but can't find onward passage within three weeks? They'll be deported to Latvia, or, more likely, back to Poland. Then they may be in a worse position than if they'd stayed in Latvia. I'd be responsible!"

Nellie was tempted to offer anodyne words of comfort, but she understood the risks to the refugees as well. Normally, by this time of year, the amount of shipping through the Baltic grew, both in number of vessels and variety of destinations. However, the war, and specifically Germany's recent annexation of Denmark and Norway, had reduced traffic on this route. The chances of the refugees making it safely across the

Atlantic lessened every day.

Steeped in diplomatic protocols and procedures, Richard allayed his fears with meticulous paperwork. They already recorded every visa applicant's name, town of origin and date of birth in the hope that their ultimate success in escaping Europe could be tracked. Now Richard suggested an additional step.

"Nellie, I want you to help me interview the refugees. We should document a full background: the atrocities they've suffered, the property they've been forced to abandon, their work—everything. When this is over, reparations must be made. We can help them get justice!"

Nellie's heart swelled in response to Richard's appeal. With her facility for languages, Nellie had already picked up a smattering of Polish, and was even able to convert her schoolbook German into the Yiddish idioms most frequently used by the refugees. But, as she vigorously nodded her assent, she was not thinking of them; she was imagining working as a full partner with Richard, sitting near him every day, on his side of the desk, as they interviewed applicants. She recognized this urge for closeness was wrong: Richard had a wife and family; she was just an employee. But a deeper, more insistent voice compelled her to search Richard's face for a signal that he wanted her nearness too.

He fiddled with his glass, keeping his eyes averted.

"I'd understand if you didn't want to be involved. What we're doing is not strictly legal. The government surely wouldn't approve—"

Nellie interrupted him.

"But it was I who brought the yeshiva students here in the first place! How can you think I don't want to be involved?" Angry at herself for indulging in romantic fantasy while Richard seemed occupied with practicalities, her voice rose to shrillness.

"Look, I have diplomatic immunity; you don't. That's all I meant." He looked directly at her and leaned forward. "Nellie, you must know how I depend on you. You have... Your presence here..." He gestured vaguely around the office, then took a deep breath. "I need you with me, but I'm putting you at risk. If anything happened to you—"

Nellie grabbed his hand in both of hers, laughing with relief.

"Nothing will happen to me! You'll see. We'll work through this together!"

Chapter 27

May Day came and went, with the stream of visa applicants at the consulate undiminished. Sarah and Piotr obtained a transit visa through Sweden. In the end, they did not need the Dutch West Indies visa because their friend, now a pilot in the RAF, sponsored them for entry into Britain.

Without notice, Dani's school was closed down. The janitor padlocked the doors to the building and nailed up an unconvincing explanatory notice signed on behalf of the Education Ministry.

"Teacher retraining! Teacher substitution, more likely!" Grankat snorted in derision. "Just you wait and see. When school reopens, all the teachers will be Russian, and the only textbook will be *The Life of Lenin*."

"Well, that's better than all German teachers, and being forced to read *Mein Kampf*," responded her husband. "Anyway, Dani and I could do with a little holiday." Classes at the University had been suspended too. Being locked out of his office, with its stored years of research, all his lecture notes and half his library, was agony for Simon, but he was determined to show his granddaughter a brave face. "And at least we appear to have lost our dear friend."

He was referring to the watcher in the parked car, the presence that had appeared after Pavel's disappearance, maintaining a chilly vigil into the early hours of the morning, until satisfied that no more visitors would arrive and all occupants were in their beds. The watcher had been absent for several nights now. In a strange way, Simon was disturbed by this development. It wasn't just that he had got used to his presence; it was almost as if the spy had been protecting them somehow. He had never seen his face, and he knew that it was not one man but a team of different watchers that kept up the surveillance. But at least nothing had happened as long as he—they—were there. Now, with schools closing, Sarah and Piotr gone, and Nellie so preoccupied at the consulate, things felt as if they were shifting in unpredictable ways.

Simon had little news from the outside world except for what Nellie brought home from the consulate. He knew that in April, Germany had moved to annex Denmark and invade Norway. That seemed to have scared the Russians, because their soldiers, who had previously sauntered in twos and threes through the Riga streets like tourists, now marched in organized patrols. They had taken over the Armory in the center of the Old Town, and imposed a nightly curfew. Fresh produce and meat were scarce. The rumor was that supplies were being requisitioned for the vast Red Army massing on the border. The non-aggression pact between Russia and Germany, supposed to last a hundred years, would barely last another twelve months.

Dani and her grandparents could have used the enforced free time to take a walk in the park or stroll down to the river—the weather had finally turned pleasant. But by unspoken agreement they remained inside, waiting for the evening and Nellie's return from work. The friends who used to fill the apartment with laughter and music, stuffing themselves with Kat's ragouts and clinking glasses with Simon, seemed to have evaporated. Simon knew better than to reach out to them. The more outspoken were in hiding, and even the nonpolitical were wise to avoid contact with a suspect intellectual. Instead, Simon spent hours fiddling with the radio, searching for the elusive signal from the BBC World Service but finding only static or bursts of brassy music, as Germany and Russia tried to outdo each other in jamming the radio waves.

The tension was worse for Kat. She was always the more gregarious of the couple, and she missed the comradery of their former life. She took to playing Brahms and Beethoven on the phonograph—just the slow movements—standing at the window, swaying to and fro, wringing her hands. She pined for Sarah with a sharpness she had not experienced when Nellie set off for Holland ten years before. She loved both her daughters, but Sarah, her baby, was her image and her echo. Parting with her felt like losing a limb; she kept looking for her, listening for her voice. Nellie was always more her father's child, but now, with Sarah gone and their circle of friends dispersed, Kat leaned on Nellie as her link to the world, and, like her husband, she tried to be brave for Dani's sake.

****

The moment Nellie walked in, Kat knew something bad had happened. The skin around Nellie's eyes had a drawn, papery look, and her mouth was a thin line, not the usual smile of greeting.

"What is it, *cara*? What's happened?"

"Oh, Mama, this is a bad day! Just let's everyone sit

down, and I'll explain."

Simon and Dani joined them in the entrance hall, and they all moved together into the sitting room, shepherding Nellie like a sick lamb between them.

"I'm not sure where to start. I'll just tell it as it happened. As soon as I got to the consulate this morning, there was a telegram from the Swedish consul saying he had been ordered by his government to immediately stop issuing all transit visas. Without transit visas, the visas we're giving the refugees are useless. We had to explain that to the people waiting. It was so awful to see the hope go out of their faces.

"But then, about noon, we started to get reports from Holland via the embassy in Kaunus—Rotterdam was bombed last night!"

Rotterdam was where Nellie and Dani had lived until a year ago—close to the Loesseps grandparents' home. Dani remembered them as white-haired, rosy-faced little people, smiling at her and nodding like a pair of matched wooden dolls.

"Are Oma and Opa all right?" The familiar terms rose easily to Dani's lips.

"I don't know. Let's pray they are." Nellie lifted her eyes from Dani's face to her father's. "The Germans didn't try to breach the Maginot line. They came through the Ardennes into Belgium and Holland—so much for neutrality!"

Simon knew the French and British armies were concentrated on the Rhine, relying on the supposedly impregnable Maginot line of defenses to halt any western offensive by the Germans. Apparently, the Germans had attacked the virtually undefended Low Countries instead and planned to cut off the Allies from the north.

"The Netherlands will fall. No wonder the Swedes are nervous. With Norway invaded and Denmark annexed, they can't risk any appearance of aiding Germany's adversaries." His analysis was crisp and to the point, but his voice shook. "Will your consul be recalled?"

"I don't know. Richard is at his wits' end. Besides dealing with the visa applicants, and trying to get some accurate information out of his government, he's coping with his wife. Since Marta died, she seems to be having some kind of breakdown. She won't leave her room and won't have anyone but Richard look after her. He asked if I'd bring Dani with me tomorrow. Berta has been left to fend for herself for far too long, and she needs some company."

It was almost nine months since Dani had last visited the consulate or seen Berta. She felt a rush of excitement, tinged with anxiety. Would Berta remember her? And what was a "breakdown"? She tried to imagine the immaculate Madame breaking into pieces, and failed.

"Be careful," Ekaterina stretched out to grip Nellie's arm.

"What do you mean?" Nellie asked, surprised.

Kat attempted a laugh. "I don't know. I just felt a shiver or something—a premonition? Everything seems so...up in the air." She stood and moved toward the kitchen. "Let's eat."

"Don't worry, Mama," Nellie called after her. "Dani will be fine with me."

Chapter 28

A card in Dutch, Lettish, Russian, and Polish was pinned to the consulate's massive front doors: *"In view of the current situation, all consular services, including the issuance of visas, have been suspended until further notice."*

Dispensing with the formality of waiting to be admitted, Nellie took a heavy iron key from her bag and let herself and Dani in. Over the winter, Dani had idealized the consulate, creating in her memory an elegant palace of airy rooms and sparkling windows. The reality she saw that May morning was much more ordinary. The black-and-white marble floor of the entrance hall was scuffed and dusty; the rows of empty chairs gave the place a forlorn look, as did the offices either side, pocket doors pulled open to reveal desks piled with papers, boxes on the floor overflowing with files.

Berta sat halfway up the stairs, nursing her favorite doll, whose name Dani remembered was Elizabeth. She smiled shyly as she stood and came down to meet her friend.

"Hello," Berta whispered. "Can we play that game where you're the papa and I'm the mama?"

"Yes! Let's make a house behind the sofa like we used to." But one look in the salon stopped Dani in her tracks. The drapes were closed and the dark shapes of the furniture looked threatening. A stale smell of unemptied ashtrays and long-dead flowers pervaded the air. "Let's go play in the garden. It's a sunny day."

Then she noticed that Berta was still in her nightdress. She took the younger girl's hand and led her upstairs to find some clothes. As they crossed the bedroom landing, she heard voices from behind a closed door: the consul's low placating tone, and his wife's shriller note. She could not make out the words, and as Berta made no comment, they continued on to the nursery at the back of the house. Between them, they found clean underwear and a blouse and skirt that didn't look too crushed. Abandoning the search for socks, Berta put on a pair of last year's sandals that looked painfully small, and they headed down again, passing Ivan laboring up with two dining chairs, muttering, "Upstairs, downstairs, upstairs. Why don't they make up their minds?"

The garden, at least, was not disappointing. A couple of beds near the kitchen door had been cleared, ready for Ivan's vegetable planting. Other than that, the garden was a profusion of spring growth. In the center stood a flowering cherry tree, each breezy gust dispensing a shower of petals. Yellow and purple irises, some taller than either girl, crowded at the base of the high brick walls enclosing the garden. Even the weeds—buttercups and dandelions, thick on the grass and forcing their way up between the paving stones of the path—looked joyous and welcoming.

They played together in the "flower snow," as Berta called the cherry blossoms, throwing handfuls into the wind and letting them fall onto their hair and shoulders. Then they got down to the serious business of make-believe. Time passed quickly, and Nellie surprised them when she called that it was time for lunch.

They joined Nellie and the consul at the kitchen table. Ivan refused an invitation to sit with them, preferring to eat standing up at the sink. They ate hard-boiled eggs and bread and jam; it felt like a picnic.

"Were you able to get everything on the list, Ivan?" Nellie asked.

"No fish to be had. They say there's a Soviet warship blocking the mouth of the Daugava, and the fishing fleet can't go out. I got two rabbits off a fellow who came in from the country, though. He said he had to walk the last six miles, couldn't get a ride. The fuel shortage is keeping people off the roads. I got most of the rest."

While Berta and Dani concentrated on eating, the consul and Nellie discussed the news garnered from the Ambassador in Kaunas, who was in patchy communication with the Hague.

"Even though there are still a few Dutch army units resisting, capitulation can't be far off. The Queen and the royal family have fled to London. There doesn't seem to be a functioning government anymore, so no instructions whether to stay put or go home," Richard summarized the situation glumly. He dropped his voice with a glance at the girls. "Margriet is desperate to go. She says she won't leave her room unless it's to leave Latvia entirely. I don't know what to do." He sighed and stared down at his plate. "She's devastated by Marta's death. I didn't realize they were so close. I've tried to get her to see reason, if just for Berta's sake."

"Don't worry, Papa. Dani can look after me," Berta whispered.

Dani felt a rush of pride. This was something she could do to help. Her mother had her work, and now Dani had her own mission. Nellie and the consul both smiled at the child, as she nodded solemnly.

"Yes, I can look after Berta."

The next few days passed in a weird calm. Dani accompanied Nellie each day to the consulate and played with Berta. The routine echoed the previous summer, except that Madame kept to her room, allowing only her husband to enter with trays of temptingly arranged food and clean linens. Had Margriet known that it was Nellie who carefully cut the crusts off her toast, or tucked a blossom into her napkin ring, she would not have been pleased.

The atmosphere in the house was more casual than a year ago. Meals were taken around the big kitchen table. There was little office work to be done, so Nellie took on a different role, making shopping lists for Ivan, doing the cooking and some light laundry and cleaning. The consul, who split his time between his wife and monitoring the telephone and radio for news, protested.

"Please, Nellie, you're not paid to do that. If in fact you will be paid at all," he added. But Nellie suspected he liked to watch her as she polished and dusted, humming to herself, her hair tied back in a scarf. She imagined he enjoyed this small taste of routine domesticity, given the dismal news that filtered in from the wider world, and his wife's intransigence.

"It's no problem, Richard. I like to keep busy."

On the fourth day, a brief message from the Ambassador to Lithuania informed Richard that the Netherlands' army had surrendered. He called Nellie into his office.

"The Foreign Ministry is under German control now. I'll be ordered back to Holland to account for myself. This—" he waved a hand to indicate the building—"belongs to Germany now." He took off his glasses and began to polish them on a handkerchief. His cheeks were wet.

Nellie felt stunned, although the news was expected. She sank down into the chair across the desk, the chair where for weeks a procession of refugees had perched to tell their stories.

"At least Margriet will be pleased," Richard continued. He gave a bitter laugh. "I wonder if she understands what life will be like under Nazi rule. Probably not."

Nellie stared around the room at the files piled high on every surface, each one containing the details of a refugee's life.

"What should we do with these?" she asked.

Richard stood abruptly. "Oh, God. We have to destroy them! Don't you see, if these files fall into Nazi hands, we've provided a description of every Jewish community and family the visa applicants belong to."

"But I thought the records would help them after the war, when they come home…" Nellie's voice faltered as she realized they had both indulged in a fantasy. The war was just beginning, and who knew when it would end, who would be the victors, who would survive to come home.

She and Richard had sat close beside each other, scribbling down people's pasts as if they had the power to guarantee their future—a delusion fueled by her desire to be Richard's partner, in work if not in life. A hot wash of shame poured over her.

****

Berta and Dani were happy to help with the last consular duty that remained. Ivan made a bonfire in the garden, and the consul and Nellie carried out all the papers deemed too sensitive to remain after the office's anticipated closure: mostly the records of the Jewish refugees to whom Dutch West Indies visas had been issued. Berta and Dani danced around the flames like witches, chanting spells of made-up words, chasing down the windborne scraps that escaped complete cremation, and flinging them dramatically back into the fire. Richard and Nellie stood side by side watching them.

"Do you think the visas worked, Richard? Will any of those poor people get out?"

"I don't know. We gave them a start. I wish we had been able to issue more of them."

"I counted nine hundred and forty-two files," Nellie indicated the smoldering bonfire. "That's nine hundred and forty-two people on their way to safety. You should be proud."

"No, it's you who should be proud. You're the one who brought the first refugees here, and you worked just as hard as I did on the visas."

They lapsed into silence. Nellie would remember this moment all her life: the smoke curling up into the pale sky, the children's laughter, and Richard standing close beside her. She experienced deep melancholy mixed with a sense of accomplishment. The last few weeks had been the most important of her existence, not only because of the work they had done, but also because of the profound connection forged between her and the man next to her. She felt Richard's fingers brush the back of her hand; it was not an accident. She turned her hand to touch, then hold his, and lifted her face to meet his eyes.

"Nellie," he murmured, as he leant down toward her. Over his shoulder, she caught sight of movement in one of the upper windows of the consulate, a pale blur of a face against the dimness within.

"Margriet!" Her voice was low and urgent. She turned back toward the cavorting children, but their hands remained clasped. Nellie's heart raced, and she could hear Richard breathing deeply, as if struggling to find words.

"Nellie. You can't imagine how—" but Nellie interrupted him, moving to catch hold of her daughter.

"Dani! Don't get so close to the flames!"

Part Five: *2003*

Chapter 29

When Sammy died only a year after he sold the shops and retired, friends told Dani it seemed so unfair. She didn't say anything. She knew they meant well, but life wasn't fair; life just happened. Of course, she missed him and wanted him back, but she didn't blame anyone—God or the National Health Service—for his death. He could have died at twelve years old in the bombing raid that killed his parents in 1941, and then they would never have met or had fifty-four years together.

She could have died that same year, lined up on the edge of a ditch with her mother and other Jews and Communists: they were all the same to the Nazis. After the USSR collapsed and Latvia became an independent country again, Dani read about what happened in Riga after the Germans invaded: the roundups, the forced marches out to the forest, the bullets in the back of the head. No cattle trains to labor camps and gas chambers in Poland and Germany, none of the meticulous record-keeping that condemned the Nazis after the war. Just indiscriminate slaughter.

Sammy asked Dani, after the fall of communism, if she wanted to go back and see where her mother came from, maybe visit the old apartment where she had lived with the Kutners. They had traveled abroad together several times, always to somewhere warm: Malta, the Costa Brava, to Morocco once. Always staying in nice hotels where they were treated like royalty. "We deserve it," Sammy would say. After all, they worked hard all year. Dani did the bookkeeping for the business. Sammy built it up from one TV shop to a chain of eight electrical appliance stores around the London area. By the time he sold, the venture was moving into personal computers and mobile phones. It was all above Dani's head, and above Sammy's too, if he was honest, but, as his Aunt Helen used to say, Sammy could sell ice to Eskimos. And he hired good people, youngsters who understood the new technologies. Several of the cousins got a start working in Sammy's stores. Or maybe it was the cousins' kids? The years went by so fast...

Dani didn't want to return to Latvia, or even to Holland. She still resisted thinking about the war. Her mother's image out the back window of the car, growing smaller and smaller as they drove away, still gripped her and blocked other, possibly gentler, memories. Sammy was patient. He never pushed her. She told him some of it, and he pieced together the rest from talking to Sarah and Pete.

Sarah and Pete died within a year of each other. Pete was quite famous in music production circles; he had his own recording studio and all the well-known groups wanted to work with him. Sarah's synagogue string quartet grew into a respectable semi-professional chamber orchestra. In 1994, the orchestra toured Poland and Germany, visiting some of the cities she was supposed to play in 1939 with the Latvian National Symphony before Hitler ruined the plan. Dani kept in touch with Victoria and Katherine. Victoria had moved to Canada. Katherine lived in Scotland with her husband and stepchildren. They wanted Dani to come and stay with them, but she was nervous about the journey, and Scotland was so cold in the springtime. Maybe in the summer.

Fifty-four years together: they had gone by so fast. It wasn't all a bed of roses. Her miscarriages, year after year. But then their beautiful David arrived. He was now a successful lawyer. He married as soon as he left university. His wife Isabel was a lawyer too, although working part-time at present doing clinics at the Legal Aid Society. Isabel wanted to be home when Natalie got back from school. Dani's granddaughter was twelve years old, and talented. She inherited the musical gene from Sarah and Grankat, and played the violin like an angel. Intelligent too: she won a scholarship to Godolphin and Latymer, the same school Sammy's brainy Aunt Barbara had taught at years ago.

Giving up the house was hard. It was always too big for them—Sammy's dream house, not Dani's—but giving it up meant losing her independence. She never wanted to be a burden on anyone. In the end, David and Isabel persuaded her it was better to move while she was still active, not wait for a crisis to force her out. They had renovated their basement flat, and she was quite settled there now. Natalie dropped in after school, and Dani ate dinner with the family most nights. She felt useful too, picking up a bit of shopping for Isabel, and being home for deliveries or tradesmen when she was working.

Dani had a lot of time to herself. She sat by the sliding glass doors at the back and watched the birds. The front of the flat was a bit dark—visitors had to go down some steps from the street level—but the back opened straight onto the garden. She kept the bird feeders full so even in winter it was lively within the brick walls covered with creepers and bushes on three sides, a big old apple tree at the far end.

She was sitting looking out into the garden when she remembered the tree at the consulate, a flowering cherry. Dani and Berta had scampered around it as the petals fell on them. The old man, Ivan, bent over his potato plants. She hadn't thought of that garden for over sixty years—probably since she left Riga—but the picture came clear as crystal. And the people too: Berta and Ivan. It was like unlocking a door and turning on the light in a dark room. Soon Dani remembered other things: the smell of Grankat's goulash, the feel of her hand in her grandfather's as they walked to the French bakery on the corner.

She started crying. She didn't know why she was sitting there bawling like a child, just the feeling of all those years stretching out between then and now, all the faces she'd never see again. Ivan was certainly dead now. The Kutners too, in some Siberian gulag long ago. When Dani finished crying and had blown her nose a couple of times, she felt lighter somehow. All that time shying away from the past, facing stubbornly forward— she realized she was denying the good as well as shutting out the bad. She felt the need to share her newfound memories with someone. If Sammy had been alive, he'd have listened and nodded and found something positive to say. He always made her feel perceptive and wise.

When Natalie came in after school, she gave her grandmother a quick hug, then went to the refrigerator to look for a snack. Dani followed her into the tiny kitchen.

"Natalie, I'd like you to help me with something. What do you know about Latvia?"

Natalie tipped her head to the side and frowned, a familiar expression. She was thinking hard.

"Well, you come from there, and it's near Russia, right?" She shrugged. "That's about it, I'm afraid."

"Half right. It *is* near Russia. I don't really come from there but I spent a year there at the beginning of the war." Dani wondered how much to say. Natalie was smart, and knew about the Holocaust, but she didn't want to scare her. "Lately I've been thinking about those days, and remembering stuff I'd forgotten. Just little stuff, details about my family. I'd like to write it down, but you know me." She laughed and Natalie grinned. Everyone knew Dani was good at numbers but terrible with writing. "Could you help me with that little computer of yours?"

"My laptop, you mean?" For Natalie's last birthday, her parents had given her the machine, and she had shown Dani some of the things she could do with it.

"Yes, help me write…" Dani struggled for a word to describe what she wanted.

"Your memoir?" Natalie supplied.

"Yes, that's it! A memoir. I'm not sure if it'll make much of a story, just a collection of memories, but I want to record them somehow. Will you do it?"

"Sure, Gran. We can start now, if you like. I've got my violin lesson at five thirty, but I'll go and get my laptop right away."

That was how they began, just half an hour after school. She'd talk and Natalie would tap away, sometimes asking questions, sometimes telling her to slow down so she could catch up. The more Dani talked the more she remembered. Trivial things, really, like how they all had to crowd into the kitchen to eat when Sarah or Piotr was teaching a student in the dining room, how Grankat sang opera while she peeled potatoes, reading Berta's fairy-tale books while the younger girl took a nap. And Berta's doll.

So many times Dani had been on the point of throwing the old suitcase away—the little brown case she had brought to England, packed with her few belongings, the doll wedged on top to fill the space and stop her parents' framed wedding photograph from banging about. At the last minute, when they moved from the apartment to the house in Muswell Hill, she had pulled it out from under the bed they were leaving behind for the next tenants. And after Sammy and she were married, she stuck it in the back of a closet. She supposed she hung on to it because it was the only thing she had from Riga. The photograph, reframed and carefully restored, always stood in pride of place in her home, but she forgot about the suitcase for years at a time.

She didn't even remember the doll was inside when she showed the suitcase to Natalie. They had been working on the memoir for a week or so when she thought of the case. The construction was flimsy even when new. Now, brown cloth peeled away from the board underneath, and the hinges and clasps were stiff with rust. She finally got the case open and lifted the lid. Protected from light and dust, the doll looked new, the blush on its porcelain cheeks and the silky, yellow-gold curls as fresh as when it was made. Dani picked it up and the eyes—bright blue glass—flew open. Natalie jumped backward with a gasp.

"Look, two dresses." Dani remembered the morning

she helped Berta with her packing. She'd wanted to take all her dolly's outfits, but Dani suggested she dress it in layers to save room in her own suitcase. Underneath the pink satin party dress, the doll wore a blue sailor suit.

Natalie examined the doll with interest. "So, this was yours when you were a child?"

"No," Dani replied. "It belonged to my friend Berta, the consul's daughter." She read the questioning look in Natalie's eyes. "I'm not sure how I ended up with it. I can't remember…"

But now she had started thinking about those distant days in Riga, she was not going to stop. That was why, when she saw the article about Richard Vandercam in the magazine in the doctor's waiting room that February afternoon, she kept it. She was ready—primed—to discover more, to fill in the gaps in her still patchy memory of the Riga time, and to discover what happened next to the consul and his family.

Chapter 30

It had rained earlier in the day, but now just streaks of cloud, tinged pink by the setting sun, hovered over the distant mountains. Although it was March, Berta had opened the tall glass doors that took up half of the southwestern wall. In a few months, the perfume from the lavender and rosemary bushes along the edge of the terrace would overwhelm everything else, but this evening she enjoyed the subtler scents of rain on the grass, and the new leaves on the chestnut and plane trees around the house.

She loved this view. Over her years of living at La Bergerie, she had pared away the furniture in the main room where the animals were stabled in the house's former life, so that nothing detracted from it. The scrubbed oak kitchen table, rescued from a farm sale, was placed in the center of the room, so that she could look up from her work and take in the expanse of the valley shading off into the gray of the Pyrenean foothills. Two shabby overstuffed armchairs flanked the massive stone fireplace. Guests, if any, usually came in summer when most activity was out of doors, so this was more than enough seating. A few family photographs in heavy silver frames sat on the oak beam that served as a mantel. A set of blue-and-white Delft plates, rescued from the wreckage left by the Germans who occupied her grandmother's Herengracht mansion in Amsterdam, provided the room's only ornamentation. These were arranged on the ancient dresser on the wall opposite the fireplace. There was no art on the rough plaster walls; no books other than the ones piled at one end of the table, each stuck through with multiple bright paper markers that caught the sunlight like prayer flags.

Since the cancer, Berta had pared away her life too. Keeping things simple had been a way of surviving in the moment, not giving way to the panic threatening to swamp her when she confronted loss of mobility and constant pain. Now she was in remission, the simple life had become a habit. She rarely traveled or entertained. She read, she wrote, she gardened, and she sat, sometimes for hours, looking out over the valley toward the mountains.

Berta turned her attention from the view back to her father's notebooks. Today, she was content to rest her hands on their battered board covers, reflecting on the years that had passed since his death when she had boxed them up and brought them to La Bergerie. Over thirty years of living alone in this house, longer than she had lived in Paris, or Holland, the country of her birth. After all this time, the house had become a second skin to her, as familiar as the backs of her own veined and freckled hands resting on the notebooks in front of her. The cool smoothness of the tiles in the kitchen on her bare feet in the morning, the musty smell released by the thick stone walls on damp winter days, the way the light filtered through the cracks in the shutters and lay across her bed in stripes—it was more than just her home, it was her sanctuary. At times, the building felt like a living presence that breathed in and out with her and wrapped her around with protective arms. She felt sometimes she had always lived here.

Yet when she ventured outside the property she became again *la Hollandaise*, a foreigner. The locals were not unfriendly, but they measured time differently, in generations. Their relationship to the land, forged over those generations, was paramount. A woman alone, without antecedents or descendants, was an anomaly. It would take more than the passage of years to change that.

Berta sighed and pulled the invitation toward her. Even the thought of making the trip to London exhausted her. Negotiating the airport in Toulouse would not be a problem—only one terminal, and not too much walking—but the interminable corridors and mob scene at London Gatwick would be a nightmare. The promised car to meet her would be a chatty volunteer in a Toyota, and involve two near-misses before she was deposited at her not-quite-luxury hotel. England would still be cold and wet in April, while the mimosa was blooming here in Languedoc. Another rubber chicken dinner, she would give her talk, and then the whole process in reverse before she could crawl under the duvet in her own bed. Berta considered whether her one good suit would still fit. Her skeleton seemed to have contracted. The old chambray work shirt now hung on her like a tent. She still wore it, though. It had been washed to a comforting softness, and there was no one to see the frayed collar and ancient stains. Well, the suit would have to do; she wasn't about to endure a shopping trip as well.

Ah, Papa, only for you. Her gaze lifted to the photographs on the mantel. The formal studio portrait, taken in the sixties for some university publication, made him look uncharacteristically stern in his round-framed glasses. She preferred the snapshot of the two of them laughing into the wind on a bleak Dutch beach, her a gangly teenager, him in sport shirt and flannels. It was amazing that she still felt a pang of loss. She missed the tweedy-smokey smell when she climbed on his knee and buried her face in his chest. She shook her head. How silly for a seventy-year-old woman to be thinking of that!

Perhaps she still felt the loss because of the frequent reminders—like the invitation in front of her—of the time when her scholarly father had played the unlikely hero. After his death and her discovery of letters from survivors, more stories emerged about his service as the Netherlands' consul in Latvia at the beginning of the Second World War. He had never spoken of it. And so it had fallen to Berta, who had been barely five years old at the time, and who had no memory of those years, to recreate the drama for a stream of historians and would-be historians, as well as the survivors and their descendants. She was not entirely comfortable with this role. Of course, she was proud of her father for his courage and determination to help while most were turning their faces away from the atrocities taking place in Europe. But somehow that was not *her* Papa, not the shortsighted man with a tendency to stoop, who forgot to drink his coffee while it was hot, who disliked cocktail parties and could be quite disconcerted by some innocent approach. "I wonder who he thought I was?" he would say, after a stranger's casual comment about the weather.

As an attempt to reconcile these two characters—the wartime hero with the absent-minded professor of later years—she had recently undertaken to revise and re-edit his *magnum opus,* "Eastern European Folk Tales: Morality in a Pre-Christian Society." He had gathered the material during his diplomatic postings in Budapest,

Ljubljana, and Riga between 1933 and 1940, and had written it up in Amsterdam during the Nazi Occupation. Its publication in 1948 had established his academic career.

This was her second project based on her father's notes, and the more difficult. She had written the first, "Summers in Languedoc," during the early years of her residence here. Part history, part memoir, and part travel guide, the book described the annual visits she made with her father between 1949 and 1953. Digging through the notebooks he kept during this period had sustained her emotionally as she came to terms with bereavement and solitude. Just reading his neat script, and locating the sources he referenced, immersed her in his presence. The book's success, published first in French by her former employer and subsequently translated into Dutch, had surprised her, and royalties still drifted in. That revenue, supplemented by other translations commissioned by her old publishing house, extended her inheritance into a reasonable income.

But the current work progressed slowly. It was unlikely she would find a publisher for her efforts, but that meant little. Although her research offered no clues about her father's involvement in the escape of Jews from Latvia, she came to understand his conviction that ancient stories of ogres and changelings, stories regarded as children's fare, had some essential truth that had ensured their survival and retelling through the centuries. She felt she was honoring his memory in a more authentic and complete way than by making speeches and accepting awards for the Riga activities.

This would definitely be the last time. She extracted a sheet of writing paper from the table drawer. "I am honored to accept your invitation to speak about my father, Richard Vandercam, and his role in helping Jews escape from Poland, and to accept Temple Beth Israel's Great Humanitarian Award in his name."

Chapter 31

The evening was winding down. The officer of the Temple, who had sat next to Berta and introduced her speech, was at the door saying farewell to guests as they left. Berta felt tired out. The energy that sustained her during her address had dissipated.

"He never spoke about the war." Berta started her talk the same way she always did. She described her father as she remembered him: a shy man, at ease only with his students. They returned again and again after graduation to drink a beer and tell him about their struggles in the real world. Then she explained how, going through his papers after his death, she found the folder of letters from Jews in Israel, America, and elsewhere, telling how the visas he had issued to Dutch colonies in the Caribbean had saved their lives. "I wrote back to them and to the refugee organizations that facilitated the contacts. I was able to meet some of the survivors and their families in Israel at the Yad Vashem Holocaust Remembrance Center. It was so moving. I only wish he could have lived to see his heroism recognized at last."

Before her talk, a teenage girl had played the violin. The music had provoked more moist eyes than the speech, but that was appropriate. She played beautifully, and Berta's speech sounded, at least to her own ears, jaded from repetition. The young musician and her intense blue eyes, the swing of dark hair across her cheek, stirred memories of Berta's youth: the attic room where she gathered with her friends to listen to jazz and talk about the future. Elsa had possessed that same intensity and talent. Where was Elsa now? Had any of them fulfilled their dreams? Perhaps the current generation would do better.

Berta closed her eyes, hoping her host would return to announce the car was ready to take her back to the hotel. A small movement at her side roused her, and she turned to meet the violinist's blue eyes, but in the face of a woman her own age or older with a ruddy complexion and wild gray hair. She was dressed in a royal blue suit with black braiding and brass buttons. It had perhaps been purchased at an earlier time, before its wearer gained weight.

"I hope you enjoyed the music. Natalie is my granddaughter." Berta was surprised to be addressed in Dutch, although spoken slowly and carefully, as if the woman was unused to the language.

"Very much. She plays beautifully. Are you Dutch?" How dense, Berta chided herself. The Dutch learn other languages; other people don't choose to learn Dutch.

"Originally, yes. I came to London after the war to live with my aunt and uncle. My name is Danielle Nesse. It was Danielle Loesseps then... Dani."

Silence. The other woman held her gaze. Berta could find nothing to say, tiredness so bone-deep that even long-practiced social skills evaded her. Over the background chatter of the rapidly emptying room, she could hear the woman's rapid breathing, a soft wheeze that kept time with the rise and fall of her well-padded chest.

"You don't remember me, do you?"

"I'm afraid not. Please remind me where we met."

More silence. Berta let her gaze drift. Danielle Nesse... Dani Loesseps... The names meant nothing to her. Evidently, the woman thought they should. The rabbi was making his way back across the room. All Berta wanted was to be back at La Bergerie, alone with her books and the view across the valley, far from the demands of well-meaning busybodies intent on sharing their memories.

"My mother was your father's secretary at the consulate in Riga. You and I played together there. My mother's name was Nellie Loesseps. She died in the Holocaust." This was said in a staccato rhythm, as if rehearsed, then delivered with difficulty.

Berta felt her heart stagger. She struggled to make sense of what the woman said, but before she could find words to respond, her host arrived.

"I'm so glad you've met each other! Mrs. Nesse was a moving force behind you being here tonight. She, along with her aunt and uncle, were amongst the Jews your father helped to escape." The rabbi looked from Berta to the other woman, and then back to Berta, his smile fading as he recognized the tension between them.

Ignoring the interruption, Danielle Nesse spoke now in English and a softer voice. "It's a lot to take in: someone from your childhood, from so long ago. You really don't remember, do you?"

"No, I only know what I was told by the survivors." Berta's voice cracked. She felt raw from the shock of the woman's announcement. After struggling for years to find some real and personal memory of her father's diplomatic service, here she was, face to face, not with one of the refugees who had spent an hour or two at the consulate obtaining their precious visa, but with a regular visitor, a playmate, and the daughter of possibly her father's closest collaborator.

The rabbi was attempting to steer her toward the exit, murmuring that her car was waiting. Berta turned back to the woman.

"I need to talk to you. I have so many questions," she said, reverting to Dutch.

"Yes, we must talk, but probably this is not the time or place. When do you return to France?"

"I have a flight tomorrow afternoon."

"I'll come to your hotel tomorrow at ten. I'll get the details from Rabbi Rubin." The woman laid a reassuring hand briefly on Berta's arm, then turned to scan the room. "Where is my Natalie?"

The rabbi looked relieved, slipping a hand under Berta's elbow. She walked away with him, still half-stunned.

Tomorrow at ten, Berta confirmed to herself.

****

Back at the hotel, Berta knew sleep would be impossible without resort to the pills she hated to take. Tiredness had been replaced by a sort of jittery tension. After she undressed, she lay on the bed, attempting the deep breathing technique she had learned to help her manage the cancer pain, but after a few breaths she was almost panting in panic. One question kept bubbling to the surface of her mind: Why was her father unable to save his own secretary? It made no sense.

With a sinking feeling, it occurred to Berta that the whole thing might be a scam: was Danielle Nesse trying to extract sympathy or even compensation on the basis of an unfounded and unprovable story? Berta's eagerness to learn more about that unremembered part of her life had played straight into the old woman's hands. But Mrs. Nesse seemed sincere, and the rabbi had vouched for her. If only she could remember something—anything—about the Riga consulate.

Berta reread in her mind the letters found in her father's office, searching for clues that might substantiate the woman's story. She recalled references to a colleague, but she had assumed that was the Swedish consul who worked with her father to supply the essential transit visas. Could they have meant the consul's secretary? And during her visit to Yad Vashem, when an ancient Israeli had mentioned "a lady…an angel" helping her father, she had jumped to an image of her mother, whose luminous blondeness was captured in the photographs Berta had of her. She had been delighted to add a sympathetic element to sketchy fragments of information about Margriet, picturing her working side by side with her father to save the refugees. As Berta lay rigid and perspiring in the unfamiliar bed, she reproached herself: Not all angels are blonde. No doubt something had been lost in translation—the Israeli spoke only Hebrew. Wasn't it more likely that the lady was the consul's secretary?

The luminous green figures on the bedside alarm clock showed 2:09. The night hours stretched out interminably toward the morning and her meeting with Danielle Nesse. Berta reached for the pill bottle and a glass of water.

Chapter 32

It took Dani aback how much Berta looked like her mother. Not like Madame looked back then, of course, but how she would have looked if she'd lived to be an old woman. They shared the same build—slim and flat-chested—and the oval face and perfect posture. Berta's hair was different: thin strands that showed her scalp instead of a gleaming blonde chignon. And Berta's eyes were gray, not blue. But mother and daughter had the same demeanor, a touch-me-not reserve. In Madame, Dani came to learn that was arrogance, but in Berta it seemed to signal a kind of fragility. She had imagined giving her a hug, but abandoned that idea as soon as she saw her up close. Berta might crumble.

Natalie opened the program, playing a slow movement by Vivaldi. Dani always loved to hear her play, and she was happy for another reason: grandchildren were a safe topic to begin a conversation. Berta didn't remember Dani, even after she told her about her mother's role at the Riga consulate. Rabbi Rubin had gotten it all wrong, saying Sarah, Pete, and Dani escaped from Latvia with Dutch West Indies visas, but she didn't correct him. A couple of months ago, when she had gone to talk to him about inviting Berta to accept an award on her father's behalf, she was vague regarding her connection to the Riga consulate. The rabbi didn't know her well. She only turned up at temple for weddings and bar mitzvahs, but Sarah had been a pillar of the congregation, and her chamber orchestra brought a lot of prestige. It was natural he would make Sarah the centerpiece of the story.

Dani felt a stab of anger when Berta said she didn't remember. How could she not remember Nellie, who looked after her in those last days at the consulate when her own mother had locked herself away in her bedroom? And Dani, her best friend? They had played make-believe games together, and she'd read her stories. Berta had held Dani's hand on that dreadful journey back to Holland after her mother was left behind. But then she remembered that Berta had lost her mother too, dead almost as soon as they got home to Amsterdam. Dani used to think it was a curse to remember those terrible times so vividly, but now she thought maybe it was worse not to have any memories. It must have been so lonely.

By the time Dani agreed to go to Berta's hotel the next day, she was no longer angry; she felt sorry for Berta. For all her elegant clothes, slim figure, and cultured manners, she didn't seem happy. Compared to her, Dani's life since the war had been a bit rough-and-tumble, but she had family all around her: first, Sarah, Pete, and the girls; then Sammy and all his tribe; and now David, Isabel, and Natalie. Berta just had her father, and he had died early.

Dani tried to think about what to say at the meeting the next day. She was nervous. She didn't want to hurt Berta. She must have thought the world of her father, and probably of her mother too. Dani had her version of the truth. She had lived with it so long it was hard to see what happened from anyone else's point of view. She supposed Berta's mother might have seen it all differently. She needed to tell her, though. Berta and Dani—they were the only ones left, and neither of them were going to live forever. She would tell Berta her truth, and hope reconciliation followed.

Chapter 33

Berta was waiting in the hotel lobby well before ten. She had dressed in her customary neutral colors, a high-necked sweater to hide the gauntness of her neck, no jewelry, no makeup, her post-chemo colorless wisps of hair brushed up in a futile attempt to hide the pale scalp beneath. She had packed, checked out of her room, and ordered a car for noon to take her to Gatwick. The night before, the rabbi's wife had offered to chauffeur her again, but Berta had declined. She was tense and jittery from too few hours of sleep. And excited—maybe at last she could gain a more accurate image of her parents' early life, and fill in the gaps in her own memory. However, the question that kept her awake the night before continued to nag her throughout her preparations: Why had Danielle Loesseps' mother perished when she was in the best position, as the consul's secretary, to obtain the lifesaving Dutch West Indies visa and leave Europe before the Holocaust descended?

Exactly at ten, Berta spotted Danielle making her way across the lobby, holding onto the arm of her granddaughter Natalie, the young violinist. The previous evening, Berta had gained a superficial impression of the other woman. Now she studied her. She saw that Danielle's high color, thick curly hair, and her bright clothes—last night, the royal blue suit, today a leaf green twinset under an unbuttoned raincoat—masked the fact that she might be unwell. She leaned heavily on the girl by her side, and when they arrived in front of Berta, she was breathing hard. They exchanged greetings, and Danielle took off her raincoat and settled her stocky form next to her granddaughter on the sofa opposite. Berta offered coffee—there was a small self-service bar provided for guests in the lobby—but Danielle refused. A pause while the old woman caught her breath. Berta waited, willing to let the other woman take charge of the conversation. She was still a little nervous about the encounter and thought again that this might be a hoax. She examined Danielle's face for clues. The old woman seemed serious…resigned, even. There was no trace of malice in the dark blue eyes with their radiating wrinkles.

"I hope you don't mind me bringing Natalie. I'm having a bad day, and she's such a help coping with the buses and everything. Besides, she knows our story and wanted to meet you."

Our story. Berta experienced a twinge of resentment: this teenager knew more about her distant past than she did herself. Natalie appeared self-possessed, not at all uncomfortable with the situation. She seemed to be examining Berta. Was Natalie judging her? For what?

Danielle began speaking in a deliberate voice. "Until I spoke to you last night, I couldn't believe that you remembered nothing about me, my mother, and the time when your father was consul in Riga. You see, for me, those memories are so clear, so…" Danielle paused. "I think the reason I wanted to meet you, the award, all that—I wanted to know whether you and your father had thought about us, about my mother…"

Berta could see that Danielle was working to keep

her emotions in check, that she too was nervous. The other woman pulled herself together and continued in a brisker tone.

"I'm sure you have many questions, but I think the best way is perhaps for me to tell you what happened to me *after* Riga. I want you to know I've had a good life, no regrets, and no—well, no hard feelings toward your father—or your mother, for that matter. And I want to return this to you."

Danielle's voice regained confidence as she fumbled in the canvas tote bag she had placed on the coffee table in front of them. She pulled out a doll. Although clearly an antique from its porcelain face and elongated stuffed fabric body dressed in old-fashioned finery, it was in pristine condition with glossy yellow-gold hair and an unfaded satin dress. Danielle extended it to Berta, but Berta drew back, unwilling to touch the doll until she understood its import. Her attention had snagged on Danielle's mystifying reference to "hard feelings," and she waited for an explanation.

"It's yours. You gave it to me to hold on the way back to Amsterdam," Danielle said. "I was upset, and you gave it to me to comfort me. You don't remember that awful journey?" Berta shook her head. "I'm sorry, you've already said that. Well, I forgot to give it back to you when we said goodbye in Amsterdam. I've kept it all these years. I don't know why, really. Anyway, here it is."

Danielle held out the doll again, and Berta felt she had no alternative but to take it this time. She settled it in the crook of her arm like a real baby, examining its face, stroking the silky material of the dress.

"Elizabeth," Berta breathed the name without

thought.

"Yes! That's her name! You *do* remember!" Danielle exclaimed, smiling at Natalie.

Suspicion nudged Berta again. She was reminded of fortunetellers who seized on any minor revelation to confirm their powers. And yet it was strange that the name had come unbidden to her lips.

"You were going to tell me about your life after Riga."

Danielle nodded and took in a chesty inhalation before she began.

"My father's parents were very old, in their eighties, when I arrived in Holland in 1940. Of course, they knew my mother was Jewish, but none of their neighbors did, or if they had known, they'd forgotten. It wasn't difficult for my grandparents to explain why I had come to live with them. Everything was in flux then. The German occupation was only a few weeks old. Later, when things were more organized, it would have been difficult for them to get me the proper papers. More questions would have been asked. My grandparents told everyone my mother had been killed in the bombing when the Germans invaded. Of course, I still thought she would be joining us, but they said they'd make up some other story then. Perhaps they already knew she wouldn't be able to get out of Latvia..." Danielle's voice trailed off, and Berta had to bite her tongue to stop asking the questions that bubbled up about Riga, Danielle's mother, the consulate.

"The Occupation was hard—well, you know that— but we were in the countryside, so we had better food than many, and my grandparents were very kind, loving people. It was mostly just boring, with a few frightening moments. My grandfather died before the Liberation, and my grandmother just after. The Allies were able to find my Aunt Sarah, my mother's younger sister, and I went to live with her. She and her husband Piotr—Pete, we always called him—had escaped to England early in the war, before the Russians took over in Latvia. They had two daughters. There wasn't much money, and much of London was still in ruins from the bombing, but I had a good home. I left school as soon as I could and went to work in a flower shop. That's where I met Sammy, my husband. He came in to buy flowers for his aunt."

Danielle's expressive face crinkled into a grin. "Never a dull moment after that. Sammy had goodness knows how many aunts and uncles and cousins. There was always some wedding or bar mitzvah or other celebration. I think I ended up being related by marriage to every Jew in London!" She chuckled at the memories, and Natalie, who had been following her grandmother's story, her uncannily similar blue eyes fixed on the older woman's face, smiled too. This was her family as well, a tribe of noisy, affectionate Londoners.

How different from Berta's thinly populated life in quiet rooms and isolated landscapes. It had been her choice, at least in the latter years, yet she couldn't help envying the two sitting across from her: one old, one young, but both part of a web of relationships that nurtured them.

"Sammy owned electrical stores. David, our son, Natalie's dad, wasn't interested, so we sold them when Sammy retired. He died in 2001." Danielle looked down at her lap for a second, then up again at Berta, with a proud smile. "David's a lawyer, very successful too. He and Isabel, that's Natalie's mum, have a lovely house in

St. John's Wood"—naming one of the classier inner London suburbs—"and I've been living with them and Natalie for about a year."

She started rooting around in the tote bag again and drew out a manila envelope. "I've been writing a kind of memoir. Well, Natalie's been doing the writing on her computer. I just tell her everything I can remember up to June 1940 when I left Riga, and then we sort it out together." She broke off, the good humor with which she had sketched her life story replaced once more by apprehension. "This is your copy. When you've read it, you can write to me, or telephone. I've put my address and telephone number on the envelope, see? Is that all right?"

"Yes, I suppose so." Berta picked up the envelope. It was about an inch thick and lay heavy in her hands. This was not what she had expected. She felt deflated, but at a loss to know how to resist the other woman's agenda.

Danielle leaned forward to emphasize her next words. "I wanted you to know all about me before you read my memories of Riga. Look, in wartime, everything's topsy-turvy. No one knew how it would turn out. So many people died. I used to refuse to think about it, but then I saw that you can't bury the past. You have to honor it—honor *them*—by moving on, by living." Danielle squared her shoulders and, with a brave, almost defiant smile, said, "I lived, and I've got a lot to show for it!" She put an arm around Natalie and hugged her to her side.

Berta nodded, although she still felt confused and frustrated. She was drawn to Danielle's warmth, her lack of self-pity, and her simple buoyancy. In spite of her age and illness, Danielle had a vibrancy that contrasted with Berta's self-protective neutrality. There was a message in Danielle's narrative. Dwelling on the past was a poor idea, and the contents of the envelope were less important than seizing what today had to offer. And there was a warning too: Don't delve too deep because you may not like what you learn. Nevertheless, Berta's hand strayed to the envelope. She pulled it toward her, reluctant to let Danielle leave, yet eager to be alone with the manuscript and immerse herself in the past. But she would not let Danielle leave without getting an answer to at least one question about the Riga days.

"Please tell me, I want to know *now*, and from *you*, not from reading it—what happened to your mother? Why didn't my father bring her with us to Holland in 1940?"

Danielle sighed. Her eyes drifted across the lobby.

"She was supposed to come with us, but she was prevented. She was going to follow a day later, but she couldn't because of the Soviets. I had a couple of letters, then nothing. The Germans invaded. We never found out exactly what happened, but most likely she was rounded up in June 1941 with all the other Jews and taken to the forest and shot. There's a memorial there now. I've never seen it. I have no interest in going back."

Berta understood that Danielle had evaded answering her question directly, but in such a way that she could not press her further without seeming insensitive.

"No, neither did my father. Danielle, I'm so sorry. I know what it's like growing up without a mother." She saw a sudden tightening around the other woman's mouth and regretted her attempt at empathy. She hurried on. "I wish I remembered something about all this. I've tried and tried, but it's a blank."

"The mind protects itself, I suppose. I hope I'm doing the right thing, giving you this memoir. It might upset you, even after all these years." Danielle struggled to her feet, leaning on Natalie. Her breath came in little gasps, and her color was even more heightened than when she sat down. She seemed in a rush to get away. "Goodbye. I'm glad to have seen you again. Those days at the consulate were special for me. Anyway, please do keep in touch." As the old woman and her granddaughter made their way toward the entrance, Natalie looked over her shoulder at Berta and gave a solemn nod. Berta half-rose to go after them, gripped by a panic that she was losing her only chance to learn about her childhood. Then she remembered Danielle's memoir.

Berta checked her watch: more than an hour before she needed to leave for the airport. Should she read the memoir now, or wait until she regained the privacy of her own home that evening? She helped herself to another coffee, then moved to a quiet corner, well away from the bustle around the registration desk. She sat for a moment with her hands resting on the envelope before she drew out the sheaf of paper.

Chapter 34

Dani had lost her nerve.

That night, after she left the presentation, she had resolved to tell Berta the whole story, even if it pricked a hole in Berta's image of her father, the selfless hero too modest to speak of his wartime efforts. Then, as the night-time hours unspooled, she began to have her doubts. What if Berta didn't believe her? There was no reason why she should. She didn't know Dani. Dani had never told this part of the story before, not to Sarah and Pete, not even to Sammy. It was too painful at first, then life took over and she pushed it away, refusing to let it sour her perspective.

Natalie was the first person to hear it. They had spent a few hours together working on the memoir by that point, Dani in the chair by the glass doors to the garden, watching the birds as she spoke. More often, she sat with eyes closed, picturing the people and places she talked about, hearing the clack of the keyboard. Natalie printed out each session's work on her parents' printer upstairs, and then Dani pored over it, adding dates, shifting things around so it made more sense. The end product was still more or less random, just an old person's meandering memories, but it was satisfying to hold the pages in her hand.

When she reached that last day, when everything came apart, Natalie's fingers stopped moving over the keys. Dani turned to see what had happened. Natalie stared at her, mouth open. She looked for words to reassure the girl, as if *Natalie* was the child whose mother dwindled into the distance beyond the rear window of the car.

"It was *her* fault, that—that Madame, Margriet, whatever her name was. She could have taken your mum with you in the car. I *hate* her!"

Dani remembered Natalie's venom as she tried to relax into sleep. Whether Berta believed her or not, Dani's story would disturb her. Was it really so important she learn the truth about her parents? And that she learn it from Dani, face to face? And what if her memories were only a part of the truth? Was there another side to this she had no knowledge of?

Dani decided to take the coward's way out. She wouldn't tell Berta to her face what she remembered about that last day in Riga. Instead, she would give her the memoir, and she could make of it whatever she wanted. She could reject what was written, consider them falsehoods spun from a bitter old woman's spite. She could weigh it against her own memories and experiences, what she had been told by her father or others. Or she could write to Dani, ask questions, and they could explore the history together.

She told Natalie about her plan before they set off. She could tell by her granddaughter's pursed lips that she didn't approve. From her straightforward young person's view, you should speak out, whatever the consequences. But Natalie knew what was written in the memoir. She had printed out a fresh copy, all additions and corrections included, put it in an envelope, and handed it to Dani without comment.

Now it was out of Dani's hands. She refused to worry about it anymore. Life was too short.

Chapter 35

The first few pages of Danielle's memoir described the Kutner family and their *art nouveau* apartment on Elizabetes Street in Riga. Berta could hear the adult woman's voice in the child's impressions.

"There was always a lot of noise, whether it was Grankat belting out an aria in the kitchen or one of Sarah's violin students repeating a shaky scale in the sitting room. And the arguments! All kinds of people dropped in, especially at dinner time, and everyone had an opinion about politics or art, even the weather. But they all agreed Grankat's goulash was the best they'd ever tasted."

Berta's interest was piqued when Dani wrote about her first visit to the consulate.

"It was all a muddle, really. The consul thought Mama had come about a job, but actually it was just to register us as Dutch citizens. Anyway, she took the position as his secretary, and that's how I came to spend almost every day that spring and summer at the consulate."

May, 1939. Berta would have been four. She suppressed the urge to skip ahead to find references to herself. It was clear the mansion in which the consulate was housed impressed Dani—the massive double doors from the street, the sweeping stone staircase from the entrance hall, the second-floor salon that stretched the width of the building. But she reserved her most detailed descriptions—and deepest awe—for "Madame," the consul's wife, Berta's mother.

"She dressed in pastel colors, silky fabrics that whispered when she walked. Well, she didn't walk as much as float, her head held high and still. Her hair was shiny and smooth, always in place, the opposite of Mama's and mine. Her domain was the salon. After lunch, Berta and I spent an hour with her there before Berta's nap. There were always fresh flowers in vases, and table lamps turned on even during the day. Madame played cards with us sometimes, but the only game Berta knew how to play was Snap, and that got boring. Madame let us stay and play with Berta's dolls as long as we were quiet and didn't disturb her. She would write in her journal or read magazines."

There were several more pages of reminiscences from that last summer before the war: the servants Ivan and Marta, one Russian, the other Dutch; the offices on the ground floor separated by an entrance hall tiled in black-and-white; and the overgrown walled garden at the rear of the mansion where the little girls played their imaginary games.

The tranquil routine came to an abrupt end on the September day the war started.

"We were all in the salon. The consul and Mama had come upstairs to listen to the announcement on the radio. I think the grownups had forgotten we were there, playing our games behind the sofa. The consul was worried, talking about what would happen next. Then Madame became furious about something, I didn't understand what. She didn't shout, not like my Kutner grandparents when they got angry. Her voice just turned

to ice, and the look she gave Mama was like throwing a knife. That was the last time I went to the consulate for many months."

The start of the war, but also the beginning of the school year. Dani's memoir turned to the challenge of fitting in at school while speaking only rudimentary Lettish and Russian. The high point of her day was when Nellie, released early from work as the northern nights drew in, picked her up from class to complete the journey back to the apartment together. But the winter darkness permeated the Kutners' home too. The ragtag crowd of students, writers, and artists whose shouts and songs had kept Dani awake during the summer no longer showed up for supper. With hindsight, Dani recorded, the self-imposed curfew amongst the intellectual class to which the Kutners belonged resulted from Soviet Russia's increasing control of the Baltic states. At the time, the child Dani was only conscious of quiet where there had been noise, and a sense of waiting for something to happen.

The rabbi's visit to the apartment was a marker in that tense time of waiting. He came to ask Nellie to persuade the consul for assistance with some Polish refugees.

"Mama said, 'The consul's a good man. I know he'll want to help.' "

****

Berta had not heard her name being paged in the hotel lobby, absorbed as she was in Danielle's memoir. A desk clerk had to come over and touch her arm.

"Your car's here, Mrs. Vandercam. Can I help you with your luggage?"

Berta suppressed an impulse to wave her off and

continue reading. Instead, she rose and made her way over to the entrance. She handed her overnight bag to the waiting driver, then almost fell into the back seat of the car, eager to get back to the memoir. A hotel porter rushed after her, holding the doll she had forgotten. Berta climbed out of the car again, the young driver watching with a grin, while she fitted the doll in between folded clothes and a toilet bag in her case. She could tell the driver had consigned her to the category of "dotty old lady."

He closed the trunk with a thud.

"Ready to go now, love?"

Berta nodded, not responding to the condescension in his voice. She shuffled into the back seat again and found her place in the manuscript.

****

Danielle's memory of the next months was vague about dates and sequence. She remembered there was deep snow on the ground when the rabbi called—"*For weeks it had been too cold to go outside and play in the park.*" Nellie began working long hours, often coming home after the rest of the family had eaten. It was all somehow to do with the refugees. Dani had not met any refugees, and she resented the demands on her mother's time that they imposed. Sarah and Piotr left to live in England. Piotr wanted to fight the Germans, but it was the Russians who had invaded Latvia. Grandkat was sad. The silver lining, if any was to be found: schools were closed down and Dani could stay home with her grandparents—her grandfather's university had also been shuttered.

Berta straightened the pages on her knees as her eyes scanned the south London suburbs streaming past the car's windows. She tried to gauge how soon they would arrive at the airport and how much more of the story she could absorb before they did so. Although Danielle told her story in a straightforward, conversational manner, without pathos or melodrama, Berta sensed the encroaching shadows in the narrative. From her own knowledge, in early 1940 Germany was preparing its sweep through western Europe. Once that was accomplished, the Nazis would turn on Russia. The pact with Stalin, forged in secret in 1939, and which gave the Soviets an unfettered entrée to the Baltic states, would collapse in 1941. But Berta's research told her little of what happened to Latvia in the interim, either on the national scale or to the individuals she cared about.

"Winter was behind us when I went back to the consulate again. Everything was different. Marta, Madame's maid, was dead, and Madame had locked herself away in her room. The entrance hall was full of empty chairs, the mud on the checkerboard tiles showing where the refugees had waited. Ivan was still the same, pretending to be grumpy but finding time to show us new things growing in the garden. Berta and I spent most of our time out there now, or in her bedroom with her toys and books. The salon was dark. It smelled stale and we didn't want to play there anymore.

Ivan did the shopping and Mama did the cooking. We all—except Madame, of course—ate at the kitchen table. That was nice. Ivan made a big bonfire one day. Berta and I danced around it, and Mama and the consul stood and watched us, laughing. That was the last happy day."

Berta had read about three-quarters of the manuscript. The car was speeding south on the M-23 now. They would be at Gatwick Airport soon. Although she knew she was approaching the crux of the story and perhaps answers to the questions that had plagued her, she slid the pages back into the envelope. She needed time to assimilate what she had already read: new and conflicting images of her mother, and the key role Nellie played in introducing the refugees to her father. Also, she was afraid she would not be able to control her emotions if she continued reading. Crying in front of the patronizing young driver would be humiliating. With the manuscript back in the envelope, she stared out at the springtime countryside—green fields dotted with cows, tidy cottages, and hedgerows white with blossom. After a few minutes, she closed her eyes and dozed.

****

Berta was still holding the manuscript when she arrived at the gate for her flight to Toulouse.

"Only two items of hand luggage allowed."

She stared blankly for a couple of seconds at the gate agent. He gestured impatiently at the package she was holding to her chest, and started to repeat his litany in French.

"*Seulement deux pièces—*"

"Yes, yes, I'm sorry." She stuffed the envelope containing the memoir into an outside pocket of her roll-on case, aware of the disapproving grunts and sighs of the passengers lined up behind her. The gate agent, noting her age and air of distraction, must have regretted his brusque tone. He spoke again, his voice lower and more respectful.

"You can ask a flight attendant to get it out for you once the plane reaches cruising altitude." No, she planned to spend the brief flight resting and reflecting, saving the rest of the story until she was home.

The flight arrived on time in France. She reclaimed her car from the parking deck, and maneuvered it carefully through the surface streets to the autoroute. There, she stuck stubbornly in the slow lane, concentrating on her driving as cars and trucks flashed by. At last, she reached her exit, and, a dozen or so kilometers later, began the slow, winding climb out of the flat lands toward the Pyrenees. The sun was sinking after another clear spring day.

At the crest of the first ridge of foothills, there was a panorama of her valley and the further peaks on the Spanish border. She had often pulled in there, taking a few minutes to exchange her preoccupation with whatever purpose had taken her away for the anticipation of the calm waiting within the familiar stone walls of her house. It was a special place because she and her father had stopped here that first summer of exploring the region together. Her father pointed out the ruined castle in the distance, one of the last strongholds to hold out against the bishops' armies that had crushed the Cathars in the thirteenth century.

"The Catholic church could not allow the sect to survive. The Cathars' simple faith was a challenge to the establishment. Those who did not starve to death in the siege were burned at the stake as heretics."

Fifteen-year-old Berta had been shocked that the peaceful vista was the site of such brutality.

"Did *all* the Cathars die? Didn't *any* of them escape?"

"Perhaps. I hope so…" Her father's voice had trailed off as he turned his gaze again to the distant mountains. Now, she wondered whether he was remembering the long hours interviewing refugees, handwriting visas into their passports, adding the flourish of a seal and signature, shaking grateful hands, and greeting the next applicant. Maybe his fascination with this area and period of history had roots in his wartime experiences—the Cathars and the Jews, both persecuted for their religion.

Prompted by the incursion of another memory, she slowed the car and pulled into the small parking area. Much as she wanted to be home, she needed to follow her thoughts through without the distraction of negotiating the steep descent into the valley. Just after the war, Papa had insisted on a day trip to Rotterdam. They had spent little time in the bomb-scarred city. She remembered that the object of their journey was an abandoned cottage in the countryside where Papa hoped to find people he'd known in Latvia. Of course—Nellie and Dani! Berta recalled her father's disappointment when he learned the child had been taken by relatives, and, "No, not the mother; she never came," a woman in the village had said. Her father had looked stricken.

Nellie. Danielle's memoir had contained only the briefest physical description of her mother, but Berta had no difficulty summoning up an image: a rosy face, a head of dark, irrepressibly curly hair, a figure of less than average height but with curves in contrast to the blonde slenderness shown in photographs of her own mother. A combination from this morning's meeting with old Dani and young Natalie. Nellie and Margriet had been approximately the same age, but physical opposites. Had Papa been attracted by that contrast?

No. Her father's reticence about his secretary suggested something other than a fleeting physical attraction. He had shared an intense season with Nellie, worked long hours for a cause greater than either of them, and then he had left her in Riga to an uncertain fate at best. His guilt must have been overwhelming.

Berta began to understand that her father's decades-long silence about helping Jews in Riga was not—or not just—the modesty of a well-bred gentleman. Certainly, during the Occupation it would have been extremely dangerous to speak of it. But all the years afterward? Had he tried to find out what happened to Nellie? He had never been back to the Baltics, but had he at least made inquiries beyond that brief excursion to the cottage outside Rotterdam? Or had he suspected from the start that Nellie following "in a day or two," as Danielle was led to believe, would be virtually impossible?

Berta could imagine the agony her father felt as news of the fate of Jews in Latvia emerged after the war. An agony no doubt renewed when he started receiving letters from Jewish survivors who had escaped thanks to the Dutch West Indies Visa. For another man, the pain of memory might then have been relieved by speaking out at last, and honoring the woman whose role was as heroic as his. But Berta knew her father too well. He bore his grief and his guilt in silence, a private penance. He had modeled for Berta a stoicism that she had adopted as her own, and now, facing the last years of her life alone, she regretted. So many words unsaid, feelings unexpressed.

She started the car and began the steep descent around a succession of hairpin bends. She was eager now to be home and to finish reading Danielle's memoir. Arriving at La Bergerie, Berta wasted no time in unpacking. Remembering she had consumed little beyond coffee since waking in the London hotel that morning, she prepared a plate of the crumbly local sheep's cheese, crackers, and a handful of hazelnuts. She poured a glass of red wine and put a match to the crumpled paper and kindling piled ready in the grate. Then she sank into the armchair and found her place in Dani's manuscript.

"...That was the last happy day."

Part Six: *1940*

Chapter 36

When they left the consulate that evening, Dani was still excited from the bonfire in the garden. She sported sooty marks on her face as she danced around Nellie on the path home across the park. Even the Russian soldiers lounging around the old bandstand, cigarettes dangling from their lips, could not dampen her giddy mood. She returned their mocking salutes, and giggled when they aimed incomprehensible comments after her.

Nellie, however, was pensive. Very soon, Richard and his family would return to Amsterdam. She would no longer have a job. The intensity of the previous months would dissipate like mist. She could foresee a moment in the future when the relationship she had forged with Richard over the refugee visas would appear illusory. Was she happy or sad that they had never put their feelings into words? What could they have said anyway? Promises made in wartime were worthless. Nellie resolved to refocus her attention on her family, especially Dani.

They climbed the wide curving staircase to the second floor of their apartment building, Dani chattering something about Ivan when Nellie held up a hand to hush her. She saw that the door to their apartment gaped open.

"Wait here," she whispered, stationing Dani against

the farthest wall of the landing. A shiver of trepidation ran over her as she entered the apartment. Behind her, she heard Mrs. Zabovski, their neighbor, open her front door. Nellie glanced back and locked eyes with the woman for a second before Mrs. Zabovski retreated, closing the door. Nellie continued into the dimness of the entrance hall. As she moved forward into the sitting room, she took in the mess. Not the empty-bottles-and-full-ashtrays mess of the morning after a raucous night before. This was different. Tables overturned, drawers pulled out, books and papers everywhere. The bedrooms, her father's study, even the kitchen cupboards and the linen closet in the bathroom showed the same signs of a rough and hurried search. After a few minutes, Nellie emerged onto the landing, her face white and eyes wide.

"They're gone—no, don't go in." Instinctively Dani had moved toward the open door. Nellie grabbed her hand and crossed the hall to the Zabovskis' apartment. It took several minutes for Mrs. Zabovski to open it in response to Nellie's insistent knocking. She opened just wide enough to look around the landing, to make sure they were alone.

"What happened?" Nellie asked.

"Well, they came about lunchtime. I'd just come in from shopping. I peeped out to see what was going on. They made an awful racket. I think your ma put up a fight, you know how she is. Anyway, I saw them being taken down the stairs—your ma and pa."

"Who took them? Soldiers? Were they Russian?"

"Not soldiers, dear. Police, I think, at least the one in uniform looked like a policeman. The rest were in suits. Yes, they were Russians! Who else would it be?"

"Mrs. Z, please will you look after Dani while I go

to the police and try to find out where they've taken them?"

"Don't be silly, girl. You go to the police and they'll take you too. Then who'll take care of Dani?" Mrs. Zabovski was not a bad sort. She seemed torn between sympathy and the desire not to get involved. Now, she opened her door a little wider to reach out and touch Nellie's arm. "Why don't you come in for a moment? Have some tea and settle down a bit? I can't keep you here long, mind. Mr. Z will be home soon, and he wouldn't like it."

Nellie stood indecisively, looking back at the apartment door. Tears welled in her eyes. After all the emotion of the day, her reluctant acceptance that a crucial phase of her life was ended, and her determination formed only minutes before to face forward for her daughter's sake, she felt numb, incapable of thinking or even moving. Dani looked up at her mother, unblinking, looking for reassurance, for her to say that this was all a silly mistake, that her grandparents would be returning for dinner, laughing at all the fuss.

Dani's trusting gaze galvanized Nellie into action. She grabbed Dani's hand and pulled her across the landing and into the apartment. She didn't stop to respond to Dani's gasps when she saw the wreckage; she headed for their bedroom.

"We're each going to pack a suitcase. Take warm clothes, good shoes for walking, plenty of clean underwear..." She pulled two cases from under the bed and passed one to Dani. Then she started taking clothes out of drawers or from the floor where the searchers had flung them. Dani followed her example. They packed in silence, except for Nellie's occasional instructions.

"No, not the red sweater, the brown one, it's thicker… I think that skirt is too small for you now."

Nellie's thoughts skittered randomly. She remembered the pathetic bundles of belongings the refugees carried with them: cardboard suitcases tied with string; the layers of outer garments worn in spite of the mild spring weather because they would not fit into their luggage. And the useless treasures that could not be abandoned: a framed photograph, a clock, a wedding veil. She tried not to think of her parents, their terror as they were arrested, their captors' rough hands, the cell they now occupied. She feared that if she let her thoughts go in that direction, she would fly apart like an over-wound clock.

She knew Dani wanted to ask questions. The child was confused and frightened, but Nellie could not afford to divert her attention from the task at hand. She just kept packing. She dived into a box at the back of the closet for their Dutch passports and a bundle of letters from the Loesseps grandparents. She dashed to the bathroom to assemble their washing things. Finally, she found the photo of her and Henrijk on their wedding day. It had been swept off the nightstand, and the glass was cracked. She slid it into the center of her case, where clothes would cushion it from further damage.

"Right. We're going back to the consulate. As Dutch subjects, we'll be safe there."

They were ready to go. Only then did Nellie hesitate.

"Goodbye, old apartment," she whispered, looking around at the familiar furniture, touching the back of her father's chair where she could still see the faint impression from his head. "Goodbye…"

Chapter 37

It had taken Margriet ages to find where Richard had hidden her sleeping pills. How infuriating, how self-righteous of him to think he knew better than she when she might need them. She tipped back her head to swallow a couple, then looked around for a new hiding place where he wouldn't think to look. Aha! The secret drawer in her jewel box. No room for the vial, so she packed the remaining dozen or so tablets in a screw of tissue paper and laid them there with Aunt Helga's diamond earrings and a broken pearl bracelet. Satisfied that she had secured her stash, she lay back on the bed to wait for the drug to take effect.

She had not wanted Richard to call Dr. Felder—so humiliating for him to see her in this state—but in the end, his visit had been a blessing. He understood what she needed immediately: the drug to stop the squirrel wheel in her head, a single thought endlessly chasing its tail until she thought she would scream with exhaustion. She *had* screamed a little. Perhaps, in the aftermath of Marta's death, she had been somewhat hysterical, but she felt so isolated, as if she were imprisoned behind a wall of glass, crying out for help, and no one paying any attention, least of all Richard.

Marta's death had been so sudden. Within days of Felder's diagnosis, Marta was gone, Margriet's only friend. She had been dependent on her maid for the affection and approval she needed, day after day, to continue in this godforsaken backwater of Eastern Europe. How pathetic! Homesickness hit her like a tidal wave. Homesickness mixed with rage. Rage against Richard and his do-gooder projects, his preoccupation with riffraff refugees, and his total disregard for her. That was when Margriet had issued her ultimatum: "I'm staying in this room until we return to Amsterdam."

Her mother would not have approved; Mother always put duty above all else. But she *had* done her duty, hadn't she? She had followed Richard around to his various postings, entertained his boring colleagues, made a home for him, even produced a child for him. She was tired of doing her duty.

And the ultimatum had worked. Richard had not been this attentive since the first year of their marriage. He brought her dainty meals and sat with her, holding her hand. She sighed a little groggily. Maybe it was time to emerge and take up the yoke of duty again. After all, Richard said he expected his recall instructions daily. It would be so hard on her, without Marta, to arrange all the packing and shipping, getting someone to prepare the Amsterdam house. The tears started again, and she did nothing to stop them. She felt them leaking down her temples, through her hair, and into the pillow. The moisture felt soothing. She thought the pills were beginning to work.

Then she heard voices on the landing. She recognized Richard's, but the other was—surely not Berta at this hour? No, it was a woman's voice—the Loesseps woman! She sat up abruptly and threw off the satin quilt. How dare he? How dare *she*? She stood up and staggered for a moment, fighting the narcotics in her system. She crossed the room and flung the door open with such force it hit the wall and bounced back. She stood speechless, breathing hard, staring at Richard, Nellie Loesseps, and the girl Dani as they tiptoed toward the attic stairs.

"I'm sorry, darling. Did we wake you? Nellie's parents have been seized by the Secret Police. She and Dani are in danger, so they found sanctuary here."

Richard's placating tone enraged her further, but her voice came out as a croak. "Not in my house!" She cleared her throat and tried again. This time it was a screech. "Not in my house!"

Richard moved quickly to her and pulled her back into the bedroom, hooking the door closed behind them with his foot.

"It is not *your* house. It is the consulate of the Kingdom of the Netherlands, and I am charged to protect all Dutch subjects from foreign aggression." He must have realized how pompous he sounded, because he loosened his grip on her arms, and adopted a gentler manner. "Look, Nellie is my secretary, that's all. She's been a faithful employee, and she and Dani have been very kind to us while you've been ill. But that's irrelevant. I have an obligation to Dutch subjects, and they are both Dutch subjects."

Margriet was weeping messily now. Her head throbbed, and she felt dizzy. "It was all a sham, wasn't it? All the attention and time up here with me? Just to hoodwink me so you could sneak that woman in here. How could you?"

"Margiet, that's nonsense. Sleep now, and we'll talk in the morning. Things will be clearer then." He arranged the covers over her and wiped her face with a handkerchief. "Do you want a sleeping pill?"

She shook her head drowsily, and her eyes drooped closed. She felt Richard's weight lift from the bed, and she tried to extend a hand to keep him with her, but before her limb could obey the message from her drugged brain, she fell asleep.

Chapter 38

Nellie and Dani spent the night in Marta's room. Nellie quickly made up the bed with some old sheets stored in an oak chest at its foot, and they climbed in, Nellie curling tightly around her daughter to still her shaking. She concentrated on quieting Dani's terror, suppressing her own sobs.

The image of Madame as she had appeared on the landing—yellow hair streaming over her shoulders, shining white face with staring eyes, the pupils huge and black—had frightened Dani, supplanting the shock of her grandparents' abduction and the breathless flight back to the consulate in the gathering dusk. Where was the smooth chignon, the elegant clothes and carefully applied makeup, the bored, world-weary tone she affected when speaking to the children and servants? Dani was a little afraid of *that* woman too, even while she admired her, but she was petrified by her transformation.

And then to find herself in a bed most recently occupied by a corpse... She imagined Marta lying here, her face cemented in death into the same dour scowl she wore in life. She expected any second to feel a cold hand rise from the mattress to grab her. She fought the urge to jump out of the bed and instead huddled even closer to her mother. The muffled sound of Nellie weeping reawakened Dani's anxiety about her grandparents.

"Mama, why did the Russians take them?"

"Because your grandfather spoke and wrote about ideas they didn't like. He was a teacher—he influenced young people. The Russians are scared of people who don't think like them."

"But why Grandmother too? She wasn't a teacher or a writer."

"I don't know. Perhaps she made a fuss—you know how she is—and they wanted to keep her quiet." Nellie's voice broke.

"Where did they take them?"

"Siberia, perhaps. It's way over to the east, the other side of Russia. I've heard they resettle people there because it's so remote."

"Can we go there too?"

Nellie was silent for a while. "I don't know if we could find them, and the winters there are hard, even harder than Latvia. I think they would not want us to try and follow them. I think we should leave, go back to Rotterdam and your other grandparents."

"But the Germans are there, and the Germans hate Jews." Dani had discovered she was a Jew only recently, on the night of the rabbi's visit to the apartment. Her life had been so utterly transformed over the last year or so, this Jewish identity was just another change to which she was struggling to adjust.

"We won't tell anyone we're Jews," Nellie whispered. "We are Dutch citizens. People there will just know us as Henrijk Loesseps' widow and daughter. Oma and Opa will be so happy to have us back with them."

Nellie soothed her daughter to sleep, reminding her in a soft voice of the little domestic rituals they had enjoyed when they lived in Holland: Sunday lunch at

Oma's and Opa's, the bakery where they picked up sweet white rolls to take to their house, Opa's pipe, the pigeons he kept in a shed in the garden.

While Dani slept, Nellie remained awake, her head throbbing as she turned over the events of the day until they jumbled into a kaleidoscope of emotions—her sadness watching the refugee files burn, conscious that her time at the consulate was over; the wild elation when Richard touched her hand; and the devastating realization that her parents had been taken.

Toward dawn, she fell into an exhausted half-sleep, floating in the gray light that seeped into the room. In her semiconscious state, she could make out the framed photographs arranged on every surface. The single subject: Margriet. As a baby in a family group, a child in a white party frock, a slender girl in a swimsuit, and a bride on the consul's arm, him with an astonished look on his face, her with a serene smile. Studio portraits and snapshots, so many as to seem obsessive, the collection of a secret admirer. They seemed to crowd around her, the eyes accusing, the smiles mocking. Nellie buried her face in the pillow to escape.

Chapter 39

Margriet had not believed it at first when Richard woke her to say they were returning to Amsterdam. Something she had wanted for so long—that she had obsessed over for hours as she paced her room—was suddenly happening. Maybe she was still dreaming. Then the fog of drugged sleep lifted, and she sat up in bed. Richard had already left.

She was going home! There was so much to do, and no Marta to help her. She pushed away the wave of misery that approached whenever she thought of her maid's death, and her utter loneliness without her. She needed to be sharp now, decisive. Where were the pick-me-up pills Dr. Felder had given her to take away the morning-after effects of her sleeping drug? At least Richard hadn't thought to confiscate *them*, she thought. She pulled on her peignoir and headed for the bathroom. Extracting the pills from her cosmetics case, she caught sight of her reflection in the mirror above the wash basin.

My God! Her hair hung limp in strands around her face. She had brown circles under her eyes, and her lips were chapped. She remembered with sudden clarity the scene last night when she had confronted Nellie and her daughter sneaking across the landing outside her bedroom. What were they doing in her house? Why had Richard brought them here without saying anything to her? She gulped the pills down with water and turned to start running a bath. So much to do. Perhaps she should take another pill to make sure…

She went back through the bedroom and stuck her head out the door.

"Ivan!" she called, her voice scratchy and shrill. She swallowed and tried again. "Ivan! I need you at once!" She closed the door, irritation mounting.

A timid knock.

"Ah, finally." She motioned Ivan in. He stood, mouth agape, eyes trailing over the unmade bed, the scattered clothes. "I need the trunks." She spoke emphatically, but he seemed not to understand. "To pack. We're going. The trunks!" She mimed packing, picking up a pile of clothes and putting them down again. She pretended to carry a big object toward the door. "The trunks!"

Ivan gave a solemn nod and left the room, leaving Margriet to wonder whether he had taken in a single word.

She bathed rapidly and washed her hair. The pick-me-up had taken effect, and she moved with precision as she selected clothes to wear, styled her hair, and made up her face.

"That's better," she said to herself, assessing her reflection in the full-length mirror mounted on the wardrobe door. She heard noises on the landing: children's voices. One was surely Berta; the other must be Nellie's brat. Still here. That meant her mother was here too. Thoughts chased around Margriet's head like squirrels in a tree. They must have spent the night in the house. Where? And where did Richard sleep? Not with Margriet. With *her*? Under Margriet's own roof? Insufferable! As quickly as rage flared, a sickening sense of panic replaced it. Was he leaving her? Marta's death had taken her only friend. Was she to be stripped of her family too? Because he would surely take Berta with him; he had often implied she was inadequate as a mother. She couldn't face it. The whole world would see her as a failure. Everyone would think *she* was at fault, not perfect, dutiful, *boring* Richard.

It must not happen. Margriet would do everything in her power to preserve her marriage. She took several deep breaths, trying to calm her jittery nerves. Once they got back to Holland, surrounded by their social circle— Richard's mother, her brothers—everything would be back to normal. She would make sure of it. She just had to get him away from Riga and *that woman*. Looking again at her reflection, she told herself she was beautiful, she was intelligent, and she was charming. She *would* be charming, and a better mother. Once they were back in Holland.

****

When Nellie next came to consciousness, she could tell from the light that the day was already well advanced. She roused Dani and helped her dress before dressing herself. Fearing another confrontation with Margriet, she waited with the door cracked open to see if the coast was clear. Sounds of activity floated up from the floors below, and then she heard the sound of Ivan grumbling his way up to the attic floor. Nellie opened the door wider and motioned him in. If he was surprised to see them in Marta's old room, he didn't show it.

"What's going on?" asked Nellie, not wasting time on explanations or greetings.

"Trunks. She wants me to fetch down the trunks. It looks like the consul's finally got his marching orders.

They're off back to Holland, and Her Majesty wants to pack." Ivan gazed around the attic bedroom, previously off-limits to him, taking in the array of photographs.

"So Madame is feeling better?"

"Hmm? Yes, miraculous recovery, if you ask me. You wouldn't think she'd been too sick to leave her bed for weeks." He moved further into the room, picking up the wedding photograph and peering at it.

"But did the consul *say* they were leaving? What's he doing?" Nellie pressed him.

"He's been in his office since seven, on the telephone or tap-tapping away on that telegraph thing. He hasn't spoken a word to me."

Once Ivan left, Nellie hurried to tidy the room and repack their cases. They tiptoed down the stairs and past Madame's room. The door was closed, but there was the sound of movement inside. They sped down the remaining flights and stood in the open doorway to the consul's office. Richard was on the telephone. He looked up and smiled, gesturing for them to come in while he continued his conversation.

"Yes. ...Tonight, if possible. ...Five tickets. ...Five. ...First class, if you can get them. ....I'm not sure, but I'll arrange something. ...Hello? This line's breaking up, I'll have to phone you back. ...Hello? Damn! Please excuse me." This last was to Nellie, as he replaced the receiver.

"It's true, then? You're returning to Amsterdam?"

"Yes. Still nothing direct, but the ambassador in Kaunas has been recalled, and he got through early this morning to tell me to close up shop and get to the station in Vilnius as soon as possible." The only railroad from Riga ran north and east to Leningrad and Moscow. There was no line south or west. The closest rail terminus for those directions was in the Lithuanian capital, four hours' drive to the south. "I'm hoping Pers Lindstrom will lend us a car and some fuel. He's feeling guilty enough right now over the visas, and anyway, helping us get home hardly qualifies as aiding the Allies." Lindstrom, the Swedish consul, had been issuing transit visas to the Jewish refugees until his government put a stop to it.

Nellie's voice was tentative. "Could… Do you think Dani and I could come with you?"

"Of course you're coming! I wouldn't leave you behind. You're under my protection. I mean—that is, under the Dutch government's protection." He blushed a little.

Nellie laughed nervously. "Well, thank you, thank you. I'm so relieved. I mean, I thought… Well, it doesn't matter. What can I do to help?"

"I'm going to try to line up the car. Perhaps you could pack some food? The train journey may take days, and I've no idea whether we can buy food *en route*. Then could you explain to Ivan? He'll need to drive us to Vilnius and bring the car back here. And Berta. I haven't seen her this morning. Dani, could you see where she is, and maybe help her pack? Just one small suitcase; we'll have to be able to carry our own luggage."

Now that things were moving, the consul appeared calm and almost cheerful. His mood was contagious. In spite of the shock of her parents' abduction, the dash for sanctuary, and the horrors of the night, Nellie left the consul's office feeling an awakening of hope.

Chapter 40

As she anticipated, Dani found Berta in the garden. She persuaded her to come inside to pack. Selecting the essentials for her suitcase was not easy. Berta wanted to take not only her favorite doll, Elizabeth, but Elizabeth's extensive wardrobe too. Eventually, they reached a compromise: Elizabeth could come, but only with the clothes the doll was wearing. While Berta piled another layer of clothing on the doll, Dani packed for her, using the contents of her own suitcase as a reference.

They were on their way down to the ground floor, each dragging their own case, when they were stopped by the scene being played out below between the consul and his wife. The tension in the entrance hall was electric. Berta and Dani stood at the top of the stone staircase, watching.

"I will not be humiliated!" Madame punctuated her statement by pounding her gloved fist on the top of a steamer trunk standing with its twin in the middle of the hall. She was dressed in a pale gray suit with a narrow skirt and fitted waist. A snowy waterfall of silk filled the neckline. Her hat was a feminine version of a derby, perched at an angle over one eye. Erect as ever, she could have been posing for a fashion magazine—"How the Smart Woman Travels"—except for the clenched jaw and the quiver of rage that ran through her body.

"You're talking nonsense, Margriet. Nellie and Dani

are under the consulate's protection. I have a duty to accompany them to safety." The consul was flushed. He was trying to mask his irritation, and not succeeding.

"Don't you dare talk to me in that pompous way about duty! Your duty is to me, not her! I suppose this is why I can't take any luggage—to make room for her!"

"I didn't say you can't take any luggage, only that you can't take those trunks, just a suitcase. It's not to make room for Nellie and Dani; it's because you may have to carry it yourself when we change trains in Berlin. Please be reasonable."

"Reasonable?" Margriet's voice was taking on the dangerous ragged pitch of the previous evening. "Is it *reasonable* to expect me to travel across Europe with my husband's mistress!"

From where Dani was standing, she could not see the door to the kitchen quarters open, but she saw the consul's eyes turn to it. Seeing the direction of his glance, Margriet spun sharply toward it too. There was a pause, and then Nellie's voice, low and even.

"I am not his mistress."

Margriet turned back to harangue the consul, as if Nellie was not there. "I don't believe it. Every day, until late in the evening, you hide away with her. At lunch, you can't get away fast enough. You barely put in an appearance at dinner. Pretending you're working together! I know what *she's* working at!" Margriet jerked her head in Nellie's direction. "This story about the Soviets being after her—that's just another ploy to get her hooks into you. We're leaving this godforsaken place, and she is *not* coming with us!"

"For God's sake, control yourself! You're hysterical. Nellie and I—" Richard was shouting too now. Dani clutched Berta's hand hard, biting her lip to keep from crying out.

"You fool! You're besotted with her, admit it. You've fallen for the little Jewish tramp!"

It happened very fast. Richard stepped forward and delivered a stinging slap to Margriet's cheek. Nellie rushed toward them, and she and the consul spoke at once.

"Richard, don't!"

"Yes, it's true, I love her!"

Dani let out a whimper. Richard and Nellie looked up to where the girls were standing. Their faces showed the identical expression of horror. Margriet did not look up. Her expression was blank, but then, in the interminable seconds before Nellie reached Dani to hug her, Richard following to gather Berta into his arms, Dani saw the hint of a bitter smile cross Madame's face.

****

Nellie finished packing the basket of food they would need for the journey and pushed open the door that separated the kitchen quarters from the entrance hall. The confrontation between Richard and Margriet brought her to a halt with one hand still on the green baize door covering.

"I'm not his mistress."

Margriet ignored her. Nellie felt the raised voices wash over her, not taking in their meaning, until the punctuation of the consul's slap shocked her back to awareness. He loved her. She had known it, just as she had known she loved him, but the knowledge had been locked away behind the conventions of his marriage and her status as his employee. As if not acknowledging it out loud could make their love invisible, or at least disarm it. But now one look at Dani's face told her their feelings for each other had the power to hurt and destroy. Their love was irrefutable, but she now realized it could never find expression.

Nellie raced up the stairs to hold Dani close against her body.

"It's all right. I'm here." She looked over at Richard, whose face was buried in Berta's hair. He had to realize it too. The looks they had exchanged, the touching of hands, the subtext to their late-night conversations—all fueling a foolish dream, a soap bubble that burst when Richard struck Margriet.

Berta was gazing past her papa down the stairs, compelling Nellie to follow her eyes. Below, Margriet stood motionless, her face impassive and beautiful.

"Berta, stay here with Nellie and Dani." Richard rose and descended the steps toward his wife. Nellie could read nothing in his posture. When he arrived in the entrance hall, Margriet turned on her heel and walked into the consul's office. He followed her and shut the door.

****

The silence lasted a full minute. Margriet was determined not to be the first to speak.

"I'm sorry I lost my temper. I shouldn't have hit you," Richard said.

"No. That was…undignified." Margriet was pleased she was able to keep her voice flat and unemotional.

Richard retreated behind his desk and started turning over papers. He wasn't reading them, just avoiding Margriet's eyes.

"Berta was upset…"

Margriet saw her opening.

"Oh, poor Berta! I've neglected her dreadfully since Marta—I was just too distraught. Marta was like a mother to me. I don't think you realize how close we were. But I'll make it up to Berta. Once we're back in Amsterdam, we can be a proper family again. Away from all this…stress. You've been so busy, and I've been so lonely. Once we're home, things can go back to normal, like they were before." She stopped abruptly, aware of the theatrical tone she had adopted, and aware too that "normal" for Richard might not be so attractive.

Richard seemed to have regained some confidence.

"And I don't think you realize, Margriet, that Holland is an occupied country. There will be no returning to normal under a German administration."

"But surely—" Margriet had been about to say that her brother Gilbert was well-placed in the National Socialist Movement and could engineer a suitable post for Richard in the new government, but she stopped herself in time. This was not a moment to mention politics, knowing how different her husband's views were from her family's. "Well, I only meant that the three of us—you, me, and Berta—could be in our own home again. Together."

"Yes, but we have to get through a war zone to get there. I've arranged a car to Vilnius, and we'll take the train to Berlin, then on to Amsterdam. With diplomatic passports, we should be protected, but we have to expect delays and discomfort. Nellie's packed food for the journey—"

"Richard, I mean it. I cannot travel with her, not after you've admitted your affair. It's impossible." Margriet could see he was about to protest, so she rushed on. "Anyway, she's better off here. She's Latvian, and she doesn't have a diplomatic passport—she'll put us all in danger. Let her follow separately. We can take her daughter with us—Dani's Dutch-born, and a child. But not the mother. It's too risky. You already have tickets, yes?" Richard nodded. "Leave her ticket with her. She can get the train from Vilnius tomorrow night and be in Holland just one day later."

Richard stared down at the jumble of documents on his desk. Margriet waited for a sign that she had been persuasive.

"I'm going to talk to Nellie. See what she thinks." He walked past his wife without looking at her, and left the office.

****

Nellie shepherded the girls into her office and slid the pocket door closed. She was shaken from the exchange she had witnessed, torn between the desire to run away to hide and the need to distract the children. She found some notepaper and pencils and encouraged them to draw, then walked over to the window to stare unseeing out into the street. When she looked back, it seemed that Berta was absorbed in her doodles, except her face was pale and clenched into a frown. Dani had not even picked up a pencil. Her wide eyes followed Nellie's every move.

"Papa!" Berta was out of her seat and running toward the door before Nellie had registered the sound of it opening. Richard stood in the gap, looking suddenly older, his shoulders stooped and hands hanging at his sides.

"Nellie, could I have a word?" His voice was diminished too, and Nellie knew that he shared her realization that his outburst had shattered any chance that they could continue as before, their love protected from exposure to the harsh light of reality.

Richard was waiting for her to leave the office to speak privately away from the girls, but Nellie shook her head. She would not risk another confrontation with Margriet in the entrance hall. Instead, he came to stand by her side at the window. The dust begriming the outside of the glass showed their faces in dim reflection.

"Nellie," he started again, but she interrupted.

"Richard, I understand. It's impossible for me to travel with Margriet now."

"No! I'm going to get another car and drive you and Dani to Vilnius myself. Ivan can drive Margriet and Berta."

Nellie almost laughed at his childish desperation.

"No," she replied gently. "Your place is with your wife and child. And anyway, what happens when we all arrive in Vilnius together? You're going to arrange a separate train back to Amsterdam?"

Richard let out a long breath. "I can't leave you here."

"I will follow as soon as I can. Tomorrow, if there's a train. But, Richard,"—she turned to face him and grabbed his arm—"You must take Dani with you. She'll be safe with you with your diplomatic passport. She's just a child returning to the Netherlands, her birthplace. It might be more dangerous for her traveling with me."

Richard couldn't meet her eyes. This was what Margriet had said: the child could come because she posed no danger, but not the mother.

They had been speaking in low voices. Now Dani called out.

"Mama, when are we leaving? I want to go now."

Nellie bit her lip to keep from crying as she walked over to the desk and scooped Dani into a fierce hug.

"Dani, I need you to be very brave…"

Chapter 41

Kneeling on the back seat of the ancient black sedan the consul had borrowed from his Swedish counterpart, Dani kept her mother in view as long as possible. Nellie waved from the door of the consulate, forcing herself to keep a smile on her face, even as her shoulders heaved with sobs. Only Richard's assurances that Nellie would be following them in a day or two at the most had persuaded Dani to let go of her mother. But on the long drive south to Vilnius, that assurance did not prevent tears sliding from her eyes from time to time. First, her grandparents, then Mama. It was little more than a year since she had left Holland and everything she had known to come to Latvia. With her mother's help she had come to feel at home in the cluttered apartment with the high ceilings and view over the park. Now her world was coming apart again, this time without Mama's reassuring presence.

Margriet, Berta, and Dani sat in the back, and the consul was in the front with Ivan, who drove. The journey passed in silence, except for occasional exchanges in Russian between Richard and Ivan, mainly directions from the consul on how to manage the gears, or more urgent exclamations—"Brake!" "Keep right!" Ivan was a novice driver, and would have to complete the journey back to Riga alone after he dropped them off at the railroad station, so he needed the practice.

Dani struggled to keep her sorrow in check. Madame, on the other side of Berta, appeared oblivious, her face turned to the passing farmland and forest as the car crawled across the landscape toward the Lithuanian capital. Berta stared at Dani with solemn eyes, and after a few minutes her hand crept into the older girl's. Later, when another wave of tears overcame Dani, she handed her the doll Elizabeth to hold, all without a word. Later still, Berta fell asleep, and Dani dozed too. She was unaware of stopping at the Lithuanian border.

An attaché from the embassy met them at the station in Vilnius with the tickets. He introduced himself as Edgar Derijk. This fresh-faced youth—he must have been in his twenties but looked like a teenager—was to accompany them on the long rail journey, via Warsaw and Berlin, back to Amsterdam. The ambassador and the rest of the delegation had already left. He was put out that the party's make-up had changed without notice.

"But you said there would be five traveling. I have five tickets here, and five border passes. Who's missing?"

The consul sounded exhausted, although the nightmare journey back to Holland had only just begun. "Mrs. Loesseps will follow in a day or two. This is her daughter Dani, who will be traveling with my wife, my daughter and myself."

"But the documents are dated. I don't know if they will be valid for future travel." The boy's face crumpled in consternation. "The train leaves at eight o'clock. We can't wait. The ambassador made me personally responsible for getting you all home."

Dani felt hot tears of anger burst from her eyes, and she tugged at the consul's sleeve.

"You promised! You said she would follow us!"

He turned and placed his hands on her shoulders. "Yes, I know." He separated some of the documents, leaving the rest with the attaché. Taking Dani's hand, he led her quickly back to where Ivan was standing by the car, smoking and attempting to get his nerve up for the return journey through the long twilight of a near-midsummer night.

"Ivan, give these papers to Mrs. Loesseps. As soon as you can, bring her back here. As soon as you can, man!" He paused, then added in a lower tone, "Look after her. Keep her safe."

Ivan nodded, and then bent toward the girl. His rheumy eyes were wet, and his voice shook a little. "I'll look after her. Don't you worry."

The consul sighed deeply. "Come on, let's find our seats." They returned to where the others were standing. Picking up his own suitcase, as well as the large basket of provisions Nellie had packed for the journey, he led them onto the platform where the Warsaw train was waiting.

The train eventually left close to midnight. By that time Berta was asleep against Dani's shoulder, but the aching need for her mother kept the older girl awake. The party had a compartment to themselves. Edgar made a few attempts at starting a conversation, but even Margriet, who was adept at the social game of identifying common acquaintances and shared experiences, was unresponsive, and he soon gave up. The only noise was the chug of the steam engine and the occasional screech of the rails as the train slowed for a signal or a bend. Dim light seeping in from the corridor showed Dani that the consul, sitting opposite her, was sleepless too.

"*Meneer*?" Dani whispered. "She'll come, won't she? Tomorrow? She'll catch up with us?"

The consul leaned forward and grasped Dani's hand. "I—well, Ivan will bring her to the station as soon as he can." He was going to add more, but stopped himself. "Try to sleep."

It took the better part of the next twenty-four hours to get to Warsaw. They crossed from the Russian-occupied zone into German-held Poland about midday, after a prolonged halt. They were ordered off the train twice, while soldiers examined and re-examined their documents, barked out rough demands, or left them standing while they disappeared to consult their officers. Dani was grateful for the consul's mastery of Russian and German. He maintained an icy calmness throughout, and it appeared that his refusal to react to the bullying tactics of either side led to them being allowed to continue the journey. The lengthy periods standing at the side of the tracks gave Dani a chance to inspect her fellow travelers. There were not many. Men in suits who may have been government officials, perhaps diplomats like the consul, forced by their profession to travel into a war zone, or businessmen looking for an opportunity to profit from the chaos. Others appeared to be families of ethnic Germans from the Baltic states now relocating to the victorious Fatherland. These seemed to get an easier time of it, at least from the Germans.

On both sides of the border they saw the scars of war: half-burned out villages, fields left unplanted, abandoned carts and disabled vehicles along the roadsides. The stations they passed through were usually empty, the Polish names on the signboards defaced with

German or Russian scrawls. Once they saw a shambling procession of refugees, mostly women and children, carrying a motley assortment of belongings, but on the whole there was an impression of emptiness, a whole country left vacant after a terrible storm had passed.

The station in Warsaw, however, was bustling with activity. German uniforms crowded the platforms, and the sound of German voices echoed in the cavernous space under the glass roof. These soldiers looked pleased with themselves, well-fed and glowing with health, a contrast to the Russians Dani was used to seeing in Riga, or those they had come across on the journey so far. The little carts selling provisions to travelers seemed well-stocked, and the Poles staffing them or scurrying to and fro looked moderately well-dressed.

While the consul set off to confirm that their carriage would be attached to the Berlin-bound express, and to replenish supplies, especially water, the rest of the party stayed on the train under Edgar's dubious protection. He had started nibbling his nails nervously as soon as the train had crossed into German-occupied territory, and repeatedly told them to speak only in German. This was unnecessary, as they had no inclination to chat. Dani was relieved when the consul returned. Although he had spoken little since they left Vilnius, his presence was reassuring. From time to time, he exchanged small sad smiles with the girls, and asked them if they were hungry or thirsty. He was the one who accompanied them to the lavatory at the end of the carriage when they needed to go. Madame was completely withdrawn. She stared out of the window without comment for mile after mile, and obeyed instructions from the border guards or the train officials like an automaton. In the Warsaw station, she seemed dazed by the noise and activity, looking blankly at the German officer who, after clicking his heels together and bowing stiffly, asked if the seat across from her was taken. The consul intervened smoothly to say there were three free seats in the compartment, and the officer soon returned with two others to fill the spaces.

If they were a quiet group before Warsaw, the presence of these sharply dressed Wehrmacht officers now rendered them completely mute. Edgar was petrified, Madame retreated again into her remote state, and the consul remained watchful. Berta and Dani were too exhausted by all they had been through to do more than doze fitfully, still clutching each other's hand. The officers talked among themselves in their harsh accents in which even a chuckle sounded like machine-gun fire. After an hour or so, one pulled out a flask, and, after it had been offered to and declined by the consul and Edgar, they passed it between themselves. More time went by. Outside the train windows, the brief night passed, and soon the only sound was the Germans' snoring.

Dani must have fallen asleep too. At one point, she was jolted awake when the train shuddered to a stop, but she was asleep again before they started moving. Late the next morning, they pulled into Berlin, its imposing gray buildings stretching away into the distance. The German officers became lively in anticipation of seeing their families again, and tried to engage the girls with silly faces and sounds, as if to rehearse their roles as fathers, but Dani copied Berta's steady wordless gaze, and they soon desisted.

****

309

The journey blurred into a single interminable ordeal. Day, night, waking, and sleeping all became one. By the end of the journey, Dani was unsure if she was remembering the station in Warsaw or Berlin, or some stop in between. The same uniforms, the same loud German voices, the same self-satisfied faces enjoying victory.

But eventually they arrived at their destination: Amsterdam. It was very early in the morning, and there was no traffic on the streets. Dani waited by herself in a taxi outside an elegant old townhouse. On the other side of the street was a canal. The driver tapped his thumbs against the wheel, impatient to be on his way back to the station for another fare. At last, the consul emerged from the house alone, and they started back to the terminus. The consul had removed the letters from her Dutch grandparents and their photograph from Dani's suitcase, and gently but insistently went over them, coaching her to memorize their first and last names and their address "just in case." Another train, this time through the flat Dutch countryside; another taxi.

The day was warm and heavy with low clouds. Dani was still clutching Elizabeth, Berta's doll. She had forgotten to hand it back when Berta and Margriet had got out of the taxi in Amsterdam. She made to give it to the consul.

"Keep it," he said. "To remember us by." He turned away, but not before Dani saw that he was crying.

She recognized the road with the dyke on one side and the sparse whitewashed cottages on the other. She struggled out of the car and ran up the path. They stood there at the door as she had imagined them. Dani was as tall as Oma's shoulder now. Oma hugged her hard, then held her at arm's length.

"But where is your mother?"

The experiences of the last few days rose up like a wave and crashed down on Dani. She let loose a loud, long-pent-up wail.

Chapter 42

Not a word, not a word, not a word... The rhythm of the train mockingly repeated the phrase in her mind. Since the journey started, Richard had said not a word to her. He had spoken kindly to the girls, he had even talked briefly to the boy, Edgar or whatever his name was. But to her, not a word. It was unbearable.

That moment in the entrance hall of the consulate, when he had slapped her and admitted his love for Nellie, she had experienced a rush of feeling, a mixture of elation and fear. The elation came from knowing that she now held the moral high ground. All his posturing about consular duty, his crusade to save the Jews, his everlasting self-righteousness—all blown aside by this outburst. She knew he would have to obey her wishes. She would not have to bear the humiliation of traipsing back to Holland with her husband's mistress in tow.

The underlying shiver of fear that had run through her had been less defined. Only during the interminable hours and days of their journey had she understood: she had lost him. Not his love. She had not relied on that for a long time. Marriages could go on without love—her parents' had—as long as there was some form of mutual respect, a tacit understanding that the two of them would put an outward face of unity over the emptiness of their relationship. But she had removed the possibility of that understanding. He would not cooperate with her in a loveless but publicly successful marriage now. He was too high-minded, too inflexible for that degree of compromise. The future yawned open in front of her, alone and dark, with no social position, no round of dinners and galas where she could feed on the admiration of others to make up for her husband's indifference.

What was she, without her role as the diplomat's wife? She stared at her reflection in the train window. With care, she could keep her looks for another dozen years, perhaps. Yet the grime of travel had etched lines in her face that showed the ravages age would inevitably bring. Her chignon had become disheveled from leaning against the back of the seat; the frothy white lace at the neck of her blouse hung limp and gray now, days after she had first put it on. Her reflection terrified her with a vision of her future, but she was too scared of what she would see in her husband's eyes to turn away from the window back into the compartment.

The train stopped and shunted back into a branch line. Another delay. She vaguely understood from the German officers' talk that another train was passing on the main line and they had to wait. She continued to stare out of the window, across the twenty yards or so of open ground to the main track they had left, and to the line of trees dimly visible on the other side. It was almost five o'clock in the morning, and the short summer night was receding into dawn. She heard the approaching rattle of another train, and soon a string of cattle cars passed on the main line. She was thinking derisively that they must be very valuable cows to make the Berlin express wait, when she saw a human arm extend out from an opening near the roof of a truck. A trick of the half-light, surely. But then she saw several hands held out as if in supplication from the next car, and the next. She checked a gasp. What—who—on earth was in those trucks?

"*Juden.*" One of the Germans spoke, as if answering her unspoken question. She looked at him blankly. She knew the word meant "Jews" but still did not understand.

"*Juden.*" He repeated. "*Für arbeit ins Ost.*"

Instinctively, she looked to Richard for an explanation. He stared back at her but said nothing. His expression was profoundly sad. She read in it a reproach for everything she had ever done or said, for everything she would do or say in the future. As if *she* had crammed those people into the cattle boxes. As if *she* was sending them east to the hell she had just escaped. And still, not a word, not a word... She turned back to her reflection.

****

By the time they reached Amsterdam in the early morning of their fourth day of travel, Margriet was numb. She had not slept for more than five minutes at a time. Food and even water made her nauseous, so she had stopped eating and drinking. She stood when told to stand, got down from the train when instructed, and now leant against one of the pillars at the entrance to the Amsterdam Station where Richard had placed her before going off to search for a taxi. The girls sat, half-asleep and propping each other up, on top of their suitcases. Edgar had left already to make his own way to his parents' house, relieved to be finally done with his duty to the consul's disconcerting and ill-assorted family.

She was exhausted. If she could just sleep, then perhaps this waking nightmare would end. She remembered with almost tearful gratitude the cache of sleeping pills in her jewel box. Perhaps she could go on sleeping for days, for weeks. But then what? At some point she would have to get up and out of bed. She would have to cope not just with the cold new reality between Richard and herself, but with this new political reality of an occupied Holland. In Riga, the war had been an inconvenience, a distraction from the predictable and therefore comforting round of social events and diplomatic housekeeping. The journey back had demonstrated to her how the war had changed everything. Nothing was predictable anymore.

"Come on. Get in. We don't have much time." Richard had returned in a taxi, and was helping the girls into it. She stumbled after them. Not much time? What did he mean? She did not ask, just slumped into a corner of the back seat.

"Dani, there's a train for Rotterdam leaving in about an hour, and I've got us tickets for it. I'll take you to your grandparents. Berta, you'll stay at home with your mother. Grandmother Vandercam is there. I've telegraphed her, and she'll help you get unpacked and settled in."

Margriet was having trouble understanding Richard's words. It seemed to take several seconds before their meaning seeped into her brain. Did he mean he was leaving her? Was he going to Rotterdam with Dani to wait there for Nellie? Was this an announcement of the end of her marriage, addressed to her through the children? She felt a stirring of outrage, but the feeling was immediately swamped by exhaustion. He was leaving her. This was how it would end: not with high drama, shouting and tears, but to the click-clacking of a taxi meter, as they made their way wordlessly through the still-sleeping streets of Amsterdam.

Part Seven: *2003*

Chapter 43

Berta broke off reading to light the lamps and add a log to the fire. Outside, darkness surrounded the house. The only sound inside was the crackling of the fire. She took a long swallow of wine, steeling herself against the impending climax of the story.

I didn't understand that Mama wasn't coming with us until the last minute. Madame was already sitting in the back of the car. The consul stood by the doors to the consulate, his arm around Mama's shoulders. She was crying.

"Come on," I begged, pulling at her, but she said there was no room in the car for her.

"I'll sit on your lap. There's plenty of room."

She shook her head, and the consul told me to get in the car with Berta. When I climbed into the back seat, Madame wouldn't look at me or say anything. She stared out the other side, tapping her fingers on her purse, impatient to be off. Ivan and the consul got into the front seats, the car started, and I got onto my knees to look out the back window. Mama waved and blew kisses. I kept looking at her until we turned a corner and I couldn't see her anymore.

Tears streamed down Berta's face. Poor Dani. In less than twenty-four hours, the child had lost her grandparents, her home, and her mother. And Nellie…her father's collaborator and perhaps more. A muse, an inspiration, a soulmate—a lover?—whom he deserted to appease the jealousy of a bitter wife. Margriet must have guessed the consequences of leaving Nellie behind; Papa surely knew them. Even if he could bring himself to forgive his wife, he would never forgive himself. How could their marriage have survived the burden of guilt?

But Margriet had died. Even before the Germans invaded the Baltic states and Nellie disappeared, Berta's mother was dead.

Berta swiped away her tears, drained the glass of wine, and leaned forward to stare into the embers of the fire. Questions about her mother had gone unanswered throughout her childhood. Eventually, she had accepted her father's silence on the subject of her mother and the circumstances of her death. She had filled the chasm in her memory with a vague image of blonde perfection, too delicate to withstand the horrors of the German occupation, although Uncle Martin had supplied some contradictory details about a rebellious child who loved to dance. Now, Dani's memoir painted a compelling portrait of a cold and selfish woman, beautiful on the outside but with a hollow center. What had happened to the exuberant girl Martin had described? A "suitable marriage" to an older man she barely knew; the birth of a child she may not have wanted; exile in a country where she had no friends and could not even speak the language—a country caught on the precipice of war. Berta supposed her mother had been isolated in a situation she had neither the experience nor the disposition to handle. Berta's grandmother had hinted that the journey back from Riga killed her. Perhaps that was when the thin ice she had been skating on—her beauty and her social skills—finally cracked, plunging her into despair.

Berta's eyes began to blur with gazing into the fire. She leaned back in the chair and closed them, feeling tiredness—and all the emotion of the last twenty-four hours—wash over her. She needed time to make sense of it all. She needed sleep.

****

Drifting in the half-light beyond consciousness, Berta had an image of a steep staircase leading up from a narrow entrance hall. She knew somehow that this was the interior of the house on Herengracht in Amsterdam, the family house her parents lived in between diplomatic postings before the war. She remembered the house from the outside after it had been taken over by the Germans, when her grandmother hurried her past. Now, she saw herself, a child, climbing the stairs and walking along a corridor toward the back of the house. It seemed familiar, as dreams often do. Had she dreamt this scene before, or was she remembering something that actually happened?

Berta knew what was behind the door at the end of the corridor: a dimly-lit bedroom, the shades closed against morning light. The mahogany prow of a huge sleigh bed faced the child, too high for her to see over. She walked to the side of the bed. Her mother lay there, golden hair spilling over the pillow, hands folded on her breast like a medieval princess carved in marble on top of a tomb. The effigy opened her eyes and turned toward the child.

"Don't look at me like that. It's not my fault." She closed her eyes again, and resumed the marble pose. The child noticed the gleaming tracks of tears on her mother's cheeks. She sat down on the floor and waited. Margriet did not speak again.

Her mother was dead.

****

Sobs shook Berta's body awake. In those few minutes of fugue, she had been on a journey into a time before memory—a time when her mother was alive. Berta had so often pushed away expressions of sympathy for the lack of a maternal relationship with a quick formula: "My mother died when I was five. I don't remember her." Now, in old age, she experienced the pain of the loss as if it were fresh. Along with pain came anger at her abandonment, and bitter regret of the love she had been denied. She hugged herself and rocked back and forth until her feelings ebbed. When she opened her eyes, she was amazed to find the familiar room unchanged, the firelight still dancing, her empty glass and plate still on the hearth.

After a few minutes, she placed a guard over the fire, turned out the lamps, and went to bed.

Chapter 44

In the days following her return from London, Berta felt vulnerable, as if she had shed a protective coating and her skin was exposed to light and air for the first time. Quite ordinary scenes caused her eyes to flood with tears: the apricot trees in blossom on the road down to the village; the little Romany child playing under her mother's stall at the Friday market; even the warmth of the sun on the zinc café tabletop as she spread her fingers over it.

For the time being, she abandoned her work editing her father's *magnus opus*. She now had a more compelling link to her father's past: Danielle's memoir. She took long slow walks along the vineyard terraces, feeling her bones strengthen even as they protested. Although previously her excursions down the hill had been restricted to daily sorties into the village *boulangerie*, and a weekly supermarket trip to Foix, she now stopped at the café on the square to linger over coffee and view the scene. As April turned into May, a few tourists penetrated the valley, pausing for provisions before heading off to tour the Cathar strongholds. The weekly market, which in winter comprised a few stalls huddled at one end of the square, expanded to include local crafts and specialties. Over the years, Berta had come to know many of the locals by sight, but had exchanged no more than the obligatory "*Bonjour,*

M'sieurs-dames." Now she watched their comings and goings avidly, trying to piece together their individual stories and work out relationships from snippets of overheard conversations.

But mostly, on her walks or at the café, she thought about the past, about Riga and the journey back to Holland. She wondered about her father's relationship with Nellie. Had they been lovers? She decided not. The impression gained of Nellie from the memoir was of a passionate woman, but a loyal and honest one. Berta could not imagine her engaging in the everyday deceptions needed to carry on an affair with a married man under the nose of his wife and two inquisitive children. Similarly, her father, although he might have recognized Nellie as his soulmate, was too unworldly—innocent, even—to have acted on his desires.

Berta also pondered her mother's behavior. She understood that Margriet had not loved her as she deserved. Probably emotionally deprived as a child herself, Margriet had not been able to respond to Berta as a mother should. A dispassionate observer might determine that Margriet had failed as a wife as well as a mother, narcissism preventing her from sharing her husband's interests or understanding his values. Perhaps it was deep-seated insecurity that led her to jump to the conclusion that her husband was having an affair with a woman who understood him better than she did. And perhaps her guilt at the realization that she had needlessly separated Nellie from her daughter, combined with the knowledge that she had irretrievably lost Richard's love, drove her to suicide. Berta was certain that her mother's death, whether intentional or accidental, was the ultimate result of not being loved, and not having loved enough.

Berta began a letter to Danielle several times. She wanted to thank her for the memoir, and explain how it had helped retrieve memories from early childhood. More difficult was putting into words her admiration for Nellie and the role she played at the Riga consulate, not just in helping the Jewish refugees but in Berta's own young life offering a model of motherhood in contrast to the distant relationship Berta had with Margriet. Nellie had brought joy to her father, too. Even though losing her had clouded the balance of his life, Berta was certain he never regretted knowing Nellie, only the momentary weakness that had prevented him insisting on her accompanying them to Holland. Hardest of all was to explain feelings about her own mother, but she felt she owed Danielle an acknowledgment of the selfishness of Margriet's actions and their consequences, including for Margriet herself. Berta's lifelong habit of reticence was difficult to break. Elizabeth, the doll, watched with impassive eyes from her perch on the mantel as Berta threw each inadequate draft into the fireplace.

Three weeks after she returned home, a package arrived from England. Berta did not recognize the handwriting—it was not the same as Nellie's scrawl on the envelope containing the memoir. Feeling a chill of premonition, she went out to the terrace, holding the package unopened. The sun had not yet reached this side of the house, and the poppies against the ancient stone walls were still closed. Berta breathed in the newness of the day, wishing she could preserve the moment. After a few minutes, she unfolded a letter from Natalie wrapped around two yellowed and stained envelopes. She put these aside and read the letter.

Dear Ms. Vandercam:

I am writing to let you know that my grandmother Danielle Nesse passed away at home on May 13th. As you may know, she had been ill for some time with emphysema complicated by high blood pressure and diabetes. She died during the night. Our hope is she died in her sleep without pain. She is buried in Golders' Green cemetery next to my grandfather Samuel Nesse.

A few days before she died, my grandmother asked me to write a letter to you after she passed on. She was insistent I explain that she was at peace with what happened in Riga. I know that she was talking about her mother, who died after the Nazis occupied Latvia in 1941. We never knew the details of exactly how, where, and when she died, but Grandmother treasured two letters she received from her while she was in hiding in Holland. She wanted you to have them.

I will be performing in Carcassonne on June 21 as part of the Fête de Musique *and then attending an international youth orchestra camp. I believe Carcassonne is close to where you live. Would it be possible for us to meet? I have some old photographs of my grandmother, as well as of her parents. People say I look a lot like her when she was young. I would like to show them to you and talk about Grandmother. I miss her very much.*

Yours sincerely,
Natalie Nesse

Carrying the envelopes enclosed with Natalie's letter, Berta walked out to the edge of the terrace. She brushed her hand against the rosemary bushes and smelled the fragrance on her fingers. Later it would be hot, the first hot day of summer, but the earth had not yet acquired that scorched dusty smell, and the trees still had the fresh lime green of new growth. The mountains to the south shaded to violet, the horizon indistinct. Berta could hear machinery from somewhere in the valley, the sound rising and falling as a farmer crossed to and fro along the rows of vines.

She sat in one of the old wooden chairs at the edge of the terrace, with the sun now on her face, readying herself to read Nellie's letters. She pictured Danielle as she had seen her in London: her bravery, the jut of her chin, and the emphatic way she spoke. She also remembered, with a small feeling of shame, that morning in the hotel lobby, how she had glibly sympathized, saying she understood what it was to lose a mother. Berta felt humbled by Dani's impulse to pass these letters on to her, the last precious communications from her mother. Until now, Berta had not understood. Her own loss had been eradicated along with her memory of Margriet. And, even when that memory was restored, as it had been so recently, she experienced a different loss: not the sudden wrenching separation, but the realization of a life lived in the absence of a mother's love. It was like being born without a limb. She had known she was different, but until the last few weeks, she had not seen how that difference had stunted her life.

She examined the envelopes, grimy as if they had been passed hand-to-hand repeatedly over the months they had taken to arrive at their destination. The address was smeared by rain, or perhaps tears, the pages inside each worn to softness from constant reading, and the paper beginning to disintegrate along the fold lines. Yet the emphatic strokes of Nellie's handwriting survived.

June 14, 1940

My darling Dani,

It's now two weeks since you left, and I picture you safely settled with Oma and Opa. Please give them lots of hugs and kisses from me. I know you are being a good girl and helping them all you can. I long to be with you there, but this letter will have to suffice for now.

After leaving you at the station in Vilnius, Ivan drove all night, arriving back at the consulate by midmorning. He would have set off immediately to the Swedish consulate to see if he could extend the loan of the car and get some more gasoline for another journey to Vilnius, this time with me, but I insisted that he get some rest first. Unfortunately, while he was still asleep, the Soviets made their final move to take over Latvia. About four o'clock in the afternoon, trucks with loudspeakers mounted on their roofs moved through the Old Town telling everyone to stay inside. The curfew lasted several days while the Russians secured their grasp on the government. From the consulate we could hear occasional gunshots, but whether that was Latvian nationalists resisting or the Russians enforcing the curfew, we couldn't tell. I'm grateful for Ivan's vegetable garden: without the spring greens and early peas that are coming in we would have a very boring diet!

When the curfew was lifted, Ivan took the car back to the Swedes, but our friend Mr. Lindstrom is no longer stationed there, and his replacement was not very helpful. Even if he had agreed to lend us the car again (which he didn't) and even if there were fuel to be had (which there isn't) I don't think we can get to Vilnius. Ivan reports that there are road blocks on all the major routes out of the city. My travel documents have expired anyway, so we will just have to come up with another plan.

In the meantime, we are quite comfortable here. I have moved into Berta's old room (Marta's mausoleum was beginning to depress me!) and I'm reading my way through her library of fairy stories. I am still a little nervous about venturing outside. Thank goodness for Ivan! He has taken care of me like a mother hen. He forages in the market and manages to come back with something to eat almost every day, but we will need ration cards and identification papers soon. He is going to pretend I'm his simpleton daughter, which will explain why I don't leave the house or speak to visitors. Not that we've had any callers. I think often of the Polish refugees and wonder how many are still stuck here.

I must stop now. Ivan is taking this letter to the new Swedish consul with the hope that, even if he won't help me escape, he might put this in the diplomatic pouch and speed it on its way to you. I am also wrapping up the consul's notebooks to send to him, all his research on Baltic folklore. I know he will be missing it. Have you heard from him? If you are in contact, please send my regards.

Dani, be strong. We'll be together again soon. I love you. Mama.

The second letter was also franked in Sweden and forwarded through the Red Cross to occupied Holland. It was undated and less optimistic than the first. The last notation on the envelope showed it arrived in March 1941, but it must have been mailed several weeks earlier.

Dearest one,

Well, it looks like we are moving on from the consulate, Ivan and me. We received a second visit from the authorities yesterday, and they have given us until noon today to report to the Latvian Soviet Socialist Republic's Bureau of Housing and Labor, or some such title. Apparently, we will be assigned a place to live, and work to do which will benefit the People. I was tempted to say that we are the People too, but it is true that this place is far too big and opulent for two Russian peasants—you would laugh to see your book-loving mother dressed in a headscarf and apron, playing the part of an illiterate servant! Only workers get ration cards, so it is good that we are being set to work. Food has become a problem. We were well off during the summer and autumn, with Ivan's garden and the stores in the pantry. But they finally ran out, as did the coal for the furnace. It is very cold now, and the thick stone walls seem to ooze dampness. After we picked the last apples, we chopped up the tree for fuel. Ivan wanted to cut down the flowering cherry tree too, but I wouldn't let him. I can still see you and Berta playing in the falling blossoms. Can that really be only months ago? I know it's silly, but I feel as long as that tree stands, there is a hope that one day, when all this is over, you will play again in this garden. It doesn't matter now. The new occupants, whoever they are, can do what they want.

The trees along the Pilsetas Canal and in the Esplanade have been cut down for fuel too. I walked through the parks to the apartment building on Elizabetes Street a few days ago. There are new names next to all the bellpushes. I didn't linger. The Orthodox cathedral has been boarded up, and the fine iron railings and grills taken away to be melted down for some military purpose. You would not recognize the New Town.

We get very little news. Occasionally, the radio

works. You remember the huge walnut cabinet in the salon. For its size, it receives a very poor signal, but we did learn about the evacuation of allied troops from Dunkirk, the bravery of the RAF fighting off the Luftwaffe over the English Channel, and, most recently, the terrible bombing of London. I pray every day for your safety.

I must close this letter now. We are going to drop it off at the Swedish consulate before we report for relocation. As soon as we are settled, I will write again. I will never stop thinking of a way to get to Holland. Give my love to Oma and Opa, and above all to you. Know that your beautiful little face is in my mind every minute. Be brave and good. Have faith that things will get better.

Your Mama who loves you very much.

Berta re-read the letters, thinking now of Dani as a child, her wild dark hair falling over her face as she held a doll in a child's bedroom. Perhaps the bedroom was hers at the consulate; the doll's name was Elizabeth, of that she was sure. She let the tears come—tears for Dani, the child who survived and made a new life, who found joy in the warmth of family and community, and was now mourned by that circle of love she had created around her. Tears for Nellie, too, whose legacy of courage and kindness had lived on, not only in her daughter but in the hundreds of refugees she had shepherded through the Riga consulate. *I wish I had known her!* The thought rushed into Berta's mind, followed immediately by realization: *I did know her!* And even if she could not remember her, she would find a way to honor her.

Yes, she would meet Natalie in Carcassonne. With pleasure, she anticipated bringing her here to the house, explaining its history, coming out onto this terrace and pointing out the ruined Cathar fortress on a distant peak. She wondered if Natalie would be accompanied by her parents, Danielle's son and daughter-in-law. It would be good to talk to them, and to look at the photographs they would bring. Perhaps, after dinner, Natalie would play her violin.

In spite of her sadness at Danielle's death, Berta felt at peace. For a long time, perhaps all her life, she had held herself taut, as if ready to run. Now she realized there was no need to run. She could face the past and the future with equanimity, even with grace. She let go of her regrets, all those questions to her father that she had suppressed when she was a child, all the care she had taken not to wake his wartime memories, and, above all, the way she had protected herself from the loss of her mother by burying memories so deep they had been unreachable. It might be late in the day, but she was determined to change. She was opening up to life no matter how messy, to feelings no matter how complicated, and to memories no matter how painful.

She would talk with Natalie about Danielle's story, which was, of course, Nellie's story too; about Nellie's parents, and Marta and Ivan, Pavel, the rabbi…all those people caught by history like insects in amber.

Berta looked at the line of peaks to the south that defined the border with Spain, and thought as she often did of the Cathars. Not of the ones who starved in the sieges or the hundreds burned in a single day after the surrender, but of those few who slipped away over the mountains, who lived to pass on the story and so to honor those who perished, not as saints or as victims, but as fathers, mothers, real and substantial, loved for who they were, imperfect and human.

A word about the author...

Marian Exall is an award-winning author of mysteries and historical fiction. She grew up in England and lived in France and Belgium before emigrating to the USA, raising a family and pursuing a career as a lawyer.

She now lives in the Pacific Northwest, where she enjoys hiking, gardening and cooking. And of course writing.

Find out more at:
https://www.marianexall.com